OVER THE FALLS

RYDER BAY #1

JORDAN FORD

ISBN: 978-0-473-46485-1

For Lenore…
The reader every author needs.
You really are the best.

AUTHOR'S NOTE

This book (this series) started with a vision that I had on a beach in Australia. I saw Harley in my mind, cruising down the road on her skateboard, her blonde hair flying out behind her, and a surfboard tucked under her arm. She was strong, independent, fearless. And I immediately loved her.

That one image created an entire world, and I'm so excited to invite you into it. I hope you fall in love with Ryder Bay and the characters who live there. I don't think I'll ever be able to go to a beach again without them wandering through my mind.

My prayer is that this book will help you escape to the beach for a while. That you can laugh a little, have your heartstrings pulled and ultimately fall in love. Enjoy the journey.

I'd like to thank some key people for helping me put this novel together:
Lenore, Beth, Rachael, Kristin & my proofreading team. I love working with you all so much. You challenge me to be better, and I'm so grateful for that.

My readers who have turned my daydreams into a career. Thank you for your help. I wouldn't even be doing this job if it wasn't for you.

My family for their constant love and encouragement.

And to Jesus. You are my lifeline, my rescuer and the love of my life. Thank you for holding me up when I'm sinking and filling me with a constant hope that surpasses my understanding.

Welcome to Ryder Bay.
Happy reading!

xx
Jordan

1

THE END

AIDAN

One dive. Two fifty-meter lengths.

Less than two minutes of my life. That's it. Then it's over.

But a lot can happen in two minutes.

Your world can be made…or broken.

"Swimmers, take your mark!"

"I'm sorry."

As I step onto the block, Savannah's is the only voice I can hear. She's in the crowd somewhere, watching me. Well, not me. She'll be here supporting the entire Walton Warriors swim team. It's not just about me anymore.

Yet she still consumes me.

The cheering crowd, the officials standing poolside

to make sure no one cheats. It's all white noise and blur.

"Set!"

I crouch into my dive position.

"I know we've been together for nearly a year, but…"

And the buzzer sounds.

My legs push off the block, propelling me into the water, because that's what they've been trained to do. I slice through the surface and pump my hips and legs, gaining as much momentum as I can before rising back to the top. My arms swing in an automatic crawl. It's almost robotic now, I've been doing it for so long.

All those early mornings, the hours in the pool— length after length, drill after drill.

It's for moments like this.

And all I can hear is…

"But…"

I slice my arms through the water, five strokes, breathe. Push hard. Kick. Head down, stay streamline.

I can't focus on the swimmers either side of me. This is my race. My strongest stroke. The one Coach thinks I can place in. The one my parents are expecting me to win.

I squeeze my eyes shut, blocking out the noise.

It's dumb.

Blindness doesn't make me deaf.

Savannah's sweet voice still echoes in my brain like a fog horn.

"But…"

I open my eyes.

The tumble turn is approaching.

I reach the wall and curve my body just before I hit. Spinning around, I push hard off the tiles and propel my body forward.

I'm not in the lead.

I need to swim faster.

To win.

But my muscles are already sluggish. I still have another fifty meters to go. Such a short distance, yet it seems so far today.

Maybe even too far.

"But…"

That was the first word to ruin my life. The ones that followed were spiky nails driven into my heart. Stinging bullets that disabled me.

"I'm just not feeling it anymore."

Her words hurt then. And now, even though a few weeks have passed, they're acting like anchors. Weights attached to my chest, hindering my shoulders, sinkers dragging my ankles to the bottom of the pool.

"I don't mean to hurt you, Aidan, but there's no point staying together when this isn't going anywhere."

I squeeze my eyes against the words, wishing I could cover my ears and block them out. Wishing I could shove my fingers into my brain and scratch the words clear.

But I can't do that.

They stay.

They cling.

They slow me down.

"I'm sorry."

"But…"

The end is near, I can see it approaching. I have to push hard. I have to win. To prove I'm worthy. To prove she's made a huge mistake.

She'll be watching.

I kick harder, stretch farther than I've ever stretched before.

My lungs are burning.

My legs are cooked spaghetti.

I hit the wall.

I'm finished.

I'm done.

Whipping off my goggles, I stare up at the board, scanning for my placing.

My chest deflates, like someone's stuck a syringe into me and is sucking out what's left of my oxygen.

"It's over."

Those were her final words before she spun and left me standing by my car—shocked, bereft, alone.

It took her less than two minutes to destroy my world.

"It's over."

And I lost.

BORN TO RIDE THE WAVES

HARLEY

And it's a win for me today!

Three-foot swells at eighteen-second intervals with a light offshore breeze—near perfect surfing conditions. And those beautiful waves are hitting the Ryder Bay shoreline just when I want to be here.

Ryder Bay used to be the undiscovered jewel of the California coastline. With a point break coming off the old pier, it's the perfect surfing spot for the locals. Apparently, my grandfather was one of those guys who used to surf around here. I wouldn't really know. I never met the guy. In fact, I didn't even set foot in Ryder Bay until after he passed away and left his house to my mom.

She took the chance and moved us here when I was fourteen.

I wish I could have met him.

I wish he'd been the one to teach me how to surf. When I found that box of old photos and saw the one of him on his board, and that smile on his face, I'm pretty sure we would have been kindred spirits.

But no, I learned to surf from a guy I thought I loved. The guy who broke my freshman heart but left me with a passion for the waves. In retrospect, I got the better end of the deal...as long as I never think about how it all ended.

I push the ugly thoughts aside and can't help but smile as I sit on the water, my legs dangling over the sides of my board. A new set is rolling in. I watch it closely as I wait in the midday sunshine, dragging my hands through the salty ocean.

I glance to my left. The old pier in the distance is like a crooked finger, marking the south end of the beach. The end where my people come from—the originals who loved this little town just the way it was, before the money and the condos started coming in. I know I arrived after that development began, but I moved into the south. I am a legacy of my grandpa, and that makes me an original. No one is ever going to convince me otherwise.

I turn my gaze to the right and frown at the north end. It's changed so much, even in the three years I've lived here. It sometimes worries me how much more it will progress and develop.

Will we be overrun by buttheads who don't really understand the rustic beauty of this place?

The sound of the waves building in the distance drags my eyes back to the horizon. I can feel them coming, the energy flowing through the water. There's something almost spiritual about being out here like this.

Time seems to disappear. I have no idea how long I've been surfing today. I've already caught a ton of decent-sized waves. Sure, I've had to share a few. With surf reports like this, I was expecting that. Axel and his crew are out in force. The three of them—actually, four. There's been a new guy hanging around lately. Crew cut, olive skin, a big tattoo on one of his muscly arms. He's Shane's brother or cousin. Ripper, I think?

I don't know what kind of name that is. His real name is probably Stanley or Arthur or something, so he chose Ripper as a cool nickname.

I snort.

Although I want to mock it, I totally understand.

I've been branded with the kind of name you avoid telling people as well. Not my first. That's okay, but telling people my last name is just plain humiliating.

I glance at the crew—all guys in their early to mid-twenties. Axel seems to be their leader. He's tall, muscular, and can be damn intimidating when he wants to be. His skin is black, his eyes are so dark brown they look black as well, and when he's pissed, you don't want to look into them. He keeps his head completely shaved. There's not even fuzz up there. It's like an eight ball.

I don't know where he's from originally. He has a slight accent, which tells me he was born somewhere in Africa, but I don't know which country. My conversations with him are only ever short, shallow, and based around surfing.

He's passionate about the sport. They all are. They follow the waves. Live for them. They don't worry about pesky jobs and stupid high school. Basically, their only concern when they wake each morning is deciding which beach to hit for the best set of waves.

They have to be careful about invading other surfers' turf. From what I know, they stick to a few main spots unless the surf is dead; then they venture out looking for sweet rides farther down the coast.

On a day like today, they'll get pissy with newbies. Thankfully they leave me alone because I know the rules and I stay out of their way. I think they kind of like me, maybe think of me as their little blonde mascot or something. I hang around on the edges—not close enough to be in, far enough away to not be annoying.

There's a certain safety in my solitude.

The energy in the water shifts gears. I feel it between my fingers and squint against the sunlight. The waves are gaining serious momentum and turning into something I can surf.

I lie down on my board and start to paddle, keeping an eye on the surfers around me.

Axel's bald head flashes in my periphery.

Will we be racing for this one, or will he let me have it?

I glance his way and notice him back off. His white teeth flash for the briefest second, and I silently thank him before duck-diving underneath the first wave.

I want to get myself into a better position.

My arms start to ache as I force them to paddle harder. My body is telling me that my surfing session should wrap up soon, but to hell with that. I might take a break after this ride, but I'll be back in the water after a drink. Maybe I'll finish that banana I started eating on my skate over here. Work doesn't start for another couple of hours, and I'm not wasting a second of my time doing anything other than surfing.

Spinning my board around, I watch the wave as it rises behind me, feeling its power surging beneath me. That excited thrill I live for spirals through my body as I paddle, paddle, paddle.

My board catches the wave and I rise to my feet, laughing as I do an easy bottom turn to travel along the wave, then quickly snap my board up. Water sprays over the top of the board and I dip back down, smiling at the rush.

This is the best frickin' feeling in the world.

Flicking my board up, I go for a roundhouse cutback, then skim along the wave before building for an off-the-lip to finish. As the wave dies, I jump from my board and splash into the water.

The cold, salty ocean envelopes me and I surge to the top, capturing my board as I break the surface.

Freaking awesome!

I whoop to the sky and rest my head back on the water. My hair floats behind me, my body weightless as I soak in the moment.

There is nothing more peaceful and exhilarating than being out in the ocean.

It's where I'm meant to be.

RIDING THE EXPRESS TO HOSER-TOWN

AIDAN

First the worst, second the best… the childhood rhyme sings in my head and I finish it off with my own lyrics…*fourth—not even on the damn podium.*

I stare up at Simon's gold medal and momentarily hate him. It's just a flash, and I instantly shove the emotion aside. I don't hate my friend. I'm proud of him. He deserves the win. As does Craig with his silver and Jonah with his bronze. Walton Academy cleaned up at this year's meet. We are the crowning jewels of high school SoCal swimming.

And then there's me.

Mr. Fourth Place.

Mr. Loser.

The crowd cheers and claps while the guys pose for

photos, then climb down from the podium. Next up is the Boys' 100m freestyle relay. I'll get a medal for that.

Gold.

I should be stoked.

But as I walk around to my teammates and get ready to take the podium, my insides feel like ash. I didn't win this gold, they did. I wasn't first off the block, and I wasn't the finisher. Jonah and I were in the middle, keeping the pace, but we weren't the glory boys. We never would be.

What the hell happened?

Last year I was Simon's biggest competition. The question was always who will win this one, Simon or Aidan?

But no one ever asks that question anymore.

Swallowing the rock in my throat, I force a smile and follow the other Walton Academy Warriors up to the podium.

A cheer goes up as we stand higher than the other two schools. I gaze into the crowd and spot my parents. Mom has her phone out snapping pics while Dad says something to my surly little brother, Grayson. The kid doesn't even bother looking up from his iPad to acknowledge him, or me.

Dad rolls his eyes and looks back at us. He gives me a thumbs-up, but I can tell his smile is forced. It quickly fades, and he drops his hand. He's disappointed that I haven't been up here alone. He knows the truth just like everyone else.

In the past nine months, Aidan De Beer has gone from star athlete, dating one of the hottest girls in school, to a fourth-place, heartbroken singleton.

Oh how the mighty fall.

At least my parents don't know about Savannah dumping me yet.

It's still too fresh, and I just can't admit it to them.

I clench my jaw and lean down so the medal can be placed around my neck. I then have to force a smile while I shake the woman's hand. She's in charge of all these swimming meets, and you can tell she loves the gig.

"Congratulations, boys. You've made your school very proud this year."

Craig nods and puffs out his chest like it was all his doing. I glance at Simon, who gives me a triumphant grin, but there's no arrogance attached to it. Si's the best. I won't be surprised if he ends up on an Olympic team one day. I used to dream of that kind of thing too, but with the way my life is going, I'll be lucky just to get on a college team.

Do I even want that?

Maybe next year, when I'm a senior and Simon is gone, I'll have the chance to rank in the top three, but I don't want to go getting my hopes up.

I have to face the truth.

I'm Aidan De Beer. Life seems set on screwing me over at the moment.

And I can't see that changing anytime soon.

The bus ride back to school is somewhat painful. Excitement is making the chatter loud and irritating. There are a ton of medals floating around the bus this year. The girls cleaned up pretty good as well. Gold, silver or bronze in almost every event. The other schools must hate us.

But I guess we've earned it.

We've worked hard.

Trained our asses off.

Some of us obviously didn't work hard enough, though. I cringe and gaze out the window, lamenting the fact that my nickname as a kid was Dolphin Boy. Mom used to call me that all the time, because she couldn't get me out of the water. It was my playground, my happy place, until it turned into work and constant training. An endless slog...just to come in fourth.

Fourth!

My insides bunch and knot, giving me a stomachache.

The bus is curving around the highway, heading north to Ryder Bay.

It's been my home for about five years now.

We moved there shortly after my aunt and uncle. They convinced my parents that Ryder Bay was the hottest new location to live. Typical real estate agents, I guess. They hooked my parents up with a sweet house overlooking the ocean. It's pretty damn nice. I won't complain.

And Walton Academy's not too bad either. That was my parents' main concern when shifting from San Francisco. Where would their precious boys attend school? Ryder Bay schools didn't have the best reputation, and there was only one high school option—Ryder Bay High, a small, old, run-down school at the southern end. Could it cater academically? Would any of the schools have the right facilities to really stretch their sons and prepare them for a successful future?

For Uncle Jeff, it was an easy sell. "We're sending Skylar to Walton Academy, an elite private school only thirty minutes north of Ryder Bay. It caters from kindergarten all the way up to twelfth grade and boasts some of the best academic results in the state."

Sold.

So my parents made the big move. And with the help of his brother, my dad started up his own investment company to cater to the rich, who Uncle Jeff was recruiting to the area in droves.

The amount of building and development that has happened at the north end of the beach is kind of crazy. I often wonder how the people who have lived here for years feel about it.

Maybe they hate it.

Maybe that's why we stick to the north and they stay in the south.

"Yeah, we're gonna party tonight!" Craig yells,

punching his arms into the air. He turns to face me, slapping my shoulder and whooping.

I force a smile while my insides rebel against the idea.

I used to love bonfires on the beach. They're not technically allowed, but Craig's dad is a cop and he lets us get away with it as long as we stick to his rules—the fire can only be in one small area of the beach, a cove at the base of the cliffs, right near the end. He'll stop by every now and again to make sure we're behaving ourselves. I'm sure he knows we're all hiding our beer cans and Solo cups when he wanders by, but as long as we never get crazy, he seems cool with it.

I like Officer Malloy. He's a good guy.

"Skylar was looking pretty damn hot today. Did you see that T-shirt she was sporting? If she raised her arms any higher, we would have gotten the full show." Jonah nudges Craig, who lets out a triumphant laugh.

My stomach clenches at the smirk on Craig's face. He's been dating my cousin for a few months now. I'm pretty sure the only reason Skylar puts up with Craig's obnoxious behavior is because he's become the most popular guy in school, and Skylar only ever goes for the best.

Too bad her idea of "best" is so damn warped.

I don't always understand my cousin. One minute she's as sweet as candy, showing actual concern for your well-being, and then the next she's acting like a first-class bitch. It's taken me years to figure out how to negotiate her, but I've learned to read her moods and when to steer clear.

She'll be in a good mood tonight, though. Her boyfriend is a winner. They'll be the star couple that everyone envies. Skylar will love that, and so she'll let Craig celebrate the way he loves best—hot and heavy.

I cringe.

Thinking about that guy pawing my petite cousin grosses me out. I've kind of been avoiding her since she started dating Craig.

That's not true.

At first I wasn't avoiding them at all, because Craig's not the reason.

Savannah is.

Since she dumped me, I've been avoiding everything to do with her. She and Skylar are best friends and they do most things together. You can't be around one without bumping into the other.

Even looking at Savannah is hard right now. I miss her so much. I want her back so badly.

But that's not going to happen.

Because she's just not feeling it anymore.

I pull my hood up and rest my head against the glass, gazing down at the ocean and wishing for the millionth time that she hadn't said those stupid words.

"I'm sorry, but…"

It felt like they came out of nowhere.

I thought we were good. We'd been at prom only two nights earlier.

I was in love.

But she wasn't…and I'd had no idea.

It was frickin' humiliating. Heartbreaking.

"You coming, man?" Craig slaps my shoulder again.

I glare at him, then shrug. "Don't know. Maybe."

He rolls his eyes and mutters something under his breath before turning back to the crowd of people who will show some enthusiasm. He soon gets a chant going, and it's clear that the Walton Warriors will be partying hard tonight.

As soon as the bus reaches school, I jump out and avoid the waiting fans, ducking around the bus and making a beeline for my car.

I spot Savannah, because I can't seem to not notice her. She's standing next to Skylar, who screams and runs into Craig's arms. He lifts her up and her legs wrap around his hips. I turn my back on the kiss-fest. It's all tongues, slobber and hands. I don't want to know.

I don't want to be reminded of how much I miss kissing Savannah.

We weren't all gropey like my cousin and Craig Malloy.

Our kisses were sweet and fun.

Sure, we got hot and heavy, and I really liked that too, but I never stepped over the mark with her. She wasn't ready, and I was okay with that. More than anything, I just liked hanging out with her. I liked having someone who thought I was the best. Who wanted to be with me more than anyone else.

"You're such an idiot," I mutter as I haul ass out of school and head for the bay.

I don't know why I'm in such a hurry to get there. It's not like I want to go home and face my disappointed parents. Sure, they'll put on the forced smiles for me, tell me I did good, but they don't really mean it. What they're really thinking is *You didn't do good enough.*

With a sharp huff, I focus on the road and soon find myself driving past the turnoff to my subdivision and heading straight for the beach.

Rather than parking in the north lot, where my friends will be showing up soon, I keep going, finding myself a spot in the south lot, all the way down by the pier. I don't come here often and almost feel like a foreign invader as I step out of my car. Yeah, Ryder Bay is a small town, but we tend to stick to our own spaces, especially when it comes to the beach.

But my end of the beach will be overrun with winners soon, and there's no place there for a loser like me.

Slamming my car door, I head for the wooden stairs and descend onto the sand. Kicking off my flip-flops, I leave them under the base of the stairs and head for the water.

I should be over water.

After my crappy day in the pool, I should be staying on dry land, but I walk to the ocean's edge anyway and stand there gazing out at the horizon, wishing I could somehow cross it. Cross it and disappear for a while.

Scrubbing a hand down my face, I resist the urge to yell out my angst.

That's not my style.

But damn, I wish it was sometimes.

I could use the release.

I settle for a loud throat clearing, then glance to my left and notice a blonde walking out of the water. She has a surfboard tucked under her arm...and she's staring right at me.

4

AN ELITE ON FOREIGN SAND

HARLEY

W hy am I staring at this guy?

Harley! Stop staring!

But I can't help it.

There's something about him that draws my attention.

Maybe it's his height and the broadness of his shoulders.

Damn, he's fine.

Jed would say that so much better than I could. I can hear his voice in my head. When I tell him this at school on Monday, he's going to say something funny or come up with some kind of acronym to describe this guy. That's what my best friend does. He talks in acronyms.

My lips twitch with a smile that quickly disappears.

Because I am *still* staring at the stranger.

I haven't seen him down at this end of the beach, which immediately makes me wonder if he's a) a tourist or b) an Elite.

My eyes narrow slightly.

Yeah, he's definitely an Elite.

A Walton Academy rich boy.

I can tell by the way he's standing. Why I think rich private school guys stand differently to anyone else, I'm not sure, but as I get closer, I can make out the Walton Warriors emblem on his T-shirt.

What the hell is he doing at the south end?

The grip on my board tightens.

He's looking at me now.

Probably trying to work out if he knows me or something. Why else would a short surfer girl be staring at him?

I clench my jaw and attempt to look away, but my eyes are drawn right back.

Maybe it's not just the fact that he's good-looking. Although I love how tall he is. The top of my head probably reaches his shoulder. I'd have to go on my tiptoes to kiss him.

My eyes bulge for a second.

Kiss him?

What the hell, Harley!

Shut up! Just stop it!

I don't kiss guys. I mean, I'm not adverse to kissing them. I've kissed before, and sometimes it was nice, but there's a certain vulnerability with the act that I don't want to put myself through again.

I don't date. Dating leads to going steady, which leads to getting hurt.

No thank you.

I'll just stick with my surfing and my skating. Things I love. Things that won't let me down.

And that's when it hits me.

That's why I'm staring.

Not because this Elite is hotter than hot sauce. Not because he's tall and broad, with a square-cut chin and dark eyebrows. It's because he looks sad.

Defeated.

And a part of me seems to understand this emotion. Without even realizing it, I feel sorry for the pretty rich boy. But that doesn't mean I want to talk to him.

Oh crap, he's moving.

He's moving in my direction.

I swallow and force my eyes straight ahead.

Why did I stare?

Why did I feel sympathy?

I glance at my wrist, but I shouldn't bother. I hardly ever wear a watch, and I already know I'm going to be late for work. I'm always late for work when the surf reports are good. I don't even know why Mrs. Kransky tolerates it. Yet I still have my crappy job scanning groceries at the Freshmart—the grocery stores with the best deals in Ryder Bay. Why shop anywhere else?

He's getting closer.

I can see him growing bigger in my periphery.

Shit! What do I do?

I can't just stare at him for what feels like an eternity and then not acknowledge the guy when he walks up to me.

Why's he walking up to me?

Turning to look at the pier, I hide my cringe, then glance back to see that he's eight feet away.

His eyes are green.

Green and sad, with flecks of curiosity.

I spot a couple of whiteheads on his chin, and for some reason it makes me feel better. He's not perfect. He's human. He's a human teenager. A rich human teenager. An Elite.

Why do I find that so damn scary?

I don't want to be intimidated by anybody.

My nostrils flare.

He's two feet away and he stops, his long toes sinking into the sand in front of me.

I like the shape of his legs. They're long and muscular, with a fine coating of black hairs. Not like a blanket, just a dusting so I can still see the tanned skin beneath. His thigh muscles flex and my pace slows even though I don't want it to.

I won't be afraid of this guy.

I won't be afraid of anyone.

Just go for casual. Casual and cocky.

"Hey." He raises his chin at me, and I realize with a sinking heart how much I like the sound of his voice.

5

RAINBOW SPIKES FOR THE STICK BOY

AIDAN

She was staring at me for so long, I figured I may as well say hello to her.

I thought I might recognize her, but the closer I get, I realize she's a complete stranger.

"Hey." She responds to my greeting in a quiet voice that screams, *Please don't talk to me.*

But maybe I'm just imagining that. She *has* been checking me out the entire way up the beach.

I run a hand through my floppy hair and try to think of something to say. My parents always taught me to ask "new friends" a question about themselves. It makes them feel like you're interested, and it's a good way to get a conversation going.

Why I want to get a conversation going with this chick, I'm not sure.

I think I'm just curious.

"Good surf today?"

This makes her stop. She turns to stare out at the water, and I can hear the instant smile in her voice. "The best. Wish I didn't have to get out of the water."

"So why are you getting out of the water, then?"

She frowns and starts walking again, mumbling over her shoulder, "Work."

Huh. I wonder what kind of work she has to do on a Saturday afternoon.

My job is after school, two days a week, teaching elementary kids how to swim. Simon hooked me up with it last year. The rec center is run by his uncle, and it's just around the corner from Walton Academy. We do four back-to-back half-hour sessions working with small groups of kids on basic swimming techniques. I actually love it. The kids are super cute and enthusiastic.

I run to catch up with the surfer girl, wondering how she earns her cash. "Where do you work?"

She gives me a pointed look, and I'm struck by the brightness of her blue eyes. They're like pale sapphires, glinting with spunk and intelligence. "Wouldn't you like to know." She lays her board down, then unzips her backpack.

I stop behind her and cross my arms, trying for casual. "I wouldn't have asked if I didn't want to know."

She grins but doesn't look at me. "My mommy told me never to talk to strangers."

"And do you always do what your mother tells you?"

This makes her laugh, and I somehow feel triumphant.

She takes a long swig from her water bottle, then turns to me, her cheeks puffed out like a chipmunk. After a loud swallow, she wipes her lips with the back of her hand and admits, "Pretty much never."

I like the way her nose wrinkles.

She has a cute nose.

It's petite to match the rest of her, with just a smattering of freckles across the bridge.

I wonder how old she is. Am I talking to a freshman or a senior? She seriously could be either one. Skylar's like that, although my cousin has a look in her eyes that screams maturity...worldliness. If she wanted to, she could strut into a bar and I bet not one person in there would think she didn't belong.

This girl in front of me isn't like that, though. She has a young freshness about her.

A sporty...

She unzips her wetsuit and starts to wriggle out of it.

It's impossible not to look. The bikini she's wearing isn't one of those flimsy string things that Skylar and Savannah wear. It's got a sporty, practical edge to it. Vibrant blue with a black trim.

That's not why I'm staring.

She practically has a six-pack. I swear this girl is one tiny ball of muscle. I bet she could kick my ass if she wanted to.

As she bends over to pull the bottom of her wetsuit off, I get a clear shot of the shape of her tanned legs, her quads flexing as she balances on one foot. I can't help a thick swallow.

Her eyes shoot to mine and I get another pointed look.

"Sorry," I murmur, my cheeks flaring as I scratch the back of my neck and force my eyes to the ocean.

I focus on the surfers out in the water. One tall black guy is catching a wave, carving it up and making it look like a piece of cake.

I watch him until I hear a little throat clearing behind me.

When I spin back, she's pulling a baggy sleeveless top over her wet bikini. Two wet circles instantly grow where her small breasts are, but it doesn't seem to bother her. She bunches her hair behind her and starts squeezing the water out of it.

I watch it drip onto the sand.

"So, I don't see you down at this end of the beach much."

"Yeah, I..." I point towards the northern end, my words trailing off as I yet again feel like an imposter.

She flicks her hair over her shoulder and places her hands on her hips. She's studying me again. I don't know what the hell she's looking for, and I can't maintain eye contact.

I'm about to sniff and say my goodbyes when she shocks the hell out of me.

"Who dumped who?"

I glance up, my mouth agape until I see her expression. Her blue gaze is deep with empathy. She knows what this feels like.

With a heavy sigh, I droop my shoulders and mutter, "Isn't it obvious?"

"Not always." She shrugs. "Dumping someone can be just as painful as getting dumped." Balling up her towel, she shoves it into her backpack. Her statement makes me wonder if she's the dumper, but her actions scream loud and clear that she was the one who was dumped, thrown completely off balance the way I was.

"I didn't even see it coming," I admit, scrubbing a hand down my face then crossing my arms again. I don't seem to know what to do with my hands right now.

She smirks, but not in a bitchy way. "What happened?"

"I guess I'm just not cool enough for her anymore or something. She said she wasn't feeling it, and there's no point staying together if there's no future in it."

"Huh." She nods and gives me a closed-mouth smile. There's a kindness to it and my lips twitch in response, one corner rising to acknowledge her. Pulling her backpack on, she picks up her board and rests the end in the sand. "So, I'm guessing you looking lost down here means you're no longer part of the Elite, then?"

Okay, so we have a name down here.

I wonder if they know we refer to them as the hippies.

She's still staring at me, waiting for an answer, so I let out a scoffing laugh that's short and hard, unable to look her in the eye when I say, "Still part of it, just falling in the ranks."

"That's not necessarily a bad thing."

"Feels like a pretty damn sucky thing right now." I glance at her, my forehead bunching with a frown. I can feel it crinkling.

She shrugs. "Yeah, well, I'd see it as a chance to broaden your horizons. Get some decent perspective. Do something worthwhile with your time."

My frown deepens as I swivel my body to face her head on. "Are you telling me I'm narrow-minded?"

"Pretty much." She grins—killing my incredulity by looking so damn cute.

"Oh, yeah?" I'm losing the don't-give-into-a-smile battle and have to lick my lips to get them under control. "And what worthwhile thing should I be doing with my time?"

"You could always try surfing." Her bright eyes sparkle some more. They're kind of enchanting, which is a weird thing to think.

I rub a hand over my mouth, then go for a deadpan

look. I have no idea if I pull it off, but my voice sounds dry enough. "Surfing?"

Her smile grows a little bigger. "It's the best thing in the world, man. I can pretty much guarantee that it will dislodge that stick you have up your ass."

What the hell did she just say to me?

I'm not used to girls being so...so spiky? I don't know if that's the right word. Skylar's kind of spiky in a semi-evil way. But this chick, her spikes aren't so sharp. They're like rainbow spikes that are supposed to tease and tickle.

Once again I'm fighting a grin, and it takes all my willpower to keep my lips in line and my tone sarcastic. "You're so pleasant. No wonder you're surrounded with so many friends right now."

"Oh!" She laughs and flips me the bird. "At least I'm happier than you." Tucking the surfboard under her arm, she starts walking for the stairs.

I like the way her hips sway as she negotiates the sand.

Pausing at the base of the steps, she grabs a long skateboard from the grass.

Huh, a surfer and a skater girl. I don't know why I find that so cool.

Glancing over her shoulder, she gives me a brilliant smile and calls out, "Think about it, Stick Boy."

And I'm left in the sand, watching cutoff denim shorts and two tanned legs ascend the stairs.

I don't really know how to feel about the conversation we just had, but as my eyes track back to the waves and the surfers, a slow smile grows on my lips.

"Stick Boy," I murmur, shaking my head.

I should be insulted.

I should be frowning.

But all I can do is laugh.

Stick Boy.

No chick has ever called me that before.

Because that girl I just spoke to is like no chick I have ever met before.

6

THE GREAT DIVIDE

HARLEY

Stick Boy.

I called him Stick Boy!

I can't decide whether to shake my head in shame or laugh out loud. The look on his face when I insulted him. Classic.

"You're so pleasant," I mock his words and start laughing again.

Leaning into the curve, I round the corner on my skateboard and stop by our yellow mailbox. The paint is peeling, exposing patches of rusty metal beneath. It's kind of in keeping with our house, although the cream-colored paint peeling away from the weatherboards is exposing all manner of deterioration. I hate to think how rotted the wood must be by now.

I can't see it getting fixed anytime soon, though.

Our little house was built God knows how long ago, and I'm pretty sure it's had zero maintenance done on it since we moved in. All Mom and I have managed to do is fill it with stuff and ignore the leaks and cracks. I sometimes wonder if Grandpa would be disappointed in us, but I never knew the guy, so I try not to think about it.

Entering the cluttered carport, I rest my board against the one patch of wall that isn't taken up by a cracked mirror and an old mattress that is beginning to smell. My nose wrinkles as I park my skateboard next to it.

I don't know what the time is, but I know I'm late.

Pushing the front door open with a little help from my shoulder, I glance at the clock above the stove and swear. "Very, very late."

Looks like it'll be shower-in-a-can for me this after-noon. Rushing through the house, I pinch my nose against the lingering stench of smoke in the air.

Great. Mom's home.

She's probably sitting on her unmade bed, her eyes glued to some talk show while she puffs away on her cigarette.

I don't bother to call out a hello. She probably doesn't want me to interrupt her show anyway.

Grabbing the stick of deodorant off the bathroom windowsill, I lift each arm and rub plenty under each pit, then go a step further and snatch Mom's aerosol can and give myself a quick spray across the torso. The watermelon scent hits my skin and masks the salt and sweat.

Yes, I'm gross, but I'm late and I can't afford to get fired right now.

My boss gives me a little leeway because she's cool, but if I'm *too* late, I'll get a grilling. And if I want to eat half-decent food, then I need to earn some cash.

My mom works and all. She actually has two jobs: three days a week waitressing at the Fish Shack and five nights a week working at Sugar Pop, this seedy bar about fifteen minutes south of Ryder Bay. I hate that place. I've only been there once—last year when Mom locked herself out of her car and refused to get an Uber home. Instead I had to get an Uber there to deliver the spare key.

It was like two o'clock in the morning and I was pissed.

I told her as much, and she stopped talking to me for three days as punishment.

That's Mom for ya.

I don't know if I'll ever understand that woman.

Even though we got left this place by Grandpa, I'm assuming mortgage free, money is still tight, because Mom likes the good stuff. Not the healthy stuff like fresh fruit and vegetables, but the good stuff like the latest flat-screen TV mounted on her bedroom wall, the trips to the day spa so she can get her weekly mani-pedi, and of course the expensive wine bottles in the bottom of the fridge.

I've tried to get her to spend the money on things I need, like healthy food for a growing teenage girl, but she tells me that she grew up on chips and fast food and she turned out just fine.

She should take a look in the freaking mirror once in a while.

She did *not* turn out fine, and I refuse to end up looking like her.

So, if I want to eat food that doesn't come out of a package, foods that contain vitamins, minerals and things that will feed my muscles, then I have to earn my own money and pay for it myself.

Fresh fruit and vegetables shouldn't be so expensive.

I run my fingers through my wet, salty hair and attempt a ponytail. It ends up being a hash-job, a messy bun concoction, but it'll have to do.

Throwing on my pale blue pin-striped shirt with the *Freshest is the Bestest* slogan on the back, I avoid the mirror and head out the door.

"Harley? Is that you?"

I cringe and call out, "I'm late for work, Mom!"

"Come here."

Muttering a soft curse under my breath, I head back through our little living room, jumping over Mom's stack of gossip magazines in the hallway before pushing her door open. The cigarette smoke hits me straightaway and I wrinkle my nose.

Mom doesn't seem to notice how disgusting the

habit is. A stream of smoke billows out of her mouth as she points one of her long painted nails at me. "Where you been?"

"Surfing." My expression is no doubt telling her what a dumb question that is.

"I'm working tonight."

What else is new?

"You'll have to get your own dinner."

I get it every night anyway.

Holding in my snarky replies is hard work, but I clench my jaw. I've learned that the best way to keep peace in this house is to never bite back. If I talk back to her, she gets pissy with me, and her silent treatment is louder than a rock concert. I know that sounds weird, but the icy cloud that descends on this house when she's angry is unbearable.

Looking at my mom is always kind of depressing. We're alike in features—same blonde hair, blue eyes, petite frames. Even our noses match.

But I don't want to end up looking like her.

There are bitter wrinkles around her mouth, weary bags under her eyes, and just a general sense of discontent. She blames the world for her problems, and it shows.

I sometimes wonder how I stay living under the same roof as her, but it's not like I have anywhere else to go. Besides, maybe she needs me. Maybe I need her. Because she's all I've ever known.

"I gotta get to work," I murmur, backing out of the room, desperate for fresh air and escape.

"Have fun scanning groceries." She cackles.

I clench two fists and get out the door before I'm tempted to throw something or shout that at least I don't dress like a skank and work at some bar where men spend the night pawing my ass.

Mom would probably take pride in that fact.

With an irritated huff, I grab my skateboard and hit the road. I push as hard as I can to build up quick momentum and get away from my cruddy little house and super-annoying mother.

Why did I rush to work?

I hate this job.

Hiding it is sometimes an effort, and forcing a smile as I listen to that constant beep of groceries being scanned is doing my head in today.

The ocean was sweet this morning.

The waves are calling me.

And I'm stuck in a grocery store going brain dead with the mundane.

Well, I'm actually not going brain dead. If I'm honest, my brain is working overtime playing a game of dodge 'ems.

The thing I'm trying so desperately to dodge?

Pretty rich boy.

Stick Boy.

Whatever I want to call him.

His long torso and broad shoulders keep swirling through my mind. I keep trying to push it back, but then his face will bloom right in front of me. That square chin, those full lips as they tried not to smile at me.

Ugh! Harley, stop it! You're being ridiculous.

Clearing my throat, I square my shoulders in preparation for my next customer and try not to stiffen when I notice two teenage girls slip into my checkout.

They're not just any teenage girls.

They're Elites.

I can practically smell them coming. Their rich perfume and the way they strut, it kind of emanates from them, creating these long-reaching ripples that affect everyone in some way or another. I bet the guys drool over these two in their skimpy shorts and tanks tops. Their long hair is flowing down their backs like two dark waterfalls that curl and wave in just the right places.

They're both kind of gorgeous.

Annoyingly.

The short one has a hard, angular edge to her. She's skinny all the way and should probably be strutting a catwalk rather than standing in some cheap grocery store. The taller one is a little more average in size. She's not fat or chubby or anything, just normal-looking, with a pretty softness to her.

Soft or not, I bet she's still a bitch below the surface. Aren't they all?

What is it with today and encountering these people?

My nostrils flare as I force a friendly Freshmart smile.

The taller girl gives me a fleeting grin, her dimples flashing, but it quickly fades as the short sharpshooter fires off a quick round. "Oh, please." She rolls her eyes at me, then mutters to her friend, "Why are we shopping in this dive?"

"Because it's closer than home, and you wanted instant snacks."

"Remind me to just go with the hunger next time." She pulls a disgusted face, like even being in this place is giving her germs.

What a snob!

I try to hide my inner thoughts as they dump their groceries on the belt. I glance down at the pile of food, figuring out what I can as they inch towards me.

Freshly squeezed orange juice.

A pint of raspberries.

A bag of carrot and celery sticks.

And a bar of chocolate.

Huh. So they want to be healthy, but just can't quite resist the chocolate. Although it is dark. Okay, points to the rich girls for eating well.

Again, I keep the thoughts to myself as I scan the large bar of chocolate and slide it into the bagging area.

I'm on my own today and will need to bag these up once I've put them through. I don't mind so much. At least I don't have to make small talk with someone I work with. That's always so exhausting. Laughing at Roger's lame jokes or nodding and smiling at Tammy's endless stories about her super-hot, super-sweet, super-sexy boyfriend. Or the worst, listening to Nelly's puppy woes as she tries to train not one but *three* beagles. Ugh. Painful.

"Did you scan that twice?" The petite girl with large green eyes and an arrogant smirk tips her head at me.

"No." I give her a closed-mouth smile.

"Can you check?" Her tone is sharp and snarky, and if I didn't like her before, I definitely don't like her now.

I glance at my screen, even raising my finger to scan the list.

"Not scanned twice," I confirm.

"Right. I guess you know what you're doing." It's impossible to miss her scathing tone. "It's not like you need a degree to work in a place like this, but I'm assuming you need a little intelligence."

My insides start to roil, like the building of a wave inside of me. I try to stem it, hoping to hold back the tsunami wanting to spew out of my mouth.

I bet you haven't worked a day in your life, you spoiled little brat.

"Oh, and this." The taller girl grabs a pack of gum from the aisle racks and slaps it down on the belt.

"Savvy, it's not even sugar free." The short one

flicks her friend's hand away, then looks at me. "This place does *have* sugar-free gum, doesn't it? I notice your stock is very limited here. You don't have many of the brands I'm used to buying."

"Yes," I grit out. "We have sugar-free gum. If there's not any at this counter, you could try the next aisle over." I look at her friend while I'm saying it and she goes to move, but the short brat grabs her arm to stop her.

"That's not your job, Sav." She looks back at me. "It's hers. Now, would you please serve us properly, or do I need to talk to your manager?"

My guess is that she's just bored, and tormenting me is making her feel better about life, but having to move from my place behind the register and over to the next aisle is one of the most painful, humiliating things I've ever done.

But I do it.

Because I need this job.

Snatching out three different sugar-free gum flavors, I walk them back around to my counter and hold them out. "Which one would you like?"

The short girl sighs. "Again, not the brand we're used to."

"Well, maybe you shouldn't shop here again," I snap.

Shit, I can't help it. This chick is driving me nuts!

She raises one of her perfectly manicured eyebrows

at me. "I guess it just goes to show how different people are, even in this small town."

Ryder Bay has never felt so frickin' big than in this moment. The chasm between the north and the south has just grown a few miles wider. We're so obviously divided—the rich and the poor, the snobs and the worthless.

Her green eyes challenge me to battle, and I stupidly engage.

"Yeah, I guess you and I *are* really different."

"We most definitely are." She crosses her arms and gives me a blistering glare. "I am *nothing* like you, shop girl."

I give her a hard smile. "You're right. I do my best to avoid hanging out with bitches, whereas you have to hang out with one every single day." I point at her, making it very clear who I'm talking about, then quickly swipe all three packets of gum.

The two girls in front of me are momentarily shocked into silence, so I quickly mutter the total before I can think about what I actually just said to a customer. "That'll be $11.90."

"Oh." The short girl looks like she wants to throw up on my face. She points her manicured finger at me. "You are so getting your ass fired. Where's your manager?"

Shit! I press my lips together and internally give myself a thrashing for running my mouth off.

What other people think of you doesn't matter. It's their *problem, not yours.*

How many times do I have to tell myself that before I'll just shut up and listen?

Swallowing all my pride in one big gulp, I look the stupid cow in the eye and try to sound sincere. "I'm sorry. I shouldn't have been so rude. Please ignore what I just said."

This surprises her. She was getting ready for war, obviously hungry for the fight, and I just retreated. Crossing her arms, the bracelets on her wrist clink together and she narrows those green laser beams at me.

"Just let her keep the job, Sky," her tall friend murmurs, then looks at me. "She probably needs it."

Sky smirks. "You're right, Savvy, her poor, pathetic ass probably does. I'll make you my charity case for the day and let you stay working here in this *amazing* job."

Hold your tongue. You can do it, Harley. Hold. Your. Tongue!

"Thank you," I rasp between clenched teeth. My cheeks feel like they're on fire as I quickly bag the groceries and hand them over.

With a triumphant simper, she snatches the bag from my hand and struts out the door.

I slump back against the counter and watch them walk to their lush convertible and jump in like two Hollywood starlets. Tires squeal as the rich bitches fly away from the poor, degrading coop they've just had to shop in.

I roll my eyes and try to ignore the burning sulfur climbing up my throat.

Apologizing to that girl was like downing a bottle of glass shards.

7

A SLOW TRIP TO LOSER-VILLE

AIDAN

I drive the long way home from the beach, winding my way through the southern streets before finally turning north and heading to my subdivision. It really is a different world up here.

The homes in Ryder Bay south look like they've been plucked straight from the sixties. They have hippy beach shack written all over them. It makes me conjure up images of what Ryder Bay must have looked like decades ago—free-spirited surfers living out of cars and vans, smoking pot around a beach fire.

Was that what it was like?

I turn left and drive down each cul-de-sac before getting to my street. Hopefully no one will notice me slowly meandering through our area.

Our houses are big. Two, sometimes three stories.

White. There's a lot of white in our suburb. White with tinted glass. White angles, sharp and clean. Nothing rustic about Ryder Bay's Clifton Terrace.

I slow as I pass Savannah's house. She lives about five streets down from mine. A six-minute walk. Her father's black Audi is parked in the driveway, which means he's home looking after Savannah's younger brother and sister. Which means my girl—my ex-girl—is probably not home. She's no doubt out with Skylar, doing girly shit and getting ready for Craig's celebration party.

Do I even want to go?

No.

I run a hand through my hair and accelerate out of Savannah's street.

What will people think if I don't show up? Will they even notice?

Savvy will be there, looking super hot in whatever outfit she's "thrown" together.

A grin twitches my lips. She always says that, so casual with a flick of her fingers. "Oh, I just threw this together, no big deal."

I call bullshit.

Savannah likes to look pretty. She deliberates and carefully selects whatever she's going to wear. And it pays off, because she always looks amazing.

Amazing...and no longer mine.

My forehead creases just as images of a very different girl swirl through my head. No makeup, no obvious thought put into what she's wearing. Just a sun-kissed surfer girl who's passionate about the water.

I wonder what it'd be like to feel that way about something.

I've never felt that kind of drive or passion about swimming. Maybe I did as a kid, but since I got serious with it, it's just become something I've done because I'm good at it. I don't hate it or anything, but my eyes don't dance when I talk about diving into a pool. I don't think it's the best thing in the world.

Finally reaching my street, I accept the inevitable and turn towards my place. I pull into my parking space at the bottom of our steep driveway and notice both my parents' cars are in the garage.

Great. So everyone's home, then. And they've left the door open for me.

Holding in my sigh, I grab my swim bag and get out of the car. As I walk up the internal staircase, I try to put on a brave face. I don't want to talk about the swim meet.

Actually, I don't want to talk at all.

Closing the door that opens to the foyer as quietly as I can, I wince when my twerp brother comes sauntering past, ready to head upstairs.

"Nice loss today." He smirks. "I'm so glad I made the effort to come."

I hold up my clenched fist in silent warning. "It's

not like you watched the races anyway, you little screen addict."

He snickers and disappears.

I shake my head and try not to despise him. He's thirteen and a little shit, but he's still my brother. Hopefully one day he'll grow out of his douche-baggery and be someone cool to hang out with.

"Aidan, is that you, honey?" my mom calls from the kitchen.

I iron out my expression, ensuring I'm in neutral before ambling down the two tiled steps and into the open-plan living area.

Our house is white too.

White and shiny, with polished tiles in the kitchen and living area and glass walls so we can look out at the ocean. Uncle Jeff scored us a really nice pad here. Mom was pretty much sold the second she walked into the living space. Cliff-top views of the Pacific—you can't really beat that.

She's at the counter, chopping bell peppers for a platter she's preparing. Cheese, crackers, hummus, dips —the works. Dad's opening a bottle of red so they can start their weekend tradition of nibbles before dinner.

We used to do it as a family, play board games together while we snacked. But not so much anymore. I'm usually heading out with my friends.

Although, I'm not sure I feel like it tonight.

Mom glances up from the chopping board, giving me a bright smile.

It's forced. I can see the strain around her eyes.

Why didn't you win today? That's what she wants to say, but instead she asks, "Where have you been?"

"Just hanging out." I shrug.

"With Savannah?"

I steal a rice cracker off the wooden tray and shove it in my mouth before I have to answer.

Dad starts pouring wine into two bulbous glasses. I watch the red liquid slosh against the sides. "I feel like we haven't seen Savvy in a couple of weeks."

"She's busy with Skylar this afternoon," I hedge.

So yeah, I still haven't told my parents that my girl-friend dumped me. They love Savannah, and they'll want to know what happened.

How the hell should I know?

She's not into me anymore. I don't know what I did or said to make that happen, and maybe I don't want to know. Maybe it's been this slow thing that's happened over time. Me in love and blissfully unaware while my girlfriend feels less and less attracted to me.

It's freaking depressing.

Mom laughs. "Knowing those two, they'll be up to their eyeballs in piles of dresses, trying to figure out what they're going to wear tonight."

My mom has a really beautiful smile. It's wide and kind of takes over her face.

I wish I could tell her the truth, but that would eliminate her grin, and I just can't bring myself to do it.

I've already disappointed my parents enough for one day.

Dad's grinning now too as he teases Mom about how bad she used to be.

"I'd be there on time to pick you up and you'd always make me wait. Sweating on the couch while your dad grilled me about where I was going to take his precious daughter."

"Oh, stop." Mom flicks a celery stick at him. He catches it and shoves it in his mouth while she tries to stand up for herself. "I wanted to look perfect for you."

"Baby, you could have been wearing a garbage bag and I would have thought you were perfect." He hands her a glass of wine and pecks her lips as if I'm not standing there watching.

I grab another couple of rice crackers and turn to leave the room.

"So, what time are you leaving, hon?" Mom says to my back.

"Not sure." I shrug and spin to face her but continue walking backwards.

"Okay, well, we're heading out for dinner at Uncle Jeff and Aunt Marlo's place. Grayson is staying over at Marty's house."

I nod, relieved to have the place to myself.

"Not sure what time we'll be home, but please just make sure you don't drink and drive, okay?"

"Mom, I never do."

"I know." She nods. "If you do want a beer tonight,

I'm okay with that, but make sure you take one from our fridge and don't have any more than that."

"Mom." I roll my eyes and tip my head back. We have this conversation every time I go out.

It's pretty cool that my parents are okay with underage drinking, as long as it's only a little, but do we have to talk about it every single time?

Part of me wants to tell her that I probably won't even bother going. Now that I know they won't be here, I don't have to make up an excuse to stay home. I can just hide out in my room playing Fortnite. It's way more appealing than hanging out on the beach watching my friends get trashed and pining for the girl I can't have.

"I'm just saying." Mom raises her hands as two white flags. "I don't want you getting drunk."

"I won't get drunk," I mutter and turn to escape.

"When you see Savvy tonight, say hi from us," Dad calls out. "We miss seeing her around here. Make sure she knows she's welcome anytime."

I wave my hand in acknowledgment before disappearing from view.

Taking the stairs two at a time, I brush past Grayson without talking to him and shut my door. As soon as that wood closes behind me, I shut my eyes and plunk down into my beanbag at the end of my bed.

My fingers tremble as I scrape them through my hair.

Shit. This is messed up.

A vibration in my back pocket alerts me to the fact that I've got a text, and probably a couple more that I ignored while driving. I yank out my phone to check them.

Craig: Party starts at eight. Be there.

Simon: You going to the party? Can you pick me up?

Jonah: Si says you can be driver tonight. Pick me up at eight.

Simon: Dude, are you there?

Me: (To all) Have to bail tonight. Have a good one.

Before I can get any reply texts, I switch off my phone and dump it on the bed behind me. Simon will get it. He's seen how heartbroken I've been over Savvy. Craig and Jonah will hassle me senseless next time I see them, but I don't give a shit.

I've been dropping in the ranks for a few months now. I don't even know when it started happening. I can't think of one specific turning point; it's been more like a slow deterioration into Loser-ville.

Savvy dumping me was the last straw.

I don't want to be around my friends while they laugh and get drunk tonight.

I just want to disappear.

Picking up the controller off the floor, I set up for a new game of Fortnite Battle Royale. If anything can distract me, it's getting lost in a fictional world where I have to kill as many people as I can to survive.

Hopefully the distraction will make me feel better.

8

BEST FRIENDS AND QUESTION MARKS

HARLEY

Monday already.

Yay!

That's sarcasm. The yay part.

I'm not one of those "I love school" kind of students.

I go to school because I need a high school diploma, and that is the only reason.

Flicking my skateboard up, I grab the end and tuck it under my arm. I have a couple of different boards—a long one, which I prefer, and then my shorty, which is the only one that fits in my locker at school.

I wrestle it into the tight space and yank out my chemistry book.

I still don't know why I have to take chemistry when I have absolutely no interest in it. I'd like to know whose brain fart it was to make all students study science. Next year will be physics. Oh joy! Thankfully I can select most of my other classes. I've decided to ignore all of the guidance counselor's advice and just take the subjects that are mildly interesting to fulfill my graduation requirements. I figure, what's the point of suffering more than I have to? I may as well enjoy my final year.

It's not like I can afford to go to college, and there's no way I'm smart enough to get a scholarship. I'm probably eligible for some financial aid, but the big question is whether Mother Dearest will make up the deficit. I guess it depends what mood she's in when I ask her.

I find it best not to think about it.

Who knows what I'll end up doing, but at least I'll have my diploma. Maybe I can eventually save up to attend a community college or something. Apparently there are some good ones in San Diego. I still have time.

Slamming my locker shut, I swing my bag off my shoulder to fit the textbook into it.

It's kind of scary to think that I only have one year and about four weeks of high school left.

I'm excited about the freedom of not studying, but if I'm honest, I'm terrified about the big question mark that looms over my future.

Yes, I have time. If I live to like ninety years old, eighteen isn't even a quarter of my life done.

I could travel, surf the globe, and get a whole bunch of life experience before figuring out what I really want to do with my life.

Surf the globe? With what money, dumbass?

I ignore the voice of practicality and figure dreaming never hurt anyone.

White beaches, blue ocean, exotic food. Oh yeah, I can see my future already.

"Morning, HQ." Jed stops beside me, breaking my fantasy but not my smile.

Jed—aka Jeremiah Elijah Dellaney—is my best friend. BMF in Jed speak—Best Male Friend. I seriously do not need the M part in the middle because I have no other friends. He is it. My best friend. My BF. Although, I think deep down he hopes I'll get some girly friends one day. It'll give him someone to flirt with.

I spin to face him, and my grin grows a little wider. He's wearing his standard horizontal stripes and a pair of black jeans. It doesn't matter what time of the year it is, what day, what season—Jed lives in black jeans and bright stripy T-shirts. He's sporting a hot pink and cobalt blue stripe today, and damn if he doesn't pull it off like a king.

"I know." He points to himself. "I look hot, you don't have to say it. FFG is working it today, baby."

I laugh and shake my head. Jed's always doing that, making jokes to cover up the fact that he's a big guy. I kind of hate that he calls himself FFG. It stands for

Funny Fat Guy. I think he does it as a way to counter the inevitable bullying.

He got it pretty bad in middle school. We weren't friends then. He didn't move to Ryder Bay until a couple of years ago. If we had been friends back then, I would have kicked their asses.

Jed's not actually that fat.

I mean, yes, he's round and he has a bit of a belly on him. There's some chub under his chin, and when he runs, things wobble. But I love him just the way he is. He's like a cuddly bear—not that I'll ever tell him that.

I didn't plan on being Jed's friend. I'm a loner. I've learned that's the safest way to live, but when he arrived sophomore year, Jed decided he wanted to be my friend, and he just hounded me until I eventually capitulated and stopped trying to ditch him around every corner.

We now eat lunch together almost every day.

And we always meet up before school for a quick catch-up.

There's still twenty minutes before the first bell rings, so we wander out to the quad. May as well catch a few rays before we're forced back inside.

"So, how was your weekend?" Jed plunks down at one of the picnic tables.

"Not bad." I bob my head. "Yours?"

"Working most of it," he mumbles.

"How's it going? Is your grams a tough boss?"

"Nah. She's cool." Jed bobs his head. His grandmother is in charge of the admin and cleaning staff at the local hospital. That's what brought them to Ryder Bay. Jed lives permanently with his grandparents. Apparently his teen mom couldn't handle things. He hasn't seen her since he was three, and he doesn't like to talk about it.

Anyway, Mrs. Dellaney moved the family to Ryder Bay when she got the job at Aviemore Hospital. It's not a huge hospital, just big enough to cater to Ryder Bay residents. I have no idea how many doctors work there, but it caters to all local emergencies and illnesses. Anything really major gets sent south to one of the bigger towns.

"You like it, though? Think you'll stick with it?" I ask. He's only had the job for a few weeks.

"Yeah, it's good enough. I mean, it's cleaning." He pulls a face. "But it's money in my pocket."

"Still saving for a car?"

"Not sure." He shrugs. "I'm wondering about saving up to do some kind of road trip after we graduate." He wiggles his eyebrows at me. "We could drive the coast. You could surf your little heart out."

"And what would you do?" I raise my eyebrows at him.

"Work on my tan and pick up hot chicks on the beach."

I giggle and shake my head. Jed is already as black as night. I love the color of his skin, and the kindness of his brown eyes.

I point at him. "To do all that, we need a car."

"Good point." Jed nods. "So I'll save for the car, and you can save for supplies and traveling cash."

"Accommodations?" I ask.

Jed doesn't even have to think about it. "We'll buy a station wagon and sleep in the back."

I actually love the sound of that and show him with an approving smile that he quickly wipes off my face. "So, how's work for you? Freshmart treating you well?"

With a harsh scoff, I scowl and tell him about the two bitchy girls I had to deal with on Saturday. "I really hate my job, but I don't know what else I'm supposed to do. I just wish I could earn some cash doing something I enjoy."

"OTD."

"What does that mean?" My forehead wrinkles as I try to work out his latest acronym.

"Oh totally, dude."

I'm instantly fighting a grin. "That's not... that's not a thing."

"Yeah, it is." He looks slightly offended. "It's *my* thing. And it's gonna catch on. You'll see."

"OTD," I say, albeit sarcastically. A smile curls my lips as I lose the battle. I can't help it. Jed can be a dork, but a very lovable one.

"Well, what about that guy you saw on the beach, the sad sack who asked you about surfing? Why don't you offer to teach him?"

I knew I'd regret telling him about that. I wish we'd

never started our text-a-thon last night, but he asked about the surf and of course I had to respond, and one text led to another.

It was annoying that I still had pretty rich boy on my brain nearly forty-eight hours after I'd spoken to him.

My nose wrinkles. "How did we go from grocery store snobs to hot guy on the beach?"

"Oh, so he's hot now?" Jed smirks. "You didn't say that in your texts last night."

I glare at him, which only makes him laugh. He has a loud, barking kind of laugh that always draws attention. I hunch my shoulders and rest my arms on the table, my glare still intact as I wait it out.

Jed clears his throat as he tries, and fails, not to grin at me.

"Come on, HQ. Stop looking at me like that." He taps my hand. "I meant why don't you offer him lessons and he pays for them? A way to earn money doing something you love."

"That's a stupid idea." I shake my head and start nibbling my thumbnail.

"No, it's not," he counters. "It's freaking brilliant."

"Well, I don't like your brilliant, stupid idea." My shoulders are tensing. I can feel it. I want to stop talking about this guy.

"Fine." Jed pulls his 'screw you' face and feigns insult. I know he's faking his anger. Jed doesn't know how to get mad at me. He probably doesn't know how to get mad at anyone. He's just that kind of a guy. Laid-back and patient to the extreme.

I roll my eyes as he refuses to look at me and then goes a step further by driving his point home. "You just keep scanning those groceries, girl. You just go ahead and earn your minimum wage when you could be charging some rich guy like fifty bucks an hour to surf dem waves."

I groan and throw my head back to the sky.

Dammit! Why does he have to be right!

Teaching someone to surf would be easy money. Good money.

Fun money.

I give in with a sigh and have to agree with my friend, but it's not really a way out of Freshmart.

That guy. Mr. Rich Boy. He'll never go for it. It wasn't like he was enthusiastic about surfing. When I told him he should try it, he didn't even look interested. But man, earning money to do what I love would be pretty damn awesome.

The bell rings, reminding me that awesome will just have to wait.

With resigned smiles, we leave our sunny picnic table and head into the gloom of Ryder Bay High School.

Thank God there's only four weeks to go before summer freedom is ours.

9

BUSY GETTING BASIC

AIDAN

Walton Academy looks like a Spanish monastery with its terra cotta-tiled roof and white walls.

More white.

How have I never noticed this before? It's like I'm surrounded by it. Every building I hang out in is white. Even the rec center where I teach after-school swimming to elementary kids. The revelation almost stops me in my tracks, which is dumb.

But why?

What makes white so great?

What the hell is so appealing about a white building?

I think about the lime-green house I drove past on Saturday afternoon, when I was avoiding going home.

And the run-down pale blue one. And then there was that yellow one with the navy trim. That one screamed vacation home. It looked empty when I drove past but would probably be overflowing with people throughout the summer months.

Ryder Bay always balloons in the summer, its edges getting round and taut as more and more vacationers fill in the spaces.

It's good for business, no doubt.

It's actually really good for the travel agency businesses too. When Ryder Bay gets too full, our crowd gets out. Many of the families who live around us will split to Europe, or go on a cruise, for the summer. We go every other year, so it means this year we'll be kicking it in Ryder Bay for the summer.

Sigh. I don't want to think about it.

It was the end of last summer that Savannah and I got together. She'd been stuck in Ryder Bay since her dad had to work at the hospital—he's a doctor—and she had to look after her siblings, Scarlett and Louis. I'd returned from our beach holiday before Skylar had. My family had spent two weeks at a luxury resort in Mexico, while Skylar and her parents had flown to France for a month. So Savannah and I hung out, like every spare second, until Skylar returned.

Then two days before school began, she kissed me.

My junior year had been nothing but a sweet ride, until it wasn't. Until I started losing races to Simon and then Craig. Did they just get stronger and faster than me while I stayed stagnant?

Is that why Savannah got over me? Because I was no longer the best?

Walking up the wide steps, I glance left in time to see Grayson disappear into the middle school area before I veer right into the high school. Next year he'll be roaming these halls with me, forced to wear a navy-blue tie with a crisp white shirt and blue blazer with yellow trim. Apparently dressing like some elite businessman will make us learn better.

Grayson will hate it.

I snicker. Right now, he's still rocking the cotton polo shirt. I can't wait to see him get pinged for having his white shirttail sticking out as he swaggers around the high school. He doesn't know what's gonna hit him.

Open archways span the outer corridors, leading off to green patches of lawn. The edges are beautifully trimmed, the vibrant grass begging you to lie down and take a nap in the sun.

Man, that's tempting.

I stayed up way too late last night playing Fortnite. It was lucky I didn't have practice this morning. Coach let us have the morning off, and our practice schedule would be pretty light for the rest of the year.

It was nice to sleep in for a change, but I'm still toasted.

I turn away from the grass and head into the school building.

My locker is on the first floor, second corridor on the right. As I round the corner, my gut sinks.

Craig is standing near my locker, surrounded by girls…and a few guys. Skylar is hanging off his arm like a piece of jewelry, and he's flashing his silver and gold medals like he was the only team member to get any.

I spot Simon as he's walking towards me, rolling his eyes. The guy's actually a little taller than me, overtook me during spring break. I don't mind so much. If Craig had beaten me on that score too, I'd be struggling with it.

Simon didn't bring any medals to school today. Knowing him, they're probably piled away in some drawer that he'll never open again.

"Hey, man." He raises his chin at me. "You all right?"

I nod.

"We missed you at the party."

I snicker and shake my head. "You probably didn't even notice I wasn't there."

"Yeah, I did. I needed a ride home," he jokes, nudging me with his elbow.

I give him a gentle shove, then point down the corridor at Craig's arrogant ass. "Unbelievable."

"I know. Like the guy's head isn't big enough already."

We both laugh and start moving towards our teammate.

I don't really want to go that direction. Savannah's down there, hovering behind Skylar like her personal assistant.

I want to catch her eye, smile at her, give her a little wink like I used to.

But apparently I'm not allowed to do that anymore, because she's no longer my girl.

I stare at her anyway until her gaze flutters past me. She bites her bottom lip and looks to the floor, her long brown hair falling off her shoulder. I wish I could brush it back the way I used to. I love her hair. It's thick but soft, with this sweet wave to it. My fingers tingle with longing. I clench my fists at my side and flinch when the bell rings above my head.

Students disperse like ants breaking formation, but I keep my eyes on Savannah while she waits for her best friend.

Skylar detaches herself from Craig, but not before giving him a hot kiss that we all have to witness. Savannah's cheeks flush pink and she looks away, tapping her finger against her arm. She's always so patient and loyal with Skylar. They've been tight ever since middle school.

"Joined at the hip." My mom always laughs about it.

When Skylar pulls away, Craig gives her a hungry smile and butt tap that makes me want to punch him.

He glances up and spots me glaring at him, then raises his chin in greeting.

"Where was your loser ass on Saturday, De Beer?"

I shrug and mutter, "Got busy."

"Got basic," he counters before sauntering off with an arrogant swagger that makes me want to double punch him.

"Morning, sunshine." Skylar winks and waves her fingers at me.

I grunt and turn for my locker while she giggles, then links her arm with Savannah's and struts off down the hallway.

I wrench open my locker, quickly changing my books and trying to ignore Craig's dig. He's just pissed off that I didn't show up to *his* party. Offended that I don't want to worship the ground he walks on and kiss his heels like everyone else at this school.

Simon gives me a pained smile that doesn't make me feel any better, so I flick my locker shut and force a grin. "Catch you later, man. I gotta hit the head before class."

We'd usually walk the same direction, as our home-rooms are pretty close together, but I choose the most out-of-the-way bathroom I can, desperate for space.

Space from everyone trying to figure out what's wrong with me.

Space from the reminder that school is not the same cool place it used to be.

10

WHERE'S A GOOD SALESMAN WHEN YOU NEED ONE?

HARLEY

As soon as school gets out, I yell goodbye to Jed and jump on my skateboard. The poor sucker is heading off to work, but lucky me is heading to the beach.

I skate home as fast as I can and am relieved to see that Mom's car is not in the driveway. She must have left for Sugar Pop already. Sometimes she does an earlier shift there.

Suits me. I don't want to have to contend with her anyway. Not when there's a sweet swell and the waves are calling me. I snuck a look at the surf report during last period. I don't want to be wasting precious time out of the water.

Dumping my backpack on the floor in my room, I

ignore the thunk of books hitting the scratched wooden boards. Homework can wait. I throw off my clothes, leaving them in a pile on the bathroom floor, and shimmy into my orange bathing suit. Out of all my swimwear, it's the driest one hanging over the towel bar.

Rushing through the house, I don't bother with my wetsuit and throw on a rash guard instead. It's warmer than it was over the weekend, and the lighter fabric should be all right at this time of day. I yank a yellow towel off the line and run for my skateboard.

A smile is stretching across my face as I power away from my house, my phone, my school bag—anything that ties me to the pressures of real life.

All I care about right now is the ocean.

I can smell the salty air before I reach the sand. It usually takes me about fifteen minutes to board to the beach, unless I choose to go the long way. I don't do that too often, but the hill that goes from the north and bends around the coastline is pretty damn fun to ride.

Not today, though.

I just need to get into the water.

After a day of sitting in a stuffy classroom, I'm ready to burn off some energy.

Dumping my board and towel in the sand, I hitch my shortboard under my arm and run to the water. As soon as that salty spray hits my skin, I feel instantly better about life.

I spend a couple of hours surfing alongside a guy with shoulder-length dreadlocks. We don't say anything to each other, just share a couple of friendly smiles and respect each other's space. The waves are consistent enough to keep me going, but they start to die off as the winds change. I catch a piddly one in before finally calling it quits and heading up the beach.

Axel and his crew haven't been around this afternoon.

Conditions must be better at Hatchet Cove. That's my guess anyway.

It's definitely more peaceful without them around dominating the waves. I glance over my shoulder and notice Mr. Dreads has given up as well. He's walking north up the beach. I don't know his name, but I've definitely seen him around. I think he works on the beach somewhere. I've seen him talking to the head lifeguard, but I haven't seen him in a uniform, so he must do something else near the water.

Rubbing my face dry, I wrap my towel around myself and perch on the top of my board. The small amount of cloud cover on the horizon is going to make for a stunning sunset. It's tempting to stay and watch it.

Stretching out my legs, I bury my wet toes in the sand and figure I might as well. Nothing but homework is drawing me home. Dinner can be leftovers from the stir-fry I made last night, unless Mom's eaten it. I roll my eyes and hope the amount of vegetables I shoved in it will have been enough to put her off.

With a contented sigh, I gaze out at the water. The pier is a crooked finger pointing out to sea—I always like to think of it that way—like an old lady telling us to not miss the vibrant orange ball that dips below the horizon each night.

I rest my forearms on my knees and link my fingers. My insides feel warm and happy as I watch the sky slowly change.

A couple walks along the beach, their feet splashing in the water while their two kids run ahead, laughing as they drag a long tail of seaweed behind them.

Other than that, the beach is kind of quiet tonight.

I don't mind so much, although it's a shame that people are missing out on this sunset.

Glancing right, I spot a tall figure walking my way. He's dressed in running gear and must be doing some kind of resistance training on the sand. I always admire that. Although this guy's not running, he's walking. Must have run out of steam.

I gaze back at the ocean but can see the guy out of the corner of my eye. He's walking towards me still. Like directly at me.

My eyebrows dip together, and I glance back to get a proper look at him.

Oh crap, it's pretty rich boy.

I swallow and try to pretend like I haven't seen him.

But he makes it impossible when he walks all the way up to me and stands at the end of my board.

"Hey." He gives me a sad smile and I know I have to be nice to him.

I just wish my heart wouldn't pinch so tight at the idea of talking to him again.

Act casual, Harley. Play it cool.

"What are you doing here?" I swipe a drying tendril of hair off my cheek. "Hiding out from your friends again?"

"I don't know." He sighs and slumps down beside me, his neon blue sneakers getting covered with sand. His broad shoulders round as he draws his knees up and rests his forearms on them.

I stretch out my legs and cross my ankles, not wanting to be sitting the same way he is. It's also a good opportunity to inch away from his bare skin.

He's wearing a sleeveless tank tonight, and damn his arms are nice. Muscly. I like the shape of them—the curve and the definition.

This irritates me, so I force my eyes away and look out at the sky. It's changed again, the colors turning from blues and purples to light pinks and orange. I love the way the light coats the bottom of the clouds. They're not always painted this way, and it's my favorite kind of sunset.

The morose guy lets out another heavy sigh and my eyes dart towards him. I give his ankle a nudge with my foot. "Come on, dude, the sun is about to set.

Look at that beautiful sky." I point to it. "You're not allowed to be sad when you look at a sky like that, so you can just take your rain cloud butt and march it back to the north end if you're going to ruin this moment for me."

An instant grin changes his entire face, lifting the corners and making his green eyes glint for a moment. Without a word, he shifts his butt in the sand, like he's getting comfortable, and gazes out across the ocean.

Silence settles between us, and I can sense his body starting to relax beside me. His shifting around has put us closer together. I can feel the heat radiating from his legs. It's hitting my cooling skin and giving me tingles.

"Wow," he murmurs, his expression one of awe as the sun dips a little lower, making the orange and yellow hues burn like gold.

"It's my happy place, you know." I keep my voice soft, not wanting to shatter this moment. "The sand. The sun." I smile. "The water."

"It used to be mine too." He tips his head, then looks at me. "The water, I mean. I'm a swimmer. Compete for my school."

"Nice," I murmur. I should have guessed that. Swimmers always have broad, muscly shoulders. Sometimes it even puts their bodies out of proportion, but not this one. He's got a great frame and structure.

A great frame and structure? Harley, shut the hell up!

Pretty rich boy lets out a hard laugh and shakes his head. "It used to be nice. I used to win everything, but in the last year…" His jaw works to the side and he lets out a brittle laugh. "I'm just not feeling it."

"Well, maybe you need to change your water."

"Huh?" He glances at me, his frown kind of adorable.

I grin at him. "You know, change chlorine for salt?"

This makes him laugh for real. "Are you saying the ocean's better than a swimming pool?"

"Hell yeah!" My voice pitches high with enthusiasm. "Natural, beautiful ocean with waves you can ride and living amazing creatures beneath you. Ocean beats pool every time."

He opens his mouth but then closes it again. I wonder if he was going to argue with me, but then he gazes back at the water for a moment before turning to me. "You really love surfing, don't you?"

"Best thing in the world." I can tell I'm smiling big-time. Even my voice sounds like its smiling. His lips twitch as he studies me and before I can change my mind, I blurt, "I can teach you if you want."

His head jerks back like I've just told him I have two extra arms hiding behind my back.

I don't know whether to be offended or not, but Jed's voice is rocketing through the back of my brain, goading me on. I could be earning cash doing something I love!

Okay, I have to sell this and make it sound good. "If you pay me."

His eyebrows, which I didn't think could go any

higher up his forehead, inch just a little farther as he asks, "Pay you?"

Wow. Great sales pitch, Harley. I internally roll my eyes at how stupid I am, then force a smile. "Yes. Surfing lessons."

"You give surfing lessons? You're a surf instructor?"

I swallow, and my head starts doing this weird bobbing thing, like I'm one of those bobblehead dolls on a car dashboard. "Well... I mean, I can be."

His eyes narrow as he readjusts his position in the sand so he's facing me. His bent knee brushes against my ankle, and it's an effort not to jerk away like I'm electrocuted.

Forget about his legs and focus on the sale!

I put on my brightest smile. "If I'm honest, you would be my first client, but a business has to start somewhere, right?"

He starts to laugh, and it looks like I can safely rule out a career in sales. I wrinkle my nose while he snickers at me, then nudge his shoulder with my fist. "Oh, come on. Surfing is cool. You want to get your mojo back and impress those prissy Elite girls? Become a surfer. Some of the guys who surf this beach are sexy as hell, and girls come down to check them out all the time." I cringe. I'm seriously messing this up and should probably shut the hell up, but I can't leave it there.

He has to know.

I have to make him understand.

"But more important than all that stuff, surfing is like..." I stretch my arms wide, trying to figure out how to put something so epic into words. "Okay, so, being one with the water, carving up a wave, feeling that energy flow beneath you...there's nothing like it. I swear, man. It'll change your life."

11

HARLEY QUESTION MARK

AIDAN

Change my life.

I kind of like the sound of that.

This girl's passion is pretty damn compelling. As the last of the sun illuminates her features, turning them bright and beautiful with its golden hue, I'm struck by just how badly I want to say yes.

Even just for the chance to hang out with her some more.

And maybe she's right. Maybe learning to surf will help me find my confidence again. Savannah and Skylar are always ogling the surfers. Maybe if I become one of them, Savvy will want me back.

In the meantime, it'll be a damn good distraction.

"Okay." I nod. "How much do you charge?"

The girl's nose wrinkles like she's only just thinking about it.

Starting a business my ass. She's doing this on the fly.

"Uh…" She shrugs. "Fifty?"

"For how many lessons?"

"One." She holds up her index finger.

I gape at her for a second then laugh. "Fifty bucks for one lesson?"

"What?" She frowns at me. "You can afford it."

"How would you even know that?" I give her a matching scowl. "You just assume because I go to Walton Academy that I'm rolling in money, I sleep on hundred-dollar bills, and use fives to wipe my ass?"

She snorts and lets out a quick laugh. It's not a cute sound to match her size, more like a low, husky giggle, but I like the melody of it.

"Okay, fine. What do you think is fair, poor man?"

I look at her, fighting a grin as we enter into serious negotiations.

Rocking back on my butt, I do some quick calculations in my head. I'm not going to borrow money off my parents. For some reason I don't want them knowing about this. If I say I'm taking up surfing, they'll want details. And details will lead to conversations about my future and how I should be spending my time, and won't that take me away from my friends, and school, and Savannah?

I swipe a hand over my mouth. I earn about ninety bucks a week teaching swimming lessons…

"I'll give you thirty bucks for two lessons a week."

She tips her head, then shrugs and says, "Make it forty and you've got a deal."

I can't help my scoff. She drives a hard bargain.

"What?" She spreads her arms wide. "If you're motivated, you'll only need like four or five lessons anyway. Then it's just up to you to practice. I'll provide a longboard to start, and then you can buy your own when you're ready to practice without me."

This makes me hesitate. Buying my own board? How the hell will I keep that under wraps?

The girl holds out her hand. "Do we have a deal?"

Screw it. I'll figure out the board thing later. For all I know, I might hate surfing.

"All right, deal." As I wrap my hand around her small digits, I get an overpowering feeling that I won't hate it. I won't hate it at all. "So, when do you want to start?"

She lets go of my hand. "You free Wednesday morning before school?"

With the swim season wrapped up, I can probably drop to training only three mornings a week, so I nod. "I can swing it."

"Good. Meet me here at six. We can squish in an hour before heading off to school."

"Okay." I nod.

She nods back and then gets up to leave.

The sun has basically disappeared now. Only a blinding beam of orange highlights the horizon.

"Just one more thing." I reach out and grab her wrist without thinking about it.

"What?" She goes still, giving me that pointed look of hers. It's impossible to miss, even in the fading light.

I let her go and stand up, brushing the dry sand on the side of my shorts. Now that I'm standing next to her, I'm aware of how much taller I am. This chick's about the same size at Skylar, only just reaching my shoulders.

"What?" She's still waiting for me to talk.

I shake thoughts of our height difference out of my mind and smile. "I think I should know the name of my surf instructor."

She laughs, and I swear there's a blush on her cheeks. "Yeah, of course. Sorry. It's Harley."

"Harley what?"

Her lips dip at the edges. "You don't need to know my last name."

"But I'd like to." She makes a face and I start to laugh. "Is it really embarrassing or something?"

She rolls her eyes and then scratches her forehead.

She's thinking of telling me. I can sense the wheels in her head turning.

"I promise I won't tell anyone. In fact, I'm kind of going to keep these surf lessons under wraps, so your identity is completely safe with me."

She gives me a dry look before rolling her eyes again.

"Otherwise I can just call you Harley Question Mark. Would you prefer that?"

"You don't have to call me Harley anything. Just Harley is fine!"

I nod but can't resist. She's kind of cute when she's flustered, so I drag this out a little more. "You know I'm going to keep guessing, right? So unless you want me to spend every lesson calling you the dumbest surnames I can think of, you should just tell me now."

"Fine!" She tips her head up to the sky, giving me a glimpse of her pretty neck before glancing back at me and mumbling, "It's Quinn."

"Quinn," I repeat, trying to figure out why that's embarrassing for her...until I put the two names together. A slow smile stretches across my face. "Your name is Harley Quinn? As in the chick from *Batman*?"

"Yes." She hisses the S. "My mother hates me."

"Any middle name?"

"Nope! And she thinks it's hilarious."

That's because it is hilarious.

I'm trying to hide my smile, but it's a pretty hard battle.

Harley Quinn.

I actually love it.

A short laugh bursts out of me before I can stop myself. "Wow. Halloween must be a no-brainer for you."

Her blue eyes narrow and she points at me. "If you're picturing me in pigtails and shorts so tiny my ass cheeks are showing, just stop. That baseball bat of hers can be lethal, you know."

"I don't doubt it." I smile.

"Oh, shut up." Her eyebrows bunch together as she laughs then lightly slaps my stomach with the back of her fingers. "What's your name, pretty boy?"

I clear my throat and pull my shoulders back. "Aidan Michael De Beer."

"Well, that sounds like a rich, poncy name." Harley's voice pitches up and down as she teases me. I like her voice. It's not super high or girly. Not soft or willowy. It's got a husky strength to it.

And she's not afraid to speak her mind.

I gaze at her for a moment before deciding to speak my own mind for a change. "You think us rich people up on the cliffs are such snobs, don't you?"

She swallows and looks to the ground, giving me a half-hearted shrug.

"Have you ever thought about how judgmental that is? What if we're nice rich people?"

She starts drawing patterns in the sand with her big toe and doesn't look up. "I guess the only people I've really met from up on the cliff have been horrible, but... maybe you're right. Maybe some of you are super cool." She looks up, thrusting out her hand again. "So, I'll make you another deal." I grin and slide my hand into hers. "You don't think of me as some scantily clad, crazy villain from Gotham City and I won't think of you as a pretty rich boy. Just Aidan."

I shake her hand with a nod. "It's nice to meet you, Just Harley. I'm looking forward to Wednesday morning already."

12

A LONGBOARD LESSON FROM THE PAST

HARLEY

Well, it's Wednesday morning.

And I'm nervous.

I've been awake since four thirty, tossing and turning as I try to figure out the best way to teach Aidan how to surf.

I'm reliving my lessons from three years ago. Remembering how "that guy"—he lost his name after what happened—taught me how to surf. Man, I'd had stars in my eyes back then. I clung to every syllable that fell from his mouth, soaked it in like he was God and I was simply one of his little minions, eager to learn, bow at his feet, do whatever he asked me to.

I would have walked on burning coals for that guy.

Clenching my jaw, I forcefully shove his image to the back recesses of my brain as I walk towards the beach with two surfboards balanced on my head. It's kind of awkward, if I'm honest. I forgot how long my old longboard is; a fifteen-minute skate is turning into a twenty-five-minute walk that's only getting slower.

I should have asked Aidan to pick me up, but 1) I don't really want him seeing my crappy house and 2) I don't want to have to explain him to my mother. She won't care what I'm up to, but if she gets even a glimpse of a hot guy on our doorstep, she'll assume he's my boyfriend and that we're sleeping together, because my mother will sleep with anyone.

She'd no doubt say something super classy, like "It's about time you got your cherry popped. You're nearly seventeen."

I shudder and am now forcing images of my mother to the back recesses of my mind. She can hang out with "that guy" and leave me the hell alone.

By the time I reach the beach, I'm actually grumpy, which is not a great way to start a surf lesson. As my feet hit the sand, the cold grains bringing me home, I start to feel a little better. Laying the boards down, I stretch out my back and listen to the water lapping onto the shore.

It's not a big surf this morning, and that's perfect.

Aidan needs baby waves to start with. When I checked the report, I was stoked to see how perfect the conditions were.

I wonder how long Aidan's been awake for. Did he

get blasted awake by an alarm, or was he tossing and turning like me?

Hopefully tossing and turning…even just a little bit. That idea makes me feel better for some reason. I don't want to be the only nervous one.

I don't want to be nervous at all.

I can do this. I can teach someone how to surf.

If it hadn't been for the ocean and my board, I would have been shattered after what went down with "that guy." The ocean saved me. I'd paddle out into the water, tears on my cheeks, heartbreak in my soul and I'd get lost, distracted, made happy by the joy of surfing.

I found a passion for something greater than myself.

The ocean has become my sanctuary, a place to hide when things get bad at home. A place to run to when the ugly memories chase me.

And now it's my turn to pass this on to someone else. I want to give this gift to Aidan. I want to help him get past that restless sense of loss and despair that comes after a breakup.

And I want to get paid for doing it.

I smile as I remember our last conversation. Twenty bucks an hour. Sweet! That's nearly double what I earn at the Freshmart. Shit, he could pay me half what I earn at that place and I still would have agreed.

"Hey, Just Harley."

An instant grin lights my face and I spin to see Aidan loping down the beach. He's in a pair of black-

and-red board shorts that sit low on his hips, with a rash guard that is hugging every muscle of his torso. It's like a second layer of skin, and I can still make out the contours of his muscles.

He's so tall. And broad. And handsome.

I scowl and internally berate myself, *Stop thinking he's handsome, princess!*

Clearing my throat, I wipe my expression clean and force my grin back into place. "Good morning."

He rubs his hands together and gives me a nervous smile. It helps me to relax.

"You ready to do this?"

"Yes." But his head is shaking.

I laugh and bend down to collect the longboard. Handing it to him, I feel an excited thrill race through me as I watch him take it and rest it upright in the sand.

"Looking good."

"You think so?" He does one of those grimace smiles, which makes me laugh again.

What's with all the laughing?

I never laugh this much.

Clearing my throat, I try to think like a professional and shift into teaching mode.

"That guy's" voice wafts through my head, and I let it stay there for a few minutes while I formulate what I'm going to say.

"Okay." I pick up my board and mirror Aidan, resting mine in the sand and holding it like I'm about to pose for a photo. "So, we're going to start off just riding a few waves lying down. You need to get used to the feel of the board on the water. We'll start in the sand to get your position right, then head out and see how many waves you can catch on your belly."

"I can do that." Aidan nods, glancing out to the ocean.

An early morning runner jogs down by the water's edge, his well-behaved dog keeping pace beside him.

Aidan's cheeks kind of flare when he notices the guy.

Scrunching up my nose, I snap my fingers to get his attention and give him the warning that was given to me when I started three years ago. "I know this is probably going to be hard, but you have to remember this above all else."

Aidan raises his eyebrows at me.

I suck in a quick breath then say, "You have to forget about anybody else on the beach and just focus on what I tell you. Even if you feel stupid doing it. Got that?"

13

SURFING IN THE SAND

AIDAN

Oh, great. She's going to make me look like an idiot.

What the hell have I gotten myself into?

Nodding is suddenly hard as my body stiffens at the idea of humiliating myself. Like I need any more reasons to feel like a loser.

"Trust me." She smiles. "It's worth getting it right here on the sand before hitting the water. You'll pick it up so much faster."

I swallow and nod. "All right. What do I have to do, then?"

"Lay your board down."

I do it right away, figuring I want to get this part over with as quickly as possible.

"Now, hold the sides of the board about three-quarters of the way up and lie facedown."

She shows me what she means and I copy her, feeling less idiotic because she's doing it as well.

"Keep your elbows back, like chicken wings." She flaps her arms and I grin, getting into it as she keeps going with her explanation.

I'm soon lifting my chin and chest in some weird yoga position.

"Oh, make sure your toes are touching the end of the board."

I wriggle my body a little farther up the longboard.

"That's it." Harley stands and checks my positioning.

She's looking pretty damn amazing in her wetsuit this morning. That neoprene is hugging every surface of her body, highlighting her toned muscles and sportiness. There's something kind of sexy about how sporty she is.

I close my eyes.

Dude! She's your surf instructor! Stop thinking about her as sexy!

"Okay, let's hit the water." Harley claps her hands and picks up her board.

I follow suit, nerves crashing through me as I watch her footprints leading a path to the sand.

Shit, I hope I can do this.

I hope I can be brilliant.

"Attach your lead first." Harley stops at the water's

edge and quickly attaches hers like she's done it a million times before…which she probably has.

I lay my board down and attach the lead around my ankle. The cold water hits my feet and I brace myself for this early morning swim. I'm used to diving into a slightly heated pool, inside four walls.

This is something else.

The salty foam tickles my ankles as I wade in, the sharp cold of the Pacific rising up my legs.

Harley wades out until the water's around her waist. I run to catch up with her and listen as she explains what type of wave I should be aiming for.

"Lay your board down and just walk it forward. These baby waves are perfect for you today." She's grinning like a happy pup.

I can't help smiling as well. Her enthusiasm is so contagious.

Harley explains the waves to me and what to look for. "So we'll spin our boards around and just ride them in. Nice and easy."

"Nice and easy," I murmur, awkwardly turning the longboard around and jumping on it when she tells me to.

"Just let the wave catch your board and ride you in," Harley calls out to me. "Hold the sides. Lift your chin and chest. That's it!" She whoops and I feel the rush as the board rides me in.

I'm not even standing yet and I'm already having fun.

I ride the wave in until it hits the sand, then stand up and turn around to do it again.

After five tries, Harley is ready to move on.

I check my watch and hope there's enough time to do a little more before I have to split for school.

"Let's go, let's go." Harley waves me up the beach and starts rushing me through. She's obviously aware of the time as well. "Okay, now we need to figure out if you're a regular or goofy foot."

"If I'm a what?"

She snickers like I'm stupid for not knowing these terms, but is then nice enough to explain them to me. "It's how you stand on the board. Kind of like...which hand is more comfortable to write with? Your right or your left? In board sports it's recommended that your dominate foot is at the back of the board as it's got the bigger job to do. I want to start that way, and if it's not working for you, you can always switch it up later." She shrugs. "Let's at least work out which foot is the stronger one and then we can go from there."

"Makes sense." I nod and wait for further instructions.

"So *regular* means your left foot is at the front of the board, *goofy* means your right foot," she keeps explaining then runs me through a few quick tests.

We soon figure out that I'm a regular foot, and then she makes me stand on the board and pretend like I'm surfing in the water. She laughs and corrects my stance, then gets me to lie down and practice the "how to stand up" move.

"Turn your foot to the side so your ankle's touching the board." She crouches down by my feet and moves my right foot for me. "Good. Okay, now lift your chin and chest, then bring your front foot forward." I do as she says. "Yes. That's it. Okay, try it again."

She makes me do it over and over until I'm getting it right every time.

"Yes!" She pumps her fist in the air and jumps excitedly. "Let's hit the water again!"

I glance at my watch and nearly tell her I don't have time, but she's already running, and I'm compelled to chase her.

She calls out instructions to me as we hit the waves, and I'm aware that this is it. This is the moment to prove that I'm not a complete waste of time.

I screw up the first wave.

Harley laughs. "Don't worry about it. Try again."

Flicking the hair off my face, I swipe the salty water out of my eyes and head back into the surf. It takes me three attempts, but on the fourth, I manage to do everything she's told me to and actually keep my balance.

I'm riding a wave.

Holy crap, I'm riding a wave!

"Yes! Go! Go!" Harley's cheering me on.

Elation blooms in my chest.

It feels freaking awesome.

Even when I wipe out and hit the water with a splash. I resurface and let out a loud whoop, punching my arm in the air. "Yeah!"

My butt hits the sand as I grab my board and stand, walking into the shallows.

"That's awesome!" Harley splashes through the water as she races up behind me and jumps on my back.

It's only for a second, but the celebration makes me warm throughout my entire body.

I spin around to face her just after she jumps back down to the water.

We're both beaming at each other, and the urge to race straight back out is nearly too strong to ignore. But I can't be late for school, and Dad always says it's best to finish on a high.

And damn, is this one serious high.

"I get it." I grin at her.

She smiles back, knowing exactly what I mean. "I thought you might. Best thing in the world, right?" She holds out her fist.

"The best." I tap my knuckles against hers and feel it again. Warmth, all the way through to my core.

14

SNIFFING THE GREENBACKS

HARLEY

That look on Aidan's face is freaking fantastic.

He has a great smile that stretches across his entire face. White teeth, no doubt straightened with braces, rest on his lower lip, and I can't help mirroring his expression.

It's tempting to suggest we head out to catch another, but our hour is most likely up. I'm not wearing a watch, but I can sense we've probably gone a little over time.

Aidan checks his watch and winces.

I shrug. "It's good to finish on a high note. If the conditions stay steady overnight, we should probably try and do this again tomorrow."

He winces again, running a hand through his wet

hair. "I really need to hit the pool tomorrow or Coach will have my ass."

"No problem." I try to ignore how sharp my disappointment is and hope it doesn't show on my face. "I'm here basically every day. I'll give you my number and any morning you can come, just text me and I'll let you know if the conditions are right for you."

"Sounds good."

I like his smile.

I like the way his body moves as he heads up the beach towards his backpack.

He stops and lays the longboard down before ripping off his rash guard and reaching for his towel.

I like the way his muscles move.

I like the tanned color of his skin.

Would you shut up!

I force my gaze away and lay my board down, yanking out my own towel and quickly drying off before getting my phone out.

Standing up, I turn to face Aidan, who is still shirtless and just as gorgeous from the front as he was from the back.

He's not gorgeous. He's just a guy. Your surf student!

He unlocks his phone and holds it out to me. I do the same and we swap, programming in our numbers. A smile twitches my lips as I label my number *Just Harley*.

When we switch our phones back, he glances at the

screen and starts laughing. I check my screen and notice *Just Aidan* typed next to his number.

"Great minds." I chuckle and slip my phone away.

"Here." He holds out forty bucks, and I hesitate for just a moment before taking it.

"That covers today and next time."

I'm super stoked that he trusts me enough to pay me in advance. I don't even bother fighting my smile. I'm actually happier that he wants a next time. I had fun today. As soon as I started teaching him, my nerves evaporated, although a small part of me was worried he didn't enjoy it, that he'd want to bail.

People bail all the time, let you down without warning. I really don't want this super-fun experience to be stripped away from me. I take the money and clutch it in my fist.

"Thanks, Harley." Aidan grins down at me and my stupid stomach flutters with butterflies. "I had a great time today."

I'm desperate to go for casual but end up grinning like an idiot instead. Clearing my throat, I look down at our sand-covered feet and tell him, "You were good. You'll be surfing in no time."

"I think I'm going to like it."

I glance up and squint against the sun. "Man, you're gonna love it."

He holds out his fist, and I pound it before he walks away.

Shit, he really is hot, and I really should not be looking at him that way.

Clenching the money even tighter in my fist, I remind myself why I'm doing this.

"For the money," I murmur, going as far as to sniff the greenbacks before slipping them into my bag. "And to help Aidan." I tip my head to the side.

He looked happy today.

I'm convinced this sport can take away his blues and make him feel better about life.

And that makes *me* feel better about life, because I'm helping someone.

"That's it," I remind myself as I crouch down to organize my gear. "That has to be it."

It's a warning more than anything.

I'm not falling into the trap of loving someone again.

That only leads to trouble.

Betrayal.

Heartache.

15

QUEEN COOL'S PARTY INVITE

AIDAN

The stone steps leading into school don't seem so long and tiresome today. In fact, nothing seems as long and tiresome when you've started your day in the ocean. Harley taught me all about surf etiquette today. Having been surfing together for a week, in an empty ocean that felt like ours, we actually had to share the waves with a few guys this morning.

For some reason, Harley wanted us to keep our distance.

"You know those guys?" I questioned her, frowning as I studied them. They looked kind of intimidating, especially the bald black guy. He glared at me like I was his next target.

"Yeah, we hang out sometimes." Harley nodded, tugging me a little farther down the beach. "They're not so bad, as long as you don't get in their way. Surfing is sacred to them, and they kind of hate newbies, so let's definitely stay in the shallows."

It was easy to agree to. I'm not ready for the big waves anyway. Thankfully the surfers paddled out to the deeper water and we ended up not interacting with them at all.

I managed a few really great rides today.

It's exhilarating.

Maybe Harley's right after all. Maybe surfing is the best thing in the world.

Man, she's easy to hang out with. Her passion for the waves is contagious. And I like her smile. Her laughter. The way she banters with me. Time takes off when we're together, and so far, I've felt a sharp disappointment every time my lessons have come to an end.

That's why Saturday was so completely cool. We surfed for like three hours, and she didn't even charge me extra. I wish we could have surfed for three hours again this morning.

I run a hand through my salty hair, water droplets hitting my white school shirt.

I'm getting used to the salty tang on my skin, the smell of the ocean lingering on me as I go about my day. The waves were so good this morning, I ended up getting out of the water really late and only had time for a quick rinse off at the beach and a shower in a can —as Harley calls it.

A grin spreads over my face as I think about her.

We've had five lessons together so far. We squeezed in an extra one on the weekend, and I'm pretty sure I'll be asking to squeeze in more.

She mentioned as we dried off this morning that as soon as I'm feeling confident on the longboard, she wants to switch me to a smaller board. That seems kind of fast to me, but I think I'll start surfing the web and doing some research so I know what I'm looking for when I start shopping.

I swivel sideways to get past a squad of giggling freshmen and head to my locker.

The grass, as always, is looking green and inviting through the archways, but I'm running late and need to get my books organized before the bell rings.

I also need to come up with a good excuse for Simon about why I bailed on his invite for an extra swim this morning. He's going to figure it out soon enough, so I should just tell him, but I kind of like keeping this surfing thing to myself. It's my thing that has nothing to do with the Walton world, and I kind of want to keep it that way.

"Hey, cuz." Skylar appears out of nowhere and steps up to my side.

"Morning." I glance down at her, struck by the fact that she and Harley are similar heights. It makes me feel like a giant sometimes, but that doesn't bother me too much. What Skylar lacks in height, she makes up for in personality. And so does Harley, but in a very different kind of way.

I look around as we walk down the hall, aware that Skylar is on her own.

No Savannah? No Craig?

Seems weird to see my cousin flying solo.

I catch a movement over her right shoulder and spot Wyatt. Facing forward, I roll my eyes.

Of course *he's* here. Skylar's probably aware of it, but she never, ever flies solo at this school.

Wyatt Mattley has had a crush on her since the second he arrived at Walton. That must have been freshman year. Skylar has shot him down plenty of times, but he still lingers in the background of her life, a loyal puppy who will never get petted or played with.

Skylar calls him a creeper and has threatened to report him, but he seems harmless enough to me. It's not like he's ever tried to touch or threaten her before, he just likes to watch her.

Okay, yeah, it's creepy, but I don't think he stalks her the way she sometimes claims.

Skylar just likes to stir shit and create drama. She's extra all the way, and I've learned to take almost everything she says with a dollop of skepticism.

"So where have you been lately?" Skylar looks up, her green eyes bright and demanding.

"What do you mean?" I play dumb, giving myself a chance to formulate an excuse.

She rolls her eyes. "You know what I mean. You've been scarce."

"I've been around." I shrug.

We get to my locker and I'm forced to stop. Simon and Jonah aren't around to cause a distraction, and for once Craig isn't either.

I can't help wondering if Skylar's planned it this way. Told them all to leave me alone so she can play chief investigator for the morning.

Resting her shoulder on the locker beside mine, she crosses her arms and gives me a pointed look. "My sources say they spotted you at the beach this morning. What's going on?"

"Your sources?" I give her an irritated frown. "Gimme a break, Sky. Are you having me followed now?"

"No, I just happened to catch the right gossip train this morning. And they said they saw you taking a shower at the beach."

I pull in a breath, relieved they didn't see me with Harley or a surfboard.

"Why are you showering at the south end?"

"What were your 'sources' doing at the south end?" I use air quotes to emphasize how dumb I think this whole conversation is.

"I don't know. I don't care." She shrugs. "What I care about is you. Showering. At the beach!"

I huff and shake my head. "It's none of your business."

Her glossy lips part, her dark eyebrows making a sharp V above her nose. "As your closest cousin, I am offended by that remark."

I roll my eyes again.

"Come on, Ace, I care about you."

I used to love it that she called me Ace. It was our thing. I was her ace cousin, the swimmer who could beat them all. But I'm not an ace anymore. And she knows it.

Now she just calls me that to mock me—I can tell by the amused glint in her eyes—and it pisses me off. I need to wrap up this conversation real quick. Not only is it annoying me, but Savannah and Skylar can only go so long without seeing each other at school.

Any minute now, Savannah will come around the corner looking for her best friend. Things are super awkward between us. Again, Skylar knows this, and her evil side obviously wants to play. I swear, if she were a Disney character, she'd be that evil chick who was keeping Rapunzel in the tower. Gothel something. I can imagine Sky going to those kinds of lengths to stay young and beautiful. She's the hottest property at this school, and she uses that power to her advantage.

Shuffling closer, she rests her shoulder against my locker so I can't open it.

I narrow my eyes at her, and she gives me a simpering grin.

I sigh. "What do you want, Sky?"

"You've had your pout. It's time to join the real world again. I'm throwing a beach party this weekend, and you have to come."

I'd heard about her planning some event. That's

what she loves to do. She must get it from Aunt Marlo. That woman knows how to put on a party.

Everyone's been talking about Skylar's beach soirée. She's calling it that to make it sound classy, but it'll just be the standard bonfire and booze-fest it always is. Loud music pumping from a Bose speaker, red Solo cups littering the sand, couples draped all over each other while they use dancing as an excuse to get vertically hot and heavy.

It's going to be a huge deal. Everything Skylar does is a huge deal.

"I'm not sure." I give her a noncommittal shrug.

She, of course, ignores this and acts as though I've just said yes. "It's on Saturday night and Savvy's going to be there. I've told her to look out for you."

I frown and gently shove her off my locker. "Why?"

"Because she misses you."

I still, hope sparking in my chest for a brief moment. "She said that?"

Sky grins. "Well, she's not going to openly admit it, but she's my best friend. I can practically read her mind. I think she regrets breaking up with you, but she figures you don't want her anymore because she hurt you. She's such a sweetie. I've told her to just talk to you, but she's too nervous. It's not like your lazy ass is going to do it, so I'm helping you two out."

I pause, my eyes narrowing as I try to sniff out some prank or ploy.

"Don't look at me like that." She frowns. "This is

legit. You know you want her back, and I'm providing you with the perfect opportunity."

I don't say anything and try to read her expression. If Savvy and I did get back together, Skylar would take all the credit. Is that why she's doing this?

Skylar rests her head back against the lockers, her dark locks smooshing against the metal. "Aidan, come on. Don't be a douche. Savvy is sad without you. You guys were great together, so do something to make that happen again." She lightly slaps my arm to really drive her point home.

My lips twitch with a grin. "Yeah. Yeah, I guess."

"So be there." She pushes off the lockers and smooths down her hair. She's getting ready to strut off down the hallway, but her eyes start to sparkle as she spots something behind my back.

I turn to my right and see Savannah waiting at the corner. She's watching us, her big brown eyes curious. I've always loved her brown eyes—those pale, nearly amber orbs with so much sweetness and soul.

"Promise you'll come," Skylar whispers and then points at me. "Say you promise."

"I promise, Sky." And then instantly wonder if I'll regret it.

Skylar's triumphant grin makes my doubts scream to the surface, but she's already strutting away. She's nearly reached Savannah's side when Craig appears around the other corner and sweeps her off her feet with a growl. She screams and then giggles, her short tartan skirt riding up as she wraps her legs around his waist.

They start making out in front of everybody, like two hungry beasts.

It's disgusting.

I turn away from it, but then can't help glancing back. Skylar's gripping the back of Craig's hair, taking control of the kiss. She'll pull away in a second, say something sassy, and then he'll drop her back to her feet.

They'll then walk to class like the king and queen of cool, their chins held high as they expect the world around them to fall into line.

Skylar's always been like that—strong and so sure of herself. Even as kids she liked to boss me and Grayson around. Being in control is her thing. I don't know how she always gets away with it, but if Skylar wants to make something happen, she will.

There's no stopping a girl like that.

A girl who gets what she wants, no matter what.

16

A PLACE TO CALL HOME

HARLEY

It's not often that I get exactly what I want, but as I tuck my phone into my back pocket, I break into a happy dance. Just a little one and super short. I'm not normally a happy dancer, but...

Aidan said yes!

He said yes!

Even though we surfed this morning and I didn't expect to see him again until Sunday, he replied to my invite for another surf.

The conditions are perfect for him, and when I saw the late afternoon report, I just had to see if he was keen for a second session. I'll make this one free of charge. It won't be a lesson, just a chance for Aidan to practice some more.

Nerves trill through me as I wait for him to arrive.

I actually asked if he could pick me up from my place, as it'll be quicker to get to the beach and we can get in at least forty minutes before the sun sets.

Mom's not home, so inviting him over isn't as scary as it normally would be. There's no way in hell I want Aidan encountering my mother. I don't know what kind of family he comes from, but I'm guessing they're whole and complete. I bet his mother is beautiful and his father is smart. He mentioned an annoying little brother the other day, and I could see it all so clearly— the all-American family with their tidy house and white picket fence. Parents with jobs you wouldn't be ashamed to tell anyone about. Meals around the dinner table, play fights between the brothers, an annual Christmas photograph, and of course a massive turkey for Thanksgiving.

It's nothing like my life.

Last Thanksgiving my mom was working, and I ended up at the beach, wrapped in a blanket and eating a limp Caesar salad from Freshmart.

We don't do family dinners around a table with lively conversation. All I've ever known is me, my mom and whichever boyfriend happens to be around at the time. Thankfully Mom's current squeeze is deployed on some aircraft carrier. I don't know which one, and I don't care. I can't stand Mr. Navy. The guy's a creep.

I think that's one of the reasons I try so damn hard to be different from my mother in every way I can. I don't want to end up old and miserable, having dated a string of losers who never stick around.

When I was a kid, I used to dream that one day my dad would show up and he'd whisk me away to a normal life. The kind portrayed on TV shows, where everyone in the house ultimately loves each other, even if they do bicker and argue sometimes. My father would welcome me into his family and I'd be brought up by his sweet wife, have siblings to play with, and even a puppy named Rocket.

But reality caught up with me soon enough. It didn't take long for me to figure out that Mom doesn't even know who my father is. She had me when she was twenty-one. Apparently, I put a big fat dent in her partying days.

Why the hell did she even keep me?

Some days, I honestly don't know.

I never knew my grandparents, so she must have done all the baby stuff on her own. Maybe she used to love me when I was cuddly and cute. Maybe she still loves me now. I'm not sure.

I try not to think about it.

All I can focus on is becoming the opposite of what she is.

Drying the last plate, I stack it in the cupboard and am satisfied the kitchen is clean enough. The living room is a total mess, but it's not like Aidan will be coming into the house, so I walk through the clutter and head to the bathroom.

I change into my blue bikini and throw a rash guard over it. Snatching a towel off the railing, I shove it into my backpack along with a dry T-shirt. Throwing on my denim shorts, I zip the fly, then jump into my flip-flops before heading out front.

It's probably best that I wait for Aidan outside. I don't really want him entering my crappy little house. It's bad enough that he'll see the outside of it.

Why the hell did I ask him to pick me up here?

I suddenly regret my decision.

Everything can't always be about maximizing my time in the water.

Yanking out my phone, I'm about to text him that I can just meet him at the beach when his car appears in my driveway.

"Hey." He grins at me, his head popping above the windshield.

Of course he owns a convertible.

I should be grateful. That tousled hair look really suits him.

"Will the boards just fit in the back seat?" He gets out of the car and starts walking towards the carport.

He doesn't seem bothered by the clutter. His eyes are on the longboard, and he looks like he's hungry for a surf.

This weird kind of elation blooms inside my chest.

He's getting into it.

He loves it, just the way I do.

I clear the butterflies out of my throat and say, "Yeah, we can make it work."

"Sweet." He picks up the board and starts carrying it to his car.

I snatch my shortboard and follow him, helping him arrange the boards so they're sticking up in the air out the back of his car.

"Nice ride," I murmur as I slide into the passenger seat.

"Thanks." He gets behind the wheel and starts up the engine.

"Was it your sixteenth birthday present?"

He stops reversing just so he can throw me a withering glare.

It makes me laugh and I wipe a hand over my mouth.

"You and your notions," he mutters, shaking his head. "It's like you think I'm some TV character from a teen drama series about rich bitches and their hot boyfriends."

I giggle at the voice he's putting on, then quickly bite back the sound. Giggling is so incredibly girly, and I hate it when a sound like that comes out of my mouth. Unfortunately, it seems to happen a lot around Aidan. The guy knows how to make me laugh, and teasing him is just so much fun.

So I keep going. "I can't help it, you've just got pretty rich boy down to an art form."

"You promised not to call me that, Harley Quinn."

I wrinkle my nose at him.

Touché.

I decide to play it safe and change the subject. "So, how was school?"

"Good." He spins the car around and starts heading for the beach.

He seems lighter this afternoon. Happier.

"What made it good?" I quietly hope he says surfing, but instead he pops my sparkly balloon with a reality pin.

"Turns out my ex regrets breaking up with me."

"Oh." I force a smile. "Well, that's cool."

"Yeah. There's a chance I might be able to kick things off again this weekend." He swallows, keeping his eyes on the road.

I'm glad. I don't want him looking at me. I have no idea what my face is doing, but my heart is deflating, shriveling up like a melting piece of plastic.

But this is a good thing.

I'm not into Aidan.

I mean, I don't want to be, so the fact that he's after his ex-girlfriend is perfect.

Now our friendship can just be about surfing, and that's all I really want out of this anyway. I bob my head like I'm not disappointed and torture myself by asking his plan of attack.

Who knew a trip to the beach could take so freaking long?

Who knew listening to plans of a bonfire beach party could hurt so bad?

As we round the corner, I spot the sparkle of the water and focus all my attention on the ocean blue. Once again those faithful waves will rescue me.

They've never let me down before.

And I can't imagine they ever will.

Unlike people, you can rely on the water.

It'll always be there, no matter who you are or what choices you make.

It doesn't change its mind about you.

It just calls you home.

17

QUESTIONS THAT DON'T WANT TO BE ANSWERED

AIDAN

Harley's gone kind of quiet. I don't know what I said to annoy her, but her lack of response over a question that she asked me is way awkward.

So I stop talking.

As soon as I park the car—which yes, my parents bought me, but not for my birthday, and as soon as Grayson gets his license, we're expected to share it—I suggest we get in the water.

This makes Harley smile, so we unload the car quickly and rush down to the waves.

As soon as the cool water hits my skin, I feel that sense of home envelop me. Harley always talks about the water being her sanctuary. For me, it's like a playground. I haven't felt so free and liberated in a long time. Rather than a sense of peace and calm, I get a rush. And I love that feeling.

Running my board out to the waves, I watch the water carefully, tracking a building wave with my name on it. I spin the longboard around and lie down, ready to start paddling. As soon as the board starts to lift me, I plow my arms through the water, gaining speed and then rising to my feet.

"Woohoo!" I yell, nearly losing my balance. I quickly correct myself, bending my knees and riding with the board.

"Go, surfer boy!" Harley yells behind me. Her laughter is free and easy.

I'm glad whatever tension was lingering in the car has been broken.

Broken by the magic of the water.

I ride the wave for as long as it will carry me, then flop into the water with a splash.

When I stand, Harley is up on her board, carving up the wave with quick swipes and turns. She's freaking awesome.

I hope I can be that good one day. Although I won't be able to do any of those tricks until I get a smaller board.

Looks like I *will* be board shopping this weekend. I'll have to ask Harley's advice. Maybe I should see if she wants to come with me.

I like that idea.

Spending a day hanging out with Harley and looking at surfboards.

Man, I kind of love it.

The thought makes me pause.

Should I love it? Or am I walking on dangerous ground?

I'm trying to win Savannah back. How would she feel about me spending the day with another girl?

I think about my ex-girlfriend's sweet face, gather up those precious memories that I've been trying to avoid. If Skylar's right and Savannah does want me back, then I can't screw it up.

But it's not like that with Harley. She's my surf instructor. A friend at the most.

"Are you coming back out or what?" Harley shouts.

I shake my head, flicking the confusing questions to the back of my mind.

Right now, I just want to have some fun.

With a grin, I push my board back out to the waves and get lost in the perfect distraction.

We stay out there until the sun is a burning semi-circle on the horizon. It's starting to get too dark to surf, and I suggest we head in. Harley doesn't fight me on it, but it's impossible not to notice the disappointment we both share. We're not ready for the fun to end.

As we're toweling off, I blurt out a question before I think better of it. "Hey, you want to have some dinner? I could murder a burrito or some tacos right now."

"Ooo, I know a great place!" She flicks the towel over her shoulders. "Why don't we drop the boards back at my place, get changed, and then we can head there? It's super cheap and only like ten blocks from my house."

"Sounds good to me." I smile at her, then follow her up the beach, all confusing questions shoved deep into the recesses of my brain.

18

CORN CHIPS, GUACAMOLE & REAL TALK

HARLEY

H anging out with Aidan is fun.

I was stoked when he suggested dinner together. I wasn't ready to say goodbye to him, and I said yes to his invitation before thought could stop me.

Was it the right thing to do?

As I dip my tortilla chip into the guacamole, I tell that question to eff off. I just need to enjoy the moment —the crunch of the chip, the creaminess of the avocado, the squareness of Aidan's chin, the husky depth to his voice. I chew and swallow before I start working my way down his body.

"So yeah, then we moved here." Aidan grabs a chip out of the bowl and scoops out a huge mound of guacamole. He's already demolished two burritos. I'm stuffed to overflowing after my fish tacos, yet we still can't stop nibbling the leftovers.

I force my eyes away from his mouth and ask, "You like it? Ryder Bay?"

He nods and finishes chewing. "It's pretty awesome. I mean, living right on the beach, you can't really beat that. Our house overlooks the water, and that view is good for the soul, you know?"

"Totally. I feel better every time I see the ocean."

We grin at each other, and Aidan's gaze lingers on my face. "I didn't feel it as deep until you showed me how. Thank you for teaching me."

I swallow, giddy nerves attacking me, making it hard to speak. In the end, I manage to rasp, "You're welcome."

My body is tingling, my stomach doing flips and jumping jacks. Those green eyes of his are way more powerful than he realizes.

"So, when did you move here? Tell me your story." Aidan takes a sip from his water glass.

I'm kind of loath to do it. I hate telling my story because it's always so sad and pathetic. How do you spruce up being raised by a single mother who could take or leave you?

"I, um..." I press my lips together and try to think of the glossy bits. "My grandfather lived here for... well, I don't know how long for, but when he died, he left my mom his house, so she took it. We arrived when I was fourteen, and I can't imagine us leaving anytime soon."

He keeps staring at me, waiting for more. I focus on the sound of the chip crunching between his teeth. What more does he want me to say?

He licks the salt off his lips. "So, it's just you and your mom?"

"Yep." My head starts bobbing and I keep my eyes on the table.

"Where's your dad?"

I shrug and for some reason admit, "I don't know who he is. I've never met him."

"I'm sorry."

He sounds genuine, so I glance up and give him a swift smile. "I don't know any different, so… you know. It's not like I have anything to compare to. I didn't even get to meet my grandfather, and other than like one or two of my mom's half-decent boyfriends, my view on older guys is pretty tainted."

"Have you ever just once wanted to find him? Or is your mom against that?"

I scoff and start dipping my chip in and out of the guacamole. "I don't think my mom knows who he is, either. There's been a lot of guys in her life."

"Ouch." He winces.

I raise my eyebrows and bite my lips together. Looking at him is impossible right now. There's a certain amount of humiliation in admitting your mom's a skank.

"I don't need a dad. I'm fine on my own."

I don't think he believes me, and I suddenly wish I'd never said it. There's a sad sympathy in his gaze, which is bugging me. Focusing back on my chip, I scrape some green dip off the edge of the bowl and shove the chip into my mouth.

"My life must seem so squeaky clean and perfect to you." Aidan shifts back in his seat. His leg brushes mine as he moves around, and I flinch away from it. The tiny hairs on his leg leave a tingling tickle that my body wants more of.

I tuck my feet back against the booth seat and start bobbing my head again. "It's pretty shiny."

He snickers. "I know I'm lucky, but it's not perfect. I mean yes, I have two parents and they love each other. I don't want for anything. I get that, and I know I probably take it for granted sometimes. But the hard part about living in a home like that is the expectations. They're so high, you know? Like I have no excuse to screw up, ever. So when I do, I just..." He swallows, his lips pulling into a tight frown. "I don't know."

"I can imagine it's hard." My voice has gone quiet all of a sudden. It seems appropriate somehow. For once, I don't feel the urge to tease him. His pretty boy speech, although a little "first-world problems" mockable, seems 100 percent genuine. He looks kind of torn up, and I wish I could fix it for him.

He glances at me, his bright green eyes tinged with

desperation. "I just wish I could break free sometimes, you know?"

"I totally know." I bulge my eyes at him. "I want to break free all the time, which is why I go to the water. Surfing has saved my life on more than one occasion." I grin.

He matches my smile and we sit there for a few minutes, silently sharing our common ground. We may come from different worlds, but we seem to understand each other. Rich or poor, north or south, none of that matters right now. We're just two people who want to catch the next ride out of home. Away from the pressure, away from the great divide, away from...

Her.

My throat instantly swells as a brunette with fiery green eyes and a scary-ass frown storms up to our table.

Who the hell is she?

And why is she about to shit all over my moment with Aidan?

My eyebrows dip to mirror her frown until she stops by our table and I suddenly recognize her—the sugar-free gum goblin from Freshmart.

"Can I help you?" I snap, my eyes narrowing to match hers.

Aidan flinches and looks over just as she stops by the table.

"Oh, shit," he murmurs under his breath.

"Why are you having dinner with my cousin?" Miss

Snark rests her hand on her hip, then juts it out like she's posing for the cover of *Vogue*.

I'd usually roll my eyes at this point, but I'm too surprised by her statement to do anything other than gape at Aidan. "Your cousin?"

He gapes back at me. "You know each other?"

My teeth slam together. He's not denying it.

Shit.

That bitch is his family?

I can barely grit out my reply. "We haven't been formally introduced."

"Uh, okay." Aidan shifts in the booth, looking like an awkward giant as he points between us. "Harley, this is Skylar. Skylar this—"

"Oh, save it," she interrupts him, then looks back to me. "We're done here. I'll cover your tab, although I'm sure you can afford a shithole like this."

I blink, shocked, but not surprised at the way she's talking. Bitch just must run through her veins.

"Hey." Aidan tugs on Skylar's wrist. "What the hell are you doing? You can't talk to her like that."

"I'm fine." I stand from the table and go eye-to-eye with her. She may look fierce, but I bet I could kick her ass. Those skinny arms of hers could be snapped like chicken bones.

"Harley?" Aidan's voice has a nervous, confused edge to it.

I glance at him, his gorgeous face wrinkled with

embarrassment. Pulling some cash from my back pocket, I dump it on the table.

"I can drive you home." Aidan goes to stand, but Skylar blocks his way. "Skylar!"

"Don't worry about it. I'd rather walk anyway." I give Skylar a pointed glare before glancing back at her cousin. "I'll catch you later."

He looks like he's going to argue with me, so I shoot away from the table, glancing back just once to mouth, "Good luck!" behind Skylar's back.

His lips twitch with a grin, which morphs into an apologetic smile.

I brush my hand through the air as Skylar takes my seat.

I don't know what the hell her problem is, but I'm not hanging around to find out.

As soon as the evening air hits my skin, I take off at a sprint. The more distance I can create between me and that witch, the better.

19

WHIPLASH

AIDAN

"**W**hat the hell is wrong with you?" I glare at Skylar, who is gazing at the tortilla chips in disgust. God forbid she have anything as vulgar as deep-fried food. I huff and push the bowl away from her. "You can't throw shade like that. You basically ran her out of here, and dammit, I shouldn't have let you do it!"

Slapping my hands on the table, I go to rise, but Skylar jumps up and shoves my shoulder. "Sit down."

I thump into my seat and glare at her.

"Oh, get over it. She's tough. She's fine. She said she'd see you later, didn't she?"

"You can be such a b—"

"That's not the point." Skylar cuts me off. She's

always been good at doing that. "The point is *what the hell, Aidan!*"

Anger and confusion are roiling inside of me. I can't decide whether to ditch my cousin and run after Harley or stick around to figure out why she's so pissed off with me.

"I'm trying to get you back together with Savvy and you're off getting tight with another girl! In case you're stupid and I have to spell it out for you, that looks really bad."

I let out a heavy sigh and slump back against the booth. "It wasn't a romantic thing, okay? She's my...friend."

"Friend, my ass," Skylar scoffs. "My source says you were getting pretty flirty over dinner."

"Who the hell is your source?"

"That's not the point."

"Skylar." My voice drops low with warning.

She rolls her eyes and flicks a lock of dark hair over her shoulder. "Okay, fine. It's Wyatt."

"Wyatt?" My voice practically cracks over the word. "Wyatt Mattley?"

What. The hell.

"He saw you showering at the beach and told me about it, so I asked him to follow you after school today." She shrugs like it's no big deal.

"You what?"

Her triumphant smirk is slightly sickening. "You know the guy will do anything for me."

"At what price?"

Her cheeks tinge pink as she starts fiddling with her left earring. "I told him I'd give him seven minutes in heaven."

I can't even form a response. Seriously! Does she have no depth to how low she'll go?

"Get that look off your face." She points at me. "What Craig doesn't know won't hurt him, so you can just shut up. It's for a good cause. Savannah's my best friend and she's miserable. She doesn't have the guts to confront you, so I have to step in and do what I must." Her long, manicured nails start tapping the shiny table-top, and she looks away from me, a guilty flush tinging her cheeks.

"What are you not telling me?" I nudge her foot with mine.

She rolls her eyes and sighs, "You'll be pissed, so I don't want to say."

I nudge her a little harder until she gives me an indignant "Ouch!"

"Say," I demand with a pointed look that could rival hers.

"Okay, fine," she mutters, crossing her arms and trying to look justified in whatever shit she's about to spill. "A couple of days before prom, Savannah admitted that she wasn't into you anymore. She was finding your relationship...boring. So I encouraged her to..." She spins her fingers in the air.

"You told her to dump me?" I jerk up in my seat.

"I thought I was being helpful!" she quickly retorts. "At least she waited until after prom, and now she totally regrets it, so I'm trying to make things right."

I let out a disgusted scoff and am two seconds away from telling my cousin exactly what I think of her meddling.

"Now can we stay on point here, please?" She snaps her fingers. "You shouldn't be off with that blonde bitch while Savannah is pining for you."

Anger rises up my throat swift and sharp. "Harley's not a bitch. She's a very nice person, and she's helping me out."

"Explain." Skylar's nostrils flare. "Because right now, all I see is you losing the best thing that has ever happened to you."

"No thanks to you," I mutter darkly.

She splays her hands on the table and leans towards me. "I am *trying* to make it right. Savannah had a moment of doubt, which I thought was legit, but we were both wrong. Let me fix this, please. You and Savannah should be together."

Shit, is she right?

Savannah *was* the best thing that had ever happened to me. I have this chance to get her back and...

I roll my eyes, wishing Skylar and Savannah weren't BFFs.

"Don't roll your eyes at me. Savannah is perfect. You guys come from the same worlds. Your parents adore her, which is why I promised not to tell them, or mine, that you and Sav are over. Shit, I don't even think her dad knows. So don't screw this up, and the lie can end this weekend!"

I let out a heavy sigh, my shoulders slumping forwards as I decide it's in my best interest to be honest with my cousin. "Harley's teaching me how to surf, okay? I was trying to figure out a way to impress Savannah, or maybe get over her. Just anything to distract me from the dull ache in my chest."

Skylar blinks, her expression morphing to one of sympathy and regret. Like, genuine sympathy and regret. The kind she rarely shows anyone, but when she does, you know she means it.

I swallow and keep going. "Surfing is a good use of my time. It's fun. It's distracting. Harley's been teaching me how."

And Skylar's expression morphs again. It always feels like whiplash when she does this to me. Skylar is this weird, confusing combination of bitch with a beating heart. When she lets that heart show itself, she's amazing. I wish she wouldn't hide it away all the time.

Her manicured eyebrows slowly rise on her forehead and she nods in approval. "That's pretty cool."

"It's *very* cool, so you can just take back your savage teardown." I scowl at her. "I can't believe you..." I shake my head and growl. "Having me followed and then coming in here and treating Harley like total shit." Skylar dips her head, looking at least a little reprimanded. I take advantage of her remorse and point my finger at her. "Next time you see her, you're apologizing."

She gasps, and the she-devil is back in full force. "Are you insane? That girl called me a bitch. To my face."

A chuckle bursts out of me before I can stop it. I love how brave Harley is. I don't know anyone else willing to stand up to Skylar that way.

"Stop laughing," she snaps. "It was humiliating."

"Well, you no doubt deserved it."

Skylar glares at me but doesn't argue. I take that as a good sign and pull my lips into line, wiping my smile away with a swipe of my knuckles. "You have to promise me, Sky. Next time you see her, you—"

"All right, fine!" She flicks her hands in the air. "*If* I ever see her again, I'll apologize, okay?"

I give her a stiff nod, suddenly swamped again by the guilt of just letting Harley walk out of here. I should have ditched my cousin and driven Harley home.

"Look, I *am* sorry for screwing things up with you and Savvy. I'm glad you still want her. You guys are good together." Skylar pulls reality back into place, reminding me where my priorities should be.

Taking Harley out for dinner was probably a bad idea. Even though it was innocent enough, it was still fun. *Really* fun, and maybe I shouldn't be enjoying myself so much in her company.

The whole guy-girl just-friends thing is so damn confusing.

"So, we're good?" Skylar nudges my foot under the table.

I bob my head and catch her eye. "As long as you apologize to Harley as well, we're good."

She smirks at me, rolls her eyes, and then pulls in a breath. "Now, can you please follow me home?" Skylar glances past my shoulder and I turn to see Wyatt hovering near the entrance. "I want to make sure Wyatt turns off onto *his* street, not mine. I know the guy is going to make me pay up on those seven minutes, and I want to hold him off for as long as I can."

"You are unbelievable." I pull my wallet out and grab Harley's money. I wanted to treat her tonight, but that would probably make it feel like a date. I hate that Skylar's right.

"I'm gonna take that as a compliment." She winks at me, and it's hard to keep my lips in line.

"Please don't," I mutter, inching towards the edge of the booth. "Now let's get out of here, Miss Sassy Pants."

"After you, Ace." She grins as we both stand up.

I give her a scathing glare and mutter, "I really hate you sometimes."

"You love me." She threads her arm around my waist, and I can't help but put my arm over her shoulders.

We've spent our whole lives growing up together,

and although I wish I could hate her, I never seem capable.

She can be annoying as hell.

But she'll always be my stupid cousin, and for that, I love her.

20

IT'S ALL ABOUT SELF-DEFENSE

HARLEY

I'm standing at the end of the pier.

Alone.

People don't venture down this far anymore. During the day you get the odd fisherman, but the pier can be spooky at night. The light at the end has been smashed in and never replaced, creating a pitch-black abyss that you have to carefully negotiate like a blind person.

The boards are old and no doubt rotting in sections. I sometimes wonder if the pier was a hive of activity when my grandpa surfed around here. It's hard to believe it now.

This crooked finger pointing out to the ocean has been forgotten about.

But it's the only place I want to be right now.

The salty air tickles my nostrils as I grip the railing

and stare out at the dark sky. The stars are twinkling above me, the new moon making them bright diamonds on a black canvas. I should be in awe of them, but tonight they don't even touch me.

I'm too upset to feel anything other than anger. And maybe a little despair. That word seems too strong and depressing, but it's real.

The way our Mexican dinner ended tonight was just another reminder that people suck. No matter how much you want to believe in them, you can't, because they can turn on you like a flash flood.

Aidan is good, but with people like Skylar in his life, there's nothing to stop him from becoming everything I don't want to be around.

"That guy" scratches the back of my brain. It's not a pleasant tickle, more of a scar-inducing reminder of the things I can't change.

All the good, sweet memories I have of him are tainted. The colorful moments in the water where he taught me how to surf, told me how amazing I was, swung me around in the salty spray and kissed me in the setting sunlight. The first time he smiled at me. The first time we spoke. He was the older guy with a crush on the freshman girl. And it was all so perfect.

I practically worshipped the ground he walked on. He was my king, and his friends were my family. But now...all of those images have turned to black and gray. Made muddy with shadows from the way he ruined it all. The way he ended it.

I can't let myself get sucker-punched like that again.

Screw Aidan and his pretty, forlorn face.

I never should have offered him those surfing lessons. What the hell was I thinking?

I'm tempted to delete his number off my phone, but I don't reach for it. Instead I lean my forearms on the rough railing and make myself remember what "that guy" did to me.

Letting someone like Aidan into my life is a really big mistake.

I won't let him hurt me.

I won't let anyone hurt me, ever again.

21

SALTY WORDS

AIDAN

I'm already looking for her before my feet hit the sand.

It's bugging me that I texted Harley hours ago and I still haven't heard back. I'm keen for another surf lesson. Keen to wipe the slate clean and make up for the shitty way last night ended. I want a chance to explain my cousin, to assure Harley that at some point Skylar *will* apologize to her.

I spent last period ignoring the teacher and covertly looking up the surf report on my phone. From what I can tell, the conditions are perfect for me today. I study the waves and see that they are. A smile is already twitching my lips. I can't wait to get out there.

I hope Harley brought the longboard with her.

I wonder if I should still suggest surfboard shopping this weekend.

Thoughts of tomorrow night's party tickle the edges of my brain. If things go the way Skylar and I are hoping, Savannah and I will be back together. Would Savvy mind if I spend the day with Harley?

Maybe she could come with us.

Why does that feel weird?

I scratch the back of my neck as I head down to the water, still scanning the beach for a petite blonde. Instead, I look up to find a guy just a little shorter than me with shoulder-length dreads and a friendly smile.

As I get closer, he spots me and raises his chin in acknowledgment.

"Hey, man." He grins.

"Hi." I raise my hand in an awkward wave. I don't think I know this guy, but he's looking at me like he knows me.

"You must be looking for the surfer girl, right?"

I smile. "Is there only one on the beach?"

"There's only one who you hang out with."

My eyebrows dip with confusion. "I'm sorry, do we know each other?"

"Oh yeah, of course. Sorry, man." He scratches his whiskers and lets out a self-deprecating chuckle before holding out his hand. "I'm Griffin. I'm the new guy at Ryder Rentals. You may not have noticed me loitering around and watching you."

I'm embarrassed to admit that I haven't. Shaking his hand, I mumble my name.

Griffin points to the bright yellow and blue shed marking the middle point of the beach. "That's my spot."

"When did you start?"

"About three weeks ago. Marshall's previous guy left, and with summer coming up, it's only getting busier. He wanted a surfer working on the beach so I can give people tips and stuff. He's actually looking for one more guy to work part time over the summer. That way he doesn't even have to think about it. You know, with him lifeguarding and all."

I bob my head. Marshall Swinton has been life-guarding at Ryder Bay since before we moved here, but he opened Ryder Rentals as a side business and just hires people to run it for him.

I look to my left, wondering when Harley's going to appear. Surely she'll show up today. The water's good... unless she's sick of surfing peewee waves and has gone somewhere better for the afternoon.

My disappointment is sharp and biting.

"You know, you're pretty good."

"Huh?" I look back to Griffin and notice the huge smattering of freckles across his face. They almost have a ginger hint to them. Actually, his dreads and short beard have a touch of red too, but the dark brown base kind of hides it.

He gives me a lopsided grin. "I'm pretty sure I

caught your first lesson. You've picked up surfing pretty fast. From what I've seen, you're a natural."

"You think so?"

He nods and looks out to the ocean. "Your body was definitely born for the water. I can see it in you."

"You been surfing for long?"

"Couple years. I get out there any chance I can get. The job is kind of hindering how much I can, but I need the money, you know?"

I nod, giving him a quick once-over. I wonder what his story is, and how much older he is than me. He could totally pass for a high school senior.

"I'm usually traveling around, don't like to tie myself down, you know? But when I arrived at this bay, I kind of fell in love with it. Think I'll stick around. At least until the summer ends."

"Sounds like an interesting life," I murmur.

"It is." A look I don't understand flickers over his face, but he quickly hides it behind an easy smile. "So hey, have you thought about a summer job?"

"Excuse me?"

"I was just wondering if you'd consider working at Ryder Rentals. Marshall said you've got good people skills, and with you taking up surfing, you'd be a good candidate. He said he was going to ask your dad if you'd be interested."

Marshall has been friends with my father ever since we moved to Ryder Bay. They hit it off after a chance meeting at Pizza Palace, and I've gotten to know the guy through family meals. He and his wife don't have any kids—I'm not sure why, because they'd make great parents. They're a really a cool couple. Griffin is lucky to be working for the guy.

I've never considered getting a summer job. I've never had one before and don't really need it.

"You should think about it." Griffin looks at me. "Earning money to hang out at the beach is pretty damn awesome. Devon prefers being up on the boardwalk with the bikes, and Marshall wants one more guy on the sand with me. It could be fun."

I'm not sure how to respond, so I just give him an awkward smile.

And then I spot Harley. She's walking down the beach, her board tucked under her arm. She's seen me talking with the new guy, and I can't tell what her expression means.

"Hey, uh, nice to meet you, Griffin."

"Yeah, you too, man." He lightly pats my shoulder, and I take off running to catch Harley before she enters the water.

"Did you get my text?" I call to her.

She stops walking but doesn't turn to face me. It's kind of annoying, but maybe she's still steamed after last night.

Shit, I shouldn't have just let her leave.

I'm about to open my mouth and apologize when she asks, "What was that about?" She raises her chin towards Griffin, who is retreating up the beach, back towards the main Ryder Rentals building, which is next to the lifeguard office. It's basically a bigger version of the shed that houses all the surf and boogie boards on the beach. It's the middle point between north and south, with big windows on all sides, so the street traffic can see the bikes available for hire.

I've been in there a few times to rent a tandem bike. It's a cluttered space, every inch used for the sole purpose of entertaining tourists and beachgoers. I try to imagine myself checking in there for work on a summer morning.

Yeah, I don't know.

Working over the summer?

Harley clears her throat to get my attention.

"Oh, uh…" I glance back at her, pointing over my shoulder. "That's Griffin. He's the new Ryder Rental guy."

"Yeah, I've seen him around," she murmurs. "He's a surfer."

"Yep." I grin. "He was saying that they're looking for someone else to work with him over the summer. It's gonna get busy with more people coming in, and Marshall wants a surfer who can give people tips when hiring out the boards, you know? He suggested I apply."

"Wow." Her eyebrows pop up while her jaw works to the side like she's fighting some kind of emotion I don't understand. "He asked you?"

My face scrunches with a frown. "Yeah, but I don't know." I shrug. "Working over the summer?"

She scoffs and shakes her head. "Some of us don't have the luxury of lazing around on the beach all summer."

My eyes snap to hers. Her blue gaze is hot and fiery, like she's yearning for a fight.

I don't want to give her one.

I want to go back to the fun and laughter of yesterday, before Skylar came along and ruined it.

"Hey, about last night—"

"You know what your problem is?" Harley snaps. "You're lazy. You're a lazy, entitled shit, Aidan De Beer."

I'm so shocked by the sudden outburst that I can't even think of a response.

"Is that what you want? To just lie around on your ass all summer? You love the water, you love the beach, and you're being given the chance to do a job that involves both. But no, the idea of actually having to work over the summer is too much for you!" Her eyes bulge, her head wobbling back and forth as she emphasizes her point. "You're going to do nothing with your life unless you find something worth getting off your ass for! All you do is mope around feeling sorry for yourself, like you're some gigantic loser!"

"A loser?" I retort. "Well, maybe I am. I had something worth getting off my ass for and she dumped me! I *lost* her!"

"Oh, so now it's your girlfriend's fault? She's supposed to be responsible for your happiness? That's bullshit!"

"What the hell do you know?"

"I know you need to find something that will ignite you." She swings around to face me head-on, nearly taking me out with her surfboard. "Not some*one*, some*thing*. You can't rely on other people because they will always let you down or leave you. The only person you can count on is yourself."

I'm starting to understand her anger.

At least I think I am.

She's pissed off with me because she thinks I let her down last night. So she's feeding me these bullshit lines in an effort to hide that fact. It feels righteously unfair. I offered to drive her home, didn't I? But she told me to stay, to sit there and endure an interrogation from my cousin.

So, I try to make it up to her. To find her today and set things right.

But she's obviously not interested.

Stepping back from her wrath, I quietly say, "Sounds kind of lonely to me."

Her glare is ice cold. "At least I'm happy."

"Or jealous," I mutter.

Her head snaps back, her eyes narrowing into an icy glare that makes me squirm. "You're an asshole."

I shake my head, figuring I've lost this one. I shouldn't have said she was jealous. Shit, I should be suggesting that *she* apply for the job if she thinks it's so great.

But I just want this battle over with.

"Look, whatever." I angle my body away from her.

"Ooooo, great finishing argument," she mocks me. "I sure as hell hope you're not on the Walton Academy debate team! It's probably way too much effort for you."

I give her a scathing smile, then flip her the bird.

She snarls at me like a wildcat before spinning on her heel and storming back up the beach.

As I take off north, I can't deny the bitter taste in my mouth. It's seeping down into my chest and turning my insides to ash. I never should have said yes to those surfing lessons.

22

DON'T MESS WITH THE ACRONYM THING

HARLEY

I get off the beach, snatching my skateboard along the way. Dumping it down on the sidewalk, I balance myself and then take off.

I can't believe Aidan has screwed up my surf session.

Dick.

When I got the text from him earlier today, it took every ounce of willpower not to respond. My fingers were itching to reply: I'll see you there!

But I wouldn't let myself do it, because I don't like him and I'm not going there.

Of course he had to show up anyway, looking hot and beautiful on that golden sand. I love the shape of his legs, his strong calf muscles. I couldn't stop staring at him as I walked towards the water. He was talking to

Mr. Dreads, and I was hoping to sneak straight past them.

But then he saw me.

And he came running over.

My heart squeezed with desire, longing, and I had to put an end to it.

Because Aidan wants his ex-girlfriend back.

And I'm not letting myself fall for anyone again.

My throat burns as I try to swallow the boulder lodged in there. I don't want to go home right now. I'm not sure what Mom's schedule is this week, but she was home when I left for the beach, and she might still be there. I don't think I can stomach one of our stilted conversations right now, so when I hit my neighborhood, I veer right towards Jed's house.

Hopefully he'll be there, listening to music up in his room or something.

His grandmother won't let girls in his room, but if she's still at work, I might be able to sneak up. His gramps is way more relaxed. He knows it's not like that between me and Jed. My BMF is like the brother I always wanted.

Sliding to a stop outside his house, I walk through the gate and rest my surfboard against the fence, then tuck my skateboard underneath it. I'm about to head to the front door when I hear my call sign.

"HQ! Up here." I glance up and see Jed sitting on the upstairs balcony.

I shield my eyes from the sunny glare and call up to him. "Hey, man."

"Why aren't you in the water?" He pulls his head-phones off, resting them around his neck, and leans his forearms on the railing.

All I can do is push my lower lip into a decent-sized pout.

"Get your butt up here." He indicates with a flick of his head. "The front door's unlocked."

I walk quietly into the house, not wanting to draw attention to myself. Jed's grandparents are pretty cool, but I'm not in the mood for adult interaction.

The fourth stair creaks loudly as I ascend, so I rush up the rest of them and race through the sunroom and out onto the balcony.

Plunking down in the sky-blue chair beside Jed, I force a smile.

He raises his eyebrows at me. "Why aren't you in the water?"

"Surf's not great," I mutter.

I'm gonna tell him—I always do—but our routine is that he has to work for it, needle it out of me. I don't know why I always play things this way, but it would seem unnatural to just launch straight into my rant.

"I call bullshit," Jed singsongs.

I give him a sideways glare and humph.

"Why aren't you in the water?" he tries again.

"I didn't feel like it." I frown.

"I call double-triple-times-infinity bullshit!" He

squeezes my knee, making me jerk in my seat and slap his hand away. "What is up with you?" He frowns, looking mildly concerned.

"Nothing." I stupidly shake my head. "I'm fine."

"You're *not* fine. You look like a GA."

GA? I haven't heard that one before, so give him a quizzical look.

"Grumpy Ass. It'll catch on." He flicks his hand through the air and my traitorous lips curl into a smile. He notices, and his own lips start to twitch. "Come on, girl. Talk to me."

"I don't want to talk to you." I nibble my thumbnail.

"Yes you do. Look at my face. This is a face that wants to listen." He leans into my space, angling his head from side to side and wiggling his eyebrows.

I snicker and realize he's won.

"Girl, open up to your BMF before I get super annoying."

"Fine!" I tip my head back so I don't have to look at Jed while I'm saying it. "I got into a fight with Aidan. That spoiled little shit has had everything handed to him on a silver platter and he just doesn't appreciate it! He's got the easiest life in the world. The easiest! He practically got offered a summer job today—a really cool one that would be so incredibly fun. But he's not sure he'll take it, because, you know, '*working over the summer?*'" I make my voice deep and mocking. "That idiot can do whatever he wants, and he'll end up doing

nothing but sit on his ass and let life just pass him by!"
I flick my arm through the air.

"It's bugging you."

"Yes, it's bugging me!" I sit up and shoot Jed an
incredulous look. I can't believe it's not bugging him
either!

"Because you like him."

"What?" I snap, then quickly look away from my
friend. "No. No I don't!"

"Yes. Yes you do. You're totally goo-goo eyes for the
guy. Every time you talk about him your voice
changes."

"No it doesn't!"

"Yes it does. It gets softer and your lips start
fighting a smile."

"Well they're not doing that now! And they
certainly weren't doing it today!"

"Yeah, I noticed." His voice softens. "What
happened last night? I didn't have time to badger it out
of you at lunch."

"I don't want to talk about it." I cross my arms and
slump against the hard wooden back. "It doesn't matter
anyway. I'm so over it. And you know what?" I give
Jed's arm a backhanded slap. "That's gross! I'm not
goo-goo eyes over Aidan De Beer. I'd have to be insane
to like that whiny, rich snot rag. He's a..." I take a
second to work it out, lifting my fingers as I count each
letter. "A WRSR."

"Okay, I think it's best that you leave the acronyms

up to me. It's my thing. You're the sporty, amazing surfer girl and I'm the funny acronym guy. Let's just leave things as they are on that score, okay?" His pointed look is kind of comical and I can't help a half-smile. "But the whole you loving Aidan thing? Let's roll with that."

"What? No. We're not rolling. It's..." I shake my head. "He's still totally into his ex-girlfriend. And I don't, and will *never*, fit into his high-class snobby world. It doesn't even matter how I feel, because it will never happen. And it shouldn't happen."

Jed lets out a sigh, then gives me a sad smile that makes me want to cry. I've never told him the details of my freshman heartbreak, but he knows I dated a senior who I was completely in love with and when it ended, I didn't just lose him, but I lost my fam as well. They let me into their group while I was dating one of them, but as soon as it was over, my status became: outcast.

I sniff and look away from Jed.

I'm done talking.

I can't believe I didn't vehemently deny that I am starting to have feelings for Aidan.

I don't want to have feelings. I want to be numb when it comes to the guy.

Clenching my jaw, I keep my eyes straight ahead, grateful that Jed's not saying anything. After a few moments of silence, he starts tapping his phone and music soon lights the air between us.

That's Jed's solution to most things.

Music.

It's part of who he is. If he's not listening to it, he's beatboxing or singing something. The guy's a walking instrument. And his cure to almost every problem is a good song.

"Rise" by Jonas Blue, Jack & Jack starts playing from his phone and I do the only thing I can. I rest my head against Jed's shoulder and let the music cover me. I guess it's the next best thing to water.

23

INDECISION ON THE WHITE TILE

AIDAN

I can't stop stewing over my stupid argument with Harley.

Even a day of playing video games hasn't helped me switch off.

Man, she was pissed.

I don't even know what to do with that. I should be used to it. I've faced off with Skylar plenty of times, but she's my cousin. It's different.

I don't want to unpack how it's different when I'm trying to get ready for Skylar's beach party. The party where I'm supposed to be resealing the deal with Savannah.

Conjuring images of my beautiful ex is usually the easiest thing in the world, but tonight thoughts of Harley keep getting in the way. I hate that she's mad at me. I hate that I couldn't fix it, right there on the beach yesterday afternoon.

Why didn't I apologize for Skylar's behavior? I could have made it right, but instead I got all salty because she was making me feel bad. I shouldn't have to take a summer job I don't need. And I don't mope around feeling sorry for myself. My life isn't always easy!

The look on Harley's face when she told me about her mom and question-mark father over our Mexi-dinner sears my mind.

Shit, my life *is* sweet. I close my eyes and shake my head.

Maybe she did have the right to yell at me like that. Maybe I should be taking a summer job. I can't expect my parents to keep paying for everything in my life, can I?

Working four hours a week at the rec center must seem so lame, and a token gesture to someone like Harley. Who knows how many hours she has to work a week to earn the same money as me?

Opening my eyes, I take a good look in the mirror, studying the angles of my freshly shaved face, the shine of gel in my styled hair.

Shit, I am a pretty rich boy.

With an irritated huff, I rest my hands on the bath-room counter.

I've had hours to obsess about this, and no matter how hard I try, I keep coming back to the same conclusion. I'm actually glad I said yes to those surf lessons. I don't want them to end. Not really.

Hanging out with Harley is fun. Surfing is liberating.

But how do I make it right?

Snatching my phone off the bathroom counter, I pull up Harley's number and stare at it, trying to figure out what to text. She was pretty riled. There's a chance she'll take one look at my name and delete it without even reading it.

I put the phone back down and gaze into the mirror. When my mom's on the warpath, the best thing to do is give her some time to cool off. It takes her about twenty-four hours to really simmer down, but Harley's had that now.

I pick my phone back up again but am interrupted by a knock on my door.

"Aidan!" Mom calls through the wood. "Simon and Jonah are here."

"Okay." I shove the phone in my back pocket and take one final glance in the mirror. I've picked Savannah's favorite shirt and am even wearing the cologne she bought me for Christmas.

"Are you walking down tonight?" Mom asks as I walk out of my bathroom.

I nod. "Yeah, probably. It's too close to drive."

"Okay. Well, take it easy on the stairs."

"Mom." I give her a pained look.

She holds her hands up. "Well, I'm sorry, but

they're steep and dangerous. Don't tell me your friends won't be drinking. I know what they're like."

"I'll look after them." I give her a reassuring pat on the shoulder.

"Don't drink too much," she warns me.

I give her a calm, "please shut up" smile, and she gives me a pointed look. "I'm your mother, I'm allowed to fuss and worry. Now be grateful I even let you go to these things."

With a short laugh, I bend down and kiss her cheek. "Catch you later, Mom."

"Home by midnight, please."

"You got it." I start to walk out the door.

"Same for Skylar," she says to my back. "Her parents are away tonight. They get back first thing tomorrow morning and expect her to be in bed, asleep. Alone."

I glance over my shoulder. "I'll do my best, but you know what she's like."

"Just call Dad if you need backup."

"Got it." I walk out the door before she can give me any more instructions.

Simon and Jonah are waiting in the family room, watching Grayson annihilate his opponents in Fortnite.

Jonah whoops, then yells, "On your left!"

I grab his jacket and start tugging him towards the door. "Come on."

We'll be here all night if we have to wait for Jonah.

Simon laughs and helps me get the guy outside. As

soon as we hit the night air, Jonah's back with us again and going on about how thirsty he is, and how many girls he's going to hook up with at the party.

Simon and I don't say anything. We just share a look behind his back and try not to laugh out loud. Jonah's mouth has always been bigger than his number of conquests.

Negotiating the stairs in the dark is a fun challenge. There are lights spread down the path and steps, but they're not exactly high beam.

I hear the party before I see it. Music is blasting from a speaker, a thick bass that's pulsing through the air like a heartbeat. It must be ear-splitting down there.

Simon leans over the railing. "It's lit, man. There are so many people."

I lean over for a quick glimpse, my eyes rounding at the swollen crowd. Skylar's really gone all out with this one. A few trucks have driven onto the hard-packed sand and are lighting up the bonfire and "dance floor."

"Bring it on." Jonah starts racing down the cliff-side steps and we hustle after him.

As soon as his feet hit the sand, he disappears around the rocks and starts looking for some arm candy. If he could have it his way, they'd be draping off him like candy canes on a Christmas tree.

Simon and I move around the boulder-like rocks at the base of the cliff and find a spot on the perimeter of the party. "No Drama" is pumping from the speakers, and I move my head to the beat.

As I gaze around the pulsating crowd, all I can think of is the swarm of bugs we unearthed in the garage a couple months ago when Dad made me help him tidy up. We lifted an old carpet square and the insects were going off.

I can't help a snicker. Skylar would kill me if she knew I was comparing her carefully planned beach soirée to squirming insects.

"You ready?" Simon slaps my shoulder and propels me forward.

We enter the fray and I look around, trying to find Savannah.

"I'll get us some drinks." Simon takes off to go find liquor while I move around the edges of the party.

Wyatt is here. Of course. He's perched on the end of a log, nursing a red Solo cup and scowling at the fire.

I wonder if Sky's delivered on her seven minutes yet. Maybe that's why he looks so pissed.

Turning away from him, I look above heads and try to find Savannah.

Simon and I always come late to these things, because being in the early crew can be awkward. But maybe we've left it a little too late tonight. Finding Savvy in this crowd is gonna be hard.

I could always text her. I go to reach for my phone, but I'm distracted by my cousin. She's in the middle of the crowd, dancing up close and personal with a guy I don't even recognize.

I frown and move closer to the fire, my eyes

popping wide as the guy leans down and shoves his tongue in Skylar's mouth. She doesn't seem to mind, matching his slobber tongue-for-tongue. His large hand envelops her ass cheek, and she lifts her leg to accommodate him.

What the...?

I spot Craig standing a few feet away from me. He's staring at the way his girlfriend is making out with someone else and doesn't seem that bothered. Hustling over to him, I stand shoulder-to-shoulder and watch the display.

"Have you guys broken up or something?"

Craig glances at me, then shakes his head. "No."

"Then why aren't you putting an end to that?" I point through the flames, trying to figure out if I know the guy who's mauling my cousin. Have I seen him before?

He's tall and tanned, with a crew cut that makes him look like a badass. He's wearing nothing but a pair of board shorts, and his muscles are on full display for all the girls to swoon over. Maybe that's why Sky's going for it. She always has to have the best.

"She's drunk off her ass." Craig lets out a harsh laugh. "But hey, she's sucking his face tonight, and she'll be sucking my dick tomorrow."

I growl and punch Craig's arm. "Dude, that's my cousin."

He just laughs at me and shoves me away from him. I can smell the alcohol on his breath as well. His eyes have that glassy, inept sheen about them. "Hey, man, she's my girl." Shit, his words are already slurring. "Tomorrow she'll wake up hungover and feeling guilty for cheating on me. I'll play nice, forgive her, and then get me some hot makeup sex. It'll be a sure thing."

I've never wanted to pummel a guy more. I lurch away from Craig, ready to go and break Skylar and Mr. Hands apart, but he grabs my shirt and yanks me back. "Don't, man. You'll get your ass whupped. Look at the size of that guy."

"She needs protecting," I growl, shaking him off me.

Craig's lips rise into a slow crocodile grin. "I won't let it go too far, swear. I'll keep an eye on her." He takes another slug from his Solo cup and I wonder how Craig will protect her when he's paralytic drunk.

With a harsh scoff, I move around the fire, looking for Simon. Maybe he can help me break up the firestorm Skylar's creating. I hate the way she uses her body to pay people off.

Earning Craig's forgiveness with a blowjob?

It makes me sick!

She needs to break up with that asshole and pull herself together.

I'm halfway around the fire and still haven't found Simon. Glancing back to the "dance floor," I notice that Skylar is now gone as well.

"Shit," I mutter, wondering if she's taken Mr. Hands into the shadows for a little more. I sure as shit hope that Craig steps up and stops that from happening.

I'm about to head across that space and start checking it out when I spot Savannah. She's sitting on a rock by the water, hugging her knees to her chest and looking lost and alone.

My heart stretches out for her before I can stop myself, and I head in her direction.

That look on her face always undoes me. She's got to be one of the sweetest people I know, and when she gets sad like this, it kind of kills me.

I wonder if she's thinking about her mom, who died a few years back. Or maybe she's wishing that Skylar hadn't ditched her to go and play shit-stirrer with the crew cut.

Whatever's going through her head, I want to make it better. I want to see those dimples when she smiles. It used to be my mission in life, to make those dimples appear. My insides warm as I picture different days together—holding her hand, lifting her onto my shoulder and spinning her around in the sand.

It's a beautiful image, until a blonde chick surfs straight through the middle of it. I force the thought aside and keeping moving.

Savannah doesn't notice me coming until I'm right beside her.

"Hey." I smile down at her, finding an awkward perch on the rock. "You all right?"

She sniffs and slashes her cheek. Shit, she's been crying. I'm gonna be having words with Skylar. How could she just ditch Savvy like this? The girl is her constant wingman whenever Skylar needs her, but when Skylar's got better things to do, Savvy just gets left out in the cold.

"I'm sorry about Sky," I murmur.

"That's okay. It's not about..." She shakes her head and looks away from me. "I'm just kind of hating this place tonight. I don't... I'm just not...feeling it." She gives me a sad smile, unaware how much her words burn me.

She wasn't feeling it with me either and I was left out in the cold. I know the breakup was Skylar's idea, but Savannah went through with it. And Sky wouldn't have even suggested it if Savannah hadn't been bored with me... us.

I clench my jaw and remind myself that Savannah wants me back. That's what Skylar said anyway, and I don't think she'd lie about that. Skylar may be thoughtless sometimes, but she does actually care about her best friend. Plus, she'd never miss the opportunity to play relationship fairy.

"I don't suppose you'd mind walking me home, would you?" Savannah's quiet voice draws my eyes back to her pretty face.

"Sure." I nod and stand tall. It's tempting to hold out my hand for her to take, but I shove it in my pocket instead.

While Savannah grabs her handbag, I glance over my shoulder, scanning the area for Skylar. She's still not around. I'll swing past once Savvy's home to make sure she's okay.

"You ready?" Savannah asks.

I nod and move in next to her. Hopefully Simon won't spend too long looking for me.

Pulling out my phone, I give him a quick heads-up.

Me: Walking Sav home. Be back later.

Simon: My heart.

Me: Shut up.

In my head, I can hear Simon laughing as he no doubt tucks his phone away and drinks both cups of beer by himself.

We walk in silence for a few minutes, and I follow Savannah when she veers away from the stairs and obviously wants to take the long way home.

Hiking up the hill can be a real bitch, but at the pace we're ambling, we probably won't even run out of breath.

"This is weird," Savannah finally murmurs. "We've been walking for like fifteen minutes and haven't said a word to each other."

I give her a smile, surprised that I hadn't noticed it.

But she's right.

It is weird.

We've got so much history together. Why aren't we talking the way Harley and I were the other night? The conversation was easy and smooth...nonstop.

"So, Skylar tells me you're learning to surf."

"Yeah." I bob my head. "It's pretty cool."

"She said you did it for me." Savannah looks up and I catch a glimpse of her pretty face as we pass beneath the streetlamp.

"Uh..." I let out a soft chuckle, confused by why I'm not taking this shot and telling her exactly how I feel.

Maybe it's because I don't know.

Is Savannah the *only* reason I said yes to those lessons? Or was it something more?

Am I really looking for something to ignite me?

Harley's words bounce around my rib cage. I run a hand through my hair, completely forgetting about the hair gel and no doubt screwing up my look.

Savannah giggles and reaches up to pat down the wild locks. "You smell nice."

"Thanks." I clear my throat. Shit, this feels like a first date.

"So, um..." A deep dimple appears on Savvy's left cheek as her lips quirk up at the edge. "Did you...do it for me? The surfing?"

"Yeah. Uh...maybe?" I shrug. "You breaking up with me was kind of a shock. I needed a distraction, but then maybe I thought you'd like me again if I could prove myself. Somehow make myself cool enough."

She cringes. "I'm sorry I did that to you. I never meant to hurt you, I just..."

I swallow and look up the hill. We're nearly at her street, and for some weird reason I don't want to talk about this.

I don't know what I want, but I didn't think getting deep with Savannah would feel this awkward. I obviously haven't thought this through—what a broken relationship reunited would feel like. Savannah's been my first and only serious girlfriend. I thought she was it. Until she wasn't.

Her hand brushes against mine, and I'm suddenly aware of how tall she feels compared to Harley.

Savannah's head reaches up to my nose, and I'm very aware of her beside me. Her long locks with a slight curl at the ends. Her sweet lavender scent from the moisturizer she religiously slathers on. She cares a lot about the way she looks. She probably spent an hour getting ready for the party tonight, and even though she's in ripped jeans and a black tank top, there's no way she would have just thrown them on. She probably picked out a couple of outfits to choose from.

I used to love that about her, but now all I can think of is Harley and how it took her less than five minutes to run into her house, throw on some dry clothes and be back in my car ready for dinner.

We turn left onto Savannah's street. Our conversation has dried up, and it's impossible to ignore how awkward this is. Savannah's no doubt waiting for me to tell her that I miss her.

And I do...sometimes.

Maybe she's waiting for me to say I want her back.

Which I do...sort of.

We reach her driveway and walk past the mailbox, stopping on the large white tile outside her front door. She's playing with the strap of her handbag, so obviously lingering.

This was our spot, for nearly a year. This is where we'd linger every time I was about to leave her. We've made out on this tile—everything from chaste kisses to heated tonsil hockey. Her body would press against mine and I'd want her so bad in those moments, but she'd always pull away. We never took things to the next level.

Why?

Because I wasn't her one?

Because she wasn't ready?

I gaze down at her now and can't help wondering if it was a sign.

We never took things to the next level because we were never meant to.

It makes me hesitate, even when she tucks her hair behind her ear then brushes her finger over her bottom lip.

"Thanks for walking me home," she whispers.

"That's okay," I rasp, then lick my lips.

She's waiting for me to make a move, but for some weird reason, I can't. "Good night, Sav."

Her brown eyes dip with disappointment, and then she nods. "Night, Aidan." Without another glance my way, she rushes to her front door and disappears inside.

"Shit," I mutter.

Did I just completely screw that up?

What the hell is wrong with me?

I hustle up the driveway, wanting to get away from the house and my shame. What kind of guy doesn't go for it with Savannah Green? She would have let me kiss her tonight, but my body wouldn't make the move.

"You really are a fucking loser," I mutter darkly, confused by the fact that everything I've been pining for suddenly doesn't feel like enough.

Once again, I'm forced to face the fact that maybe Harley is right: I'm an entitled shit who isn't satisfied with life.

My mind flicks back to the party...and Skylar.

Man, when she finds out what I didn't do with Savannah, she's gonna have my head.

It's a small show of mercy that she'll be too drunk to care right now and too hung-over to scratch my eyes out tomorrow. I've got at least one day's grace.

Whipping out my phone, I text Simon again.

Me: Skylar okay?

. . .

Simon: Aren't you supposed to be busy right now?

I roll my eyes and type back: Skylar. What's she doing?

Simon: Dancing topless by fire.

"Shit!" I pick up my pace, cursing Craig as I text: Coming back now.

Simon: Don't bother. Someone called cops. We out.

Me: Do I need to get Sky?

Simon: All good. With Craig now. Will make sure she gets home.

That doesn't sit too well with me. I don't trust Craig to get Skylar home without screwing it up. But I do trust Simon.

. . .

Me: Thanks. Tell me all tomorrow.

Simon replies with a thumbs-up emoji and I know he'll be good for it. The guy's not a gossip or anything, but he'll relay the facts as he saw them. That'll be enough for me to get a picture of what went down while I was walking Savvy home.

I stop at the end of her street. There's no point going back to the beach if the cops are gonna break things up. All I can hope is that Craig's dad is one of them. He always goes easy on us teens…unlike Officer Kimble. That chick is a hard-ass.

Turning left, I head up the hill to my place.

Mom will want to know why I'm walking in early, and I really don't feel like having that conversation. So instead, I take the walkway that leads to a small lookout on the edge of the cliff. I can't see the party or the steps from this spot, but I'm guessing it's chaos down there. I'm kind of glad not to be a part of it.

Resting my hands on the railing, I gaze out across the water, listening to its sound and wondering what Harley is doing right now.

24

A DRUG-FREE SLEEPING PILL

HARLEY

I t's been a long, lonely night.

Screw that.

It's been a long, lonely *day*.

I had to work for most of it. If anything is going to depress me, it's scanning groceries at Freshmart for an entire freaking day. I was begged into working a double shift to cover Paulo's butt. That guy gets sick way too often to be believable.

With a huff, I roll onto my back and stare up at the gloomy ceiling. My bed is unusually intolerable tonight, but I don't feel like getting up and pacing my cluttered house either.

I just want to sleep!

But I can't.

I've been trying since about eleven thirty. No dice.

I can safely label this day a full-blown SNAFU.

The surf sucked this afternoon, so I missed out on my daily exercise. It put me in a foul mood. It always does. Jed was busy with some family dinner, so it was just me and my sorry ass. Mom had already left for work at Sugar Pop by the time I walked in the door. That's been the only highlight of my day.

In an act of true self-pity, I binge-watched *Riverdale* on Netflix and ate an entire bag of popcorn, plus a tub of chocolate ripple ice cream, which goes against all my eating beliefs. It was an emotional moment of weakness that my stomach is now cursing me for.

Maybe that's why I can't sleep.

I roll onto my side, bunching the pillow under my cheek and gazing at the phone on my bedside table. The red numbers of my digital clock highlight the edges of the device, and I can't deny that my stomach has nothing to do with the fact that I can't sleep.

It's all Aidan's fault. The fact that he hasn't texted since our bust-up. The fact that I want to be mad with him, but all I've done, *all day*, is miss him. Wish we were in the water together or sharing a bowl of tortilla chips.

I don't want to like him. How many times do I have to tell myself that!

But I can't leave things as they are. It's torturing me, thinking that our last encounter was me snarling at him like some animal.

With an angry huff, I switch on my light and sit up in bed.

I check the clock: 1:18 a.m.

If I text him now, it won't disturb him. He'll be asleep, have his phone on night mode and won't get the message until the morning. If he uses night mode. Doesn't everybody use night mode? Or is that just me?

What if he's still awake?

What if the text wakes him?

"Oh, just do it! Or you'll never get any sleep."

Biting my lips together, I pick up my phone and unlock the screen.

Aidan's text from Friday is still on display.

Want to surf today? The report looks good. I read it right. I think.

My face scrunches, longing pulsing through me.

"Yeah, I want to surf," I whisper.

Aidan's the only real surfing buddy I've had since "that guy," and as scary as it is to admit, I really love having someone to hang out with in the water.

So I like him.

I can manage that, right?

All I have to do is remind myself how horrible human beings can be, and that will stop me from wanting anything more than Aidan's friendship.

"Friendship," I murmur. "A surfing buddy."

The thought makes me smile, and I start typing before I think any harder about it.

Sorry for being a bitch about the summer job thing. I didn't mean to rag on you so bad. I'm up for a surf tomorrow afternoon if the waves are good. Let me know if you want to join.

I bite my lip so hard it starts to hurt, then send the text without proofing it. I just need to get it out there.

He might respond.

He might delete.

I probably deserve the delete, but at least I've done everything in my power to get my surfing buddy back.

"Your buddy. That's it," I whisper into my pillow after I lie back down and switch off the light.

25

A SLICE OF THE BLUES

AIDAN

Harley's text is burning a hole in my pocket.

I woke up to it and wanted to reply right away, but Mom walked in before I could, ordering me out of bed and reminding me of the family lunch we have. She wanted help in the kitchen preparing salads to take with us, and every time I even reached for my phone, she barked at me to "Get on with it."

As we walk out the door, I finally manage a quick reply:

Super keen. Have fam lunch first. Will text when I head to beach.

. . .

I slip the phone into my pocket and can't help my grin. There's nothing I want to do more than go surfing with Harley this afternoon.

"Why are you smiling?" Mom asks as we walk around to Uncle Jeff and Aunt Marlo's house.

"No reason." I shake my head.

Dad snickers and tries to nudge me with his elbow, nearly dropping the platter of salmon crackers Mom prepared. "Things must be going well with you and Savannah."

Dad wiggles his eyebrows at me, then starts to laugh when I turn away.

"Oh, Luke, stop embarrassing him," Mom chides, but I can see she's fighting a smile too.

Shit, I really should have told them about our breakup already. Although, I thought after last night I wouldn't need to bother.

A confused frown wrinkles my forehead.

Why didn't I go for it last night?

And why does that question feel so damn hard to answer?

"Grayson, honey, slow down. I don't want you dropping that," Mom calls ahead.

My younger brother ignores her, charging ahead and nearly barreling straight into Officer Malloy, who is walking down the path away from Skylar's front door. He's in uniform today, his mustache neatly clipped, his police badge glinting in the sun.

"Sorry about that, Dayton!" Mom rushes past the

mailbox as Grayson dodges her glare and runs into the house.

"No problem." The man smiles although looks kind of grim too.

"Everything okay?" Dad asks, then grins. "Hope there's no problem at the De Beer residence, Officer."

The police officer's expression clears, and he puts on a smile, glancing at me before turning back to my parents. "Just checking up on a certain partygoer from last night. Things got a little crazy. My Craig is currently in bed nursing the mother of all hangovers."

Mom winces, then glances back at me.

I raise my hands and am relieved to say, "I left early to walk Savannah home. I didn't even have time for a drink."

"Sounds like you were the smart one, then." Officer Malloy raises his eyebrows before slipping on his shades and walking past me.

"Have a good shift." Mom says goodbye and we head towards the house. She's muttering something under her breath. I can't catch it all, but I'm pretty sure I hear, "…do with that girl."

I bet Mom's relieved that Skylar is only her niece and not her daughter.

"Sasha." Aunt Marlo greets her sister-in-law at the door. Her smile is bright and sunny as always, her dark hair perfectly styled, her red-and-white dress making her look like a *Vogue* model.

"Hi, Marlo." Mom laughs and kisses her cheek. "Looking gorgeous as always."

"Oh, stop. So do you." She drags Mom into the house.

Dad and I follow, laying down the food on the dining room table. Everything is set for our family lunch, and in spite of the fact that it's only family, everything is perfect. Because that's the way Aunt Marlo does things. Appearance means a lot to her. It shines through in every aspect of her life—the straightness of the cushions on each couch, the carefully selected color palette in every room, the fact that there are never smudges on the glass windows.

And I think my mom's finicky. She's got nothing on Marlo De Beer.

I don't know how Skylar copes with it.

I scan the open living area and don't spot my cousin, so I wander into the kitchen and catch the tail end of Aunt Marlo's explanation.

"So, God bless Dayton Malloy. He wasn't even on duty last night, but Craig called him in a panic, saying the cops were coming. So Dayton rushed down to the beach and gathered up a bunch of kids and personally dropped them all home."

My mom's eyes bulge. "The party must have gotten pretty wild if someone called the cops."

"I think the noise was the biggest issue, but we all know the kids would have had alcohol down there." Aunt Marlo notices me hovering in the doorway but keeps going with her story anyway. "So, this morning Dayton is visiting every teen he dropped off, and he's doing it in uniform just to really drive the point home." She shakes her head but is fighting a smile. "Skylar is looking thoroughly reprimanded. I think her migraine hangover is punishment enough, but Dayton turning up in uniform really freaked her out." She giggles. "What am I going to do with that girl?"

"Well, she's a party animal, just like her mother was," Mom teases.

Aunt Marlo gasps but then can't help laughing along with her in-law.

I cringe, hoping they don't delve into stories of Aunt Marlo dancing topless at a bar somewhere. I wonder if Skylar's mom knows just how wild her daughter got last night.

Simon still hasn't texted me the details, but I've picked up enough from overhearing that conversation. Grabbing my phone, I send my friend a quick message.

Me: Waiting on deets, man.

Simon: Just waking up. Not much to tell. Craig's dad showed up and took us home before Officer Hard Ass arrived. Jonah got stung. Parents made him spend the night at the station. Think he's grounded forever. You seen Sky?

. . .

Me: Looking for her now. Expect a visit from Malloy. He's doing rounds.

Simon: Thanks for the heads-up. See you Monday.

I sign off and slip my phone away, wondering if I should send Jonah a sympathy text. But I kind of want to talk to Skylar first.

Walking past Grayson, who of course is playing on his phone, I pick up that the dads are talking about politics, so I quickly sidestep that one and head into the den where I find Skylar curled up on the couch. She's squished right into the corner, her knees tucked against her chest. I don't think she's ever looked so small...or awful. Her cheeks are pale, her eyes puffy and red. For once, she hasn't dressed up for the occasion and is sitting there in pale blue sweats and a baggy shirt that obviously belongs to her dad.

"Hey," I softly greet her. "You okay?"

Glancing at me, she swipes a tear off her cheek and swallows. "I feel like shit."

I wince and walk down the two steps into the room. Taking a seat beside her, I follow her gaze out the window. Like us, Skylar's house looks out over the water. The den has one narrow tall window that goes from floor to ceiling. A slice of blue to break up the solid, pale gray wall.

"How much trouble are you in?" I softly ask.

She hitches her shoulder.

"How bad's the headache?"

She scoffs and slowly blinks. "Bad."

"Do you...uh...remember much about last night?"

Her slight shoulders ping tight, her entire body tensing beside me. "I was pretty drunk," she hedges.

I can't help wondering if she remembers more than she's willing to say. If she recalls dancing half-naked, making out with another guy, cheating on Craig. I want to know where she disappeared to and just how hot and heavy she got with crew cut.

Does she know Craig's expecting makeup sex, or a blowjob at the very least?

I grimace, hating the guy. Skylar shouldn't be with him. I open my mouth to tell her, but wonder if now is the best time. She seems kind of fragile, which is so unlike her. Does she really need to know that her boyfriend's a complete dick too?

Craig would kick my ass if I started meddling in his relationship with Skylar.

But that shouldn't matter.

"Hey, Sky..." I start slow, trying to figure out the best way to word things.

"How'd it go with Sav last night? I haven't heard from her this morning. Her dad probably let her sleep in, unlike mine," she grumbles. "Stupid parents woke me as soon as they walked in the door."

There's a harsh bitterness to her tone, and I can

easily sense that her mood won't allow for any extra conflict.

I'll talk to her about Craig tomorrow, when she's feeling better.

And I won't tell her how I flaked with Savannah either. That's not what Skylar wants to hear right now, so I dish out the facts and hope they're enough to appease her.

"I walked Sav home last night. We left before the bust-up."

She nods but keeps her eyes out the window. "That's good," she rasps, her voice feather soft.

It's weird seeing Skylar this way.

Shit, I shouldn't have left her. I should have made sure she was okay before taking Savvy home.

"Hey, can I get you some aspirin or something?" My lame attempt to make up for bailing.

She sniffs and shakes her head, then winces, rubbing her aching temples.

I get the distinct impression that she's done with talking. So I seal my lips and just sit with her, silently staring out at the ocean and counting the minutes until I can get out of here and hit the water.

26

SCREW DANGER & LIVE A LITTLE

HARLEY

My toes are buried in the sand, my arms crossed.

I squint against the burning sun as I gaze at the beautiful sets of waves rolling in.

There are just a couple of problems.

1. These waves will annihilate Aidan.
2. Axel and his crew are dominating out there.

I can't put Aidan into that mix. There's no way they'll tolerate a newbie. It's not like we can hang out in the shallows in these conditions. We'd be forced into the mix with those guys, and that just won't fly.

I know they've spotted us down here before. They will have worked out that I'm teaching Aidan how to surf, and they'll be okay with it, as long as he doesn't hinder what they want to do.

If he shows up, I'll have to take Aidan someplace else.

I know where'd I *like* to take him, but Axel would have my head. In thinking that, Axel is kind of busy right now, and what he doesn't know won't hurt him, right?

A smile tugs at my lips, my anticipation building as I wait for Aidan to arrive.

I was stoked to get his text this morning. I'm ashamed to say I was anxiously waiting for it. I even carried my phone around like one of those teenagers who can't be more than an inch from their device at any one time.

I've never been like that. I don't really have enough friends to need to be like that.

"Hey."

I hear Aidan's voice before I see him, and have to try and curb my grin before looking over my shoulder. "How's it?"

"Yeah, good." He stops beside me, tall as a redwood, and gazes out at the water.

I should probably take this moment to apologize, but I kind of did that in my text and I don't want to ruin the moment by getting all serious. "So, how was lunch?"

He pats his stomach. "Lunch was good." Looking

down at me with a friendly smile, he then points to the water. "But those waves look pretty big."

"I know." I scrunch up my face, then decide to just take the risk. "Did you bring your car?"

He gives me a quizzical look and nods.

"I know another place where the conditions might be better for you."

"Sure you don't mind?" He points at the ocean again. "Those waves probably have your name on them."

Aw, that's kind of sweet.

I grin and bend down to grab his longboard. "Of course I don't mind." Passing him the board, I reach down and take mine before heading back up the beach. "All you need is practice and you'll be surfing waves like this too."

"On maybe a smaller board?" he asks.

"Yeah." I ascend the stairs, talking over my shoulder as I go. "Have you looked online for any boards yet? You said you were gonna do some research."

"I was actually going to ask if you wanted to come shopping with me sometime. Help me pick something out."

My step falters, but I manage to catch myself before tripping. Hopefully he doesn't notice.

Surfboard shopping with Aidan. More "out of the water" time with him.

Damn, that's tempting.

I want to say yes. Actually, I want to holler YES at the top of my lungs, but should I?

Slowing to a stop by his car, I glance over the roof and give him a noncommittal nod-shrug. It could be read either way. If he wasn't wearing shades, I'd maybe have a better idea what he was thinking, but all I notice is his dark eyebrows dipping for just a flash as he unlocks his car.

"Or I can just look online," he murmurs. "Maybe talk to that Griffin guy. He can probably let me look at some of the rental boards."

Great. Now I feel bad.

Poor guy looks like I've just slapped him with a big rejection ticket.

I bite the inside of my cheek as he lowers the roof, then gets busy arranging the boards. I really want this afternoon to go well, but I'm screwing it up already. As Aidan slips into the car, I close my eyes and remind myself that I want him to be my surf buddy.

Do surf buddies shop for boards together?

Maybe.

I still can't find the words to tell him I'm in, though. It just feels like dangerous ground. Like I'm opening the door to heartache and saying, "Come on in."

Aidan revs the engine and reverses out of his spot. I start directing him to Hatchet Cove and hope like hell that Axel and his crew stay in the water at Ryder Bay.

I try to think of something to talk about. Anything

to kill the awkward tension that's slipped into the car with us.

"So…" I clear my throat. "How was the party?"

His right shoulder hitches. "Meh."

"Really? I thought it was your big moment to get back with your ex." He's mentioned her name before, but I can't quite remember it.

It starts with S, I think.

He sighs and runs a hand through his hair. "We left early. She wanted me to walk her home."

"Oh, okay." I swallow the sharp rocks in my throat and remind myself that this is good. Him having a girl-friend is good, because then I'm free to just be his bud and there's no weird tension.

My fingers curl into fists in spite of my resolve. I force them flat on my knees and keep talking. "Well, that's good, man. It's what you wanted, right?" I glance at him. "She won't mind you surfing with me, though, will she?"

He glances my way briefly, then locks his eyes on the road. "I just walked her home. That's it."

"So, you're not back together?"

Another heavy sigh, this time accompanied by his head hitting the back of the rest. "I don't know… if…" I narrow my eyes at him, trying to figure out what he's not saying. "We have all this history. We were together for nearly a year, but it's been broken. She broke it, and I don't know how to tape it back together again."

"How serious were you guys?" I capture a stray lock

of hair that's blowing in the wind. I try to tame it by tucking in behind my ear, then ask the burning question that I do but don't want to know. "Did you guys sleep together, or…"

He shakes his head. "Savannah wasn't ready for that."

I blink, kind of surprised by his answer. I was expecting something else.

"How about you?" He looks at me. "Any serious relationships?"

"None worth mentioning," I croak and look out my window so he can't see my face.

I've never spoken to anyone about "that guy" and how it all went down, not even to Jed. I mean, he knows about the senior who taught me how to surf, but not the rest of it. Not the ugly ending. At first, when I lost everyone, it hurt too much, and silence became my best friend. But now I just don't want to unearth it. I've moved on, gotten over the heartache. Shielded myself from anything else like it.

Until now.

Why am I doing this to myself?

So, I think shopping for a surfboard is too dangerous, but spending an afternoon at Hatchet Cove doing something I love with someone I could fall—

I cut off the thought before it can fully form in my head.

I am *not* falling for Aidan.

I just really, really, really like him.

Which is bad. Dangerous.

Yet I can't ask him to pull over, to let me out.

Because I want to be in this car with him. I want to listen to his voice as we talk about...*anything*. I want to surf with him at Hatchet Cove.

I steal a peek at Aidan. His eyes are back on the road again and a smile tugs at my lips.

Screw danger. Screw thinking so damn hard about everything.

Live a little, Harley.

Just be in the moment...with him.

27

THE PEACEFUL BLUE

AIDAN

I'll never forget this moment.

As I drive over the unsealed road, my car rocking and swaying, I'm captured by the isolated beauty of this place. And then the narrow road opens to a beach. Barely a beach, just a small patch of sand leading out to an oasis of water.

"This place is beautiful," I whisper.

"I know, right?" Harley grins at me and I'm struck by her beauty as well.

When she lets it show, her smile is sunshine. She looks like a real Californian beauty with her blonde hair, blue eyes and tanned skin. The kind of beauty I want to kiss.

She gets out of my car before I've finished studying

her, and it's a good reminder that I shouldn't really be thinking of her that way. She's just a friend, my surf instructor. It's not like she'd be interested in me that way.

Or would she?

The question sizzles through my brain, surprising and enticing me.

So far everything has been about getting Savannah back, but after my hesitation last night, maybe Savannah's not the girl I want.

I jump out of my car and start helping Harley with the boards, hyperaware of the way her body moves, the flex of her muscles as she pulls the shortboard out of the back, the shape of her body as she whips off her T-shirt, then covers her sporty blue bikini with a rash guard.

Stop staring, Aidan!

I blink, ordering my ogling eyes back into line. Gripping the edge of the yellow longboard, I remind myself that Harley doesn't even want to go surfboard shopping with me. My emotions need to get themselves in check.

Maybe that's why her noncommittal response to my invite disappointed me so much.

Because I like her...and not just as a friend.

Shit, that's probably why I couldn't kiss Savannah last night.

Because—

"So, we'll have to paddle a little farther out than

normal." Harley grabs my attention and I follow her pointing finger, looking out to the distant break she's talking about. "Those sets will be perfect for the longboard." She pauses, staring at her board while I wrestle the longboard free from the back of the car.

A slow smile is drawing her lips north.

"What?" I ask.

Her grin has now completely taken over her face, and all I can do is stare at those sparkling blue eyes of hers. "I've got an idea." She laughs, taking off her shorts and dumping them on my back seat.

Don't notice how hot she is. Don't notice!

It's impossible. I've already checked her out several times while we were surfing, appreciated her sculpted form and how strong she is.

But damn, for some reason today feels different.

She puts her shortboard back into my car.

"What are you doing?"

"Come on. This is gonna be fun." She starts running for the water, dumping her towel in the sand just before she reaches the water's edge.

"What about your board?"

"We won't need it, just bring the longboard," she calls over her shoulder, and I'm forced to follow her.

She dives into the cool ocean, her skin glistening as she pops back up and waves me in.

"What are we doing?" I push the board in and as the water gets too deep, I jump on and start paddling.

She swims over to me and captures the side of the board.

Even her eyelashes have water droplets on them. She blinks and starts kicking beside me.

"These waves are perfect for doubling up. We can surf the same board."

I give her a worried frown. "Am I good enough to do that?"

"Of course you are." She splashes my face, then duck dives under the water before I can get her back.

Playful Harley is like a dolphin, full of fun and flirt. I laugh as she swims around, then pops up to check where I'm at.

After five minutes of messing around, she swims over and helps me turn the board around.

"Okay, scooch forward. I'm jumping on the back."

I do as she says, and then she starts yelling at me to paddle. I put all my strength into it, feeling the energy surge beneath us and capture the board.

"Woohoo!" She jumps up, manning the board and riding the wave for us. "Okay, your turn, dude."

I grin and slowly rise to my feet, at first a little shaky. The board feels so different with two people on it.

"And lean forwards a little. Bend your knees," she directs me. "That's it!"

Her laughter scuttles over me and I can't help joining her. We ride the wave until our board starts to sink and we both flop off together, landing in the water with big splashes.

The cold liquid envelops me, and I float in that weightless sensation. Man, I forgot how cool it is just to be in the water—relaxed and chilled. For my entire teenage life, swimming has been about precision, training, drills. We never just messed around in the water. No wonder I got tired of it. No wonder I started losing everything.

I'm done with the rigors of swimming.

I just want to fall in love with the water again.

With a kick, I swim to the surface and rest my arms on the edge of the board.

"Holy crap, I was about to come down looking for you." Harley bulges her eyes at me. "You can hold your breath for a really long time."

I give her a modest smile. "Big lungs, I guess."

She laughs and shakes her head. "Well come on, big lungs. Let's go catch some more waves."

No argument here.

Pushing the board forward, I kick my "flipper feet," as Mom always calls them, and follow Harley into the blue.

"Man, I could stay here forever." I squint against the bright sun and close my eyes, enjoying the heat coating my wet skin.

The surf has died down for a while and I'm lying on the board, just floating in the water, while Harley balances on the end by my feet. Her legs are dangling in the water, gently kicking back and forth.

There's something very calm and peaceful about just being here like this.

Harley hasn't responded to my comment, so I open my eyes to check on her.

Her eyes are closed, her face angled towards the sun. A sweet smile is on her lips.

"Do you come here often?" I ask.

"No." She lets out a contented sigh.

"Why not? It's so beautiful."

She opens her eyes and turns to me, about to respond, when she spots something on the beach. "Oh shit," she mutters, her skin paling, her body tensing.

"What?" I turn to see what's freaking her out, nearly overbalancing and throwing us both off the board. I stop moving, lying on my side and staring at a muscly black guy who's standing on the beach and shouting at us.

"Get the hell out of the water!"

Three other guys step up behind him, their eyes locked on us like we're the enemy.

"Are they the guys from the beach? The ones you told me to avoid?"

"Time's up," Harley murmurs. "Just stay quiet and let me get us out of this."

Before I can protest, she slips off the board and starts swimming for shore.

Like hell I'm letting her face off with those guys alone. They look like a mean bunch of assholes. I start paddling, determined to reach the shore before she does.

28

POCKET KNIFE PAINTING

HARLEY

Aidan gets out of the water and I internally curse. I've already warned him about these guys. Is he stupid?

I want him to hang back so I can deal with Axel on my own. Aidan has no idea what these guys can be like. I've only told him to steer clear, not given him all the details.

Axel's crew are territorial wolves, and they have no time for punks like Aidan De Beer.

"Hey, Axel." I grab my towel, going for casual as I dry off my face.

I throw a glance at Aidan, who's eyeing them cautiously.

He's about the same height as most of these guys, but he's their junior, probably by about five years or more. I don't care how protective and badass he's trying to look, he's got nothing on these bloodhounds.

"We're just leaving." I brush past Axel, but he steps back, getting in my face.

"You don't bring strangers to the cove." His deep voice is sharp with warning.

"I'm sorry, okay." I dare to look him in the eye, but those black orbs freak me out, so I glance down at the sand. "But he's not a stranger to me."

"It's not your cove to share."

"Well, technically it's not your cove either."

Shit. Wrong thing to say.

I can sense his nostrils flaring and look up to see his wide nose quiver before he snatches my arm and yanks me against his side.

Fear spikes through me, hot and painful.

"Hey, get your hands off her! Don't touch her!" Aidan muscles up beside us, dropping the longboard at my feet. Axel immediately lets me go and turns to face Aidan head on.

Double shit!

Aidan has no idea what he's doing.

I throw myself between them with a grunt, grabbing Aidan's vibrating forearms and begging him to look down at me.

Right now, his gaze is locked with Axel's and he's going to get pummeled for it.

"Just walk away," I warn. "Let's just go."

Aidan isn't listening. He's currently locked in a

glare-off with the scariest guy I know. If he doesn't break it soon, he's going to end up with a bloody nose and who knows what other injuries.

And then the sound of scraping metal comes to the rescue.

Well, sort of.

In a black kind of way.

Aidan blinks and jerks to look over Axel's shoulder.

"Hey!" he yells, his face mottling with indignant rage.

I spin to see what's going on and notice Ripper smirking at us. His pocketknife is flipped open and he's running it along the edge of Aidan's shiny convertible.

"You shithead!" Aidan shouts at him.

This only goads Ripper on and he keeps scratching a thick line along the paint, laughing so hard that his friends join in too.

Axel stares down at me. "Get your boy out of here. And don't come back again."

"We're going." I tug Aidan's arm. "Let's go."

He gives me an incredulous look, but he can shove his righteous anger up his ass. I'm saving his freaking life right now.

"Let's go!" I snatch the longboard and march to the car, shoving Ripper out of the way so I can dump the board in the back.

Ripper goes to grab me, but Shane stops him, snatching his arm before the guy can touch me.

I slam the passenger door shut and Shane leans

down to get in my face. "This place is invitation only, bitch. You don't bring pretty boy here again, got that?"

Turning with an ice-cold look, I silently tell him I understand before glancing back at Axel. He's not impressed, and I wonder if they're going to make me pay for breaking the rules.

29

BITING WORDS & SCREECHING TIRES

AIDAN

I race down the narrow road, my beat-up car complaining at me until we reach the smooth seal of the main road. Flooring it, I speed back to Ryder Bay, my anger manifesting itself in the way I grip the wheel and negotiate the curves a little too fast.

Harley hasn't said anything, and I'm too pissed off to talk.

My insides are raging.

How dare those fuckwits mess with my car. How dare they order us out of the water like they own that freaking cove. How dare they touch Harley!

I could have killed that guy for putting his hands on her.

And that asshole that scratched up my car. I saw him reaching, his big paws going to grab her.

Something about him is so familiar. I can't think why, but I know I've seen him somewhere else.

My eyes bulge as it suddenly comes to me.

The party last night.

Skylar's hookup.

Anger spurts through me again, hot and fierce. "This is bullshit! I'm reporting that asshole."

"No, you're not," Harley snaps. "You don't take on Axel or his crew."

"Why the hell not? I have every right to. That jackass messed up my car. How am I going to explain it to my parents, huh?"

Harley scoffs like I'm stupid. "You're going to tell them that your car was parked in some random parking lot and when you returned, someone had vandalized it."

"No way!" I slap the wheel. "I'm going straight to Officer Malloy and—"

"No!" She grabs my bicep, digging her fingers into the muscle. "Don't you get it? So he arrests Ripper for messing with your precious car. Do you think it ends there? Axel's crew will pay you back and make your life a living hell for messing with one of their own."

I shake her off me and keep my eyes on the road.

Shit, she's probably right.

Dammit!

"Why the hell do you even hang out with those assholes?"

"Because they're surfers." She huffs. "It's not like

we're buddies or anything. I just see them around. They tolerate me because I know what I'm doing."

I clench my jaw, my head shaking as I softly tell her, "I don't want you seeing them again."

"Excuse me? You did not just say that."

I throw her a hot glare, which she can't see because of my shades. It'll look too dumb if I whip them off now, so I just clench my jaw instead.

"You can't tell me who I can hang out with," Harley snaps. "You're not my father."

"No, I'm your friend. A friend who cares about your well-being."

"I don't need you to care about my well-being, all right? What the hell?" She shuffles in her seat, then stabs her finger at me. "And I didn't need you to save me, Prince Charming. I told you to stay quiet and let me handle it. If you'd just shut up and did what I said, your car would probably be fine."

"He manhandled you," I argue. "You needed help."

"No I didn't. I was fine on my own."

I growl in my throat, anger spewing hot lava into my mouth. "You are so frustratingly independent! It's okay for people to help you, Harley!"

"What is your problem?" she bites back.

"I was trying to help you! And all you can do is sit here yelling at me like getting kicked out of the water and having my car vandalized is my fault!"

"It *is* your fault! You should have shut up and hung back!"

"What? And just let that guy hurt you?" My voice pitches high with disbelief. "You are one messed-up chick, you know that? You're gonna die an old, lonely hag because you push people away all the time!" I'm too riled up to even hear what I'm saying, but when she goes quiet, I glance at her face and suddenly realize I crossed a line.

Her lips are pinched tight, her expression flashing with a vulnerability that makes my chest constrict.

Shit. I did that.

With a sharp sigh, I try to make it right. "Hey, I'm sorry, I didn't mean—"

"Shut up! Screw you!" She crosses her arms and thumps back in her seat, angling her body away from me.

I clench my jaw, irritated that she won't even let me apologize.

This whole afternoon is now messed up AF, and I don't know how the hell I'm supposed to turn that around.

"Whatever." My mumbled response is lame but it's all I have. At least it'll close off the argument.

We drive the rest of the way in silence.

I glance over a couple of times to see if Harley's crying. Savannah would be a wreck after an argument like this, but not Harley Quinn. She's a statue of poise and control, her jaw set as she stares out the window, refusing to look at me.

By the time we reach her street, I've simmered

down enough to maybe try for a second take on making things right, but as I pull into her driveway, she jumps out of the car and barks, "Just stay put. I can get the boards myself. I don't need your help. I don't need you at all!"

She's really driving the stake home, unloading my car while I just sit behind the wheel like a douche. Even if I wanted to smooth things over, I have no idea how, especially when she's this riled up.

It's kind of unfair. I did the right thing standing up for her and she's punishing me for it.

Screw this.

I don't have time for this bullshit.

As soon as she's walking to her carport with the longboard, I reverse out of her driveway, my tires squealing when I accelerate down the road.

Hanging out with Harley is a stupid idea.

All we seem to do is fight.

I close my eyes for a second, reminding myself that it's not true. We were having an amazing afternoon until those surfers showed up to ruin everything.

I'm still pissed, but what if Harley's right? Will taking on that guy Ripper have really bad consequences? What if they try to hurt Harley to get back at me?

Shit, falling for this surfer chick is a really bad idea.

Wait? What?

I slam on the brakes and angle my car towards the side of the road. Gripping the wheel, I stare straight ahead and try to figure out what the hell I just thought.

"I'm falling for her now?" I whisper, kind of surprised that I'm not hearing a resounding no or any kind of defense forming in the rear of my brain. "When the hell did that happen?"

When we arrived at the cove, I was just getting used to the idea that maybe I liked her as more than just a friend, but now I'm full-on falling?

My phone dings and I reach for it, my heart twisting with confusion when I spot the message on the screen.

Savannah: Thanks for walking me home last night. I would have texted earlier but I didn't know what to say. Things feel weird between us, but I want to make them right again. Call me when you're ready to talk.

With a groan, I rest my forehead against the steering wheel and drop the phone back into the cupholder it was sitting in.

30

OVER THE FALLS

HARLEY

I t's Monday morning and I feel like death.

Sleeping last night was impossible. Sunday afternoon just kept rolling around and around in my head, like some gif that I couldn't delete from my screen.

Laughter kept turning to anger—sharp, snappy words that hurt and stung.

Snappy words that I can't seem to forget.

Why do I even waste my time with Aidan?

All we do is fight.

As I skate into school, I spot Jed sitting outside at our usual table. Flicking my board up, I tuck it under my arm and shuffle over to him. I can pass my locker on the way to homeroom. Right now, I need to unload some serious angst.

Jed's listening to music while reading a Spiderman graphic novel and fails to notice me until I plunk down opposite him and slap my bag onto the table.

With a little jump, he looks up, then slowly pulls his headphones off. Strains of "Let You Love Me" hit the air and I wrinkle my nose. For some reason, that song has always bugged me.

Jed doesn't say anything as he looks at me and I soon let out a huff and ask, "Am I frustratingly independent?"

"OTD." He nods, completely unfazed by the fact that he just replied *Oh Totally, Dude* to my question.

I let out an indignant scoff and spread my arms wide. "Well, that's a good thing, isn't it? I never rely on anybody or bother them with my problems. That's not a weakness. It's a strength!"

Jed tips his head, his bottom lip pulling into a thoughtful pout before he softly replies, "Yeah, I guess you could see it that way. Kind of a lonely strength, though."

I roll my eyes and pull the bag towards me, hugging it like a teddy bear. "Don't you start. Next thing you'll tell me is I'm going to die an old, lonely hag."

"Why would you die an old, lonely hag?" His eyebrows dip together.

"Because I push people away all the time. Apparently." I spit out the last word.

The corner of Jed's mouth rises on the left and I see

his teeth are starting to show. Hopefully my irritated glare will stop the smile from fully forming.

He snickers and wipes a hand over his mouth before giving me a serious look. "What happened?"

I grit my teeth, my nostrils flaring.

"Just tell me in bullet points." He raises his index finger. "One. You…"

"Went surfing with Aidan," I grit out.

"Two…" He holds up his next finger, and I let out a sharp huff before rattling off what happened. I keep it short and succinct, trying to justify where I was coming from and really selling my side of the story. I manage to repeat word for word what Aidan said about me, because I've freaking memorized the insults.

"Yowch." Jed cringes when I get to the end. "Sounds like a big rip."

"It was a big rip," I mutter.

"SMH." Jed shakes his head and I glare at him. Does he always have to make a joke of everything?

Pressing his hands together, he rests his fingers against his mouth like he's some therapist about to give me advice, or a pastor who's about to pray for my soul.

I fist the material of my bag and nearly tell him to shut up, but he starts talking before I can.

"You know you do it because you're scared, right?"

"What?"

"Push people away." My throat gets thick and I'm tempted to stand and split, but then Jed reaches out and gently brushes his fingers across my forearm. "It's understandable. All the people in your life that you should have been able to rely on have let you down. So now you just rely on yourself. That way no one can hurt you."

"Thanks, Dr. Phil," I mutter, shifting my arm out from under his touch. This conversation is getting way too uncomfortable for my liking.

"It's okay to ask for help. To accept someone's help. That doesn't make you a lesser person."

I roll my shoulders, irritated that my BMF is not taking my side.

"What you need to understand is that there are people in this world you can count on." He points to himself. "People who aren't going to let you down, because they love you. They'd fight fire for you. Go over the falls for you. You feel me?"

"I know *you're* okay." I blink, wondering why my eyes are suddenly stinging.

"Yeah, well I'm not the only safe bet. There might be other people in your world who would do the same thing." He covers his mouth and mumbles, "Like HRB."

I jerk up straight and give him a quizzical frown. "HRB?"

"Hot rich boy." He shrugs. "Although I feel like I can come up with something better. Now that I know he stood up for you against Axel, maybe we can work on something a little more manly, less demeaning."

It's impossible to fight my grin. "I like HRB, although it's a little *too* complimentary."

He shakes his head at me. "Anything has got to be better than your lame WRSR."

I snicker as Jed snaps his fingers and points at me. "What about GWFF?" Squeezing my eyes shut, I try to figure it out, but he gets impatient and tells me before I can. "Guy worth fighting for."

I snap my eyes open and give him a withering glare.

He laughs. "Okay, so we'll stick with HRB. It's not bad, right?"

I shrug. "It's okay."

"It's damn brilliant, woman." Jed slaps the table and then grins at me, his smile morphing to meaningful as he rests his arms on the table and leans forward. "Now he may be hot and rich—two traits I don't hold in very high esteem—but I think he cares about you, HQ. He stood up to defend you yesterday. That's pretty damn awesome."

I can't reply as I start to see things from a different angle.

I guess it was kind of sweet that he didn't want Axel hurting me. Not every guy in the world would step up like that. Some guys just walk away, leaving the wounds to heal on their own.

My swallow is thick and audible.

Getting up from the table, Jed shuffles around to sit beside me, slinging his arm over my shoulder and pulling me close. "Relying on yourself is all good, but there's still one person out there who could hurt you."

I give him a quizzical frown.

"Yourself." His smile is kind of sad and way too honest.

I look away from him, not wanting to think about the fact that he might be right.

"Have some faith, and let him in, girl. Trust me, you don't want to live the rest of this life alone." He kisses the side of my forehead. "You're one of the bravest, strongest chicks I know, so take that risk and jump over the damn falls. You won't regret it."

31

A BRAIN-HURTING TENNIS MATCH

AIDAN

It's been three days since my fight with Harley and I still haven't texted her.

I'm not sure if I should.

Every time I pull out my phone, it feels like I'm about to unlock Pandora's box. Do I really want to jump back into the fray with her?

She was pretty pissed off when we left things, and if I'm honest, so was I.

All I did was try to defend her and I didn't even get a thank-you. I shouldn't have suggested she'd die an old hag, but I had some other valid points. How are we supposed to be friends...or...?

I squeeze my eyes shut, still unsettled by the fact that I kind of want more than just friendship with the surfer girl. I've been blindsided by that revelation.

Shit, it would complicate everything.

Skylar would have my head, Savannah would be gutted, and my parents...

My parents.

Dad freaked over the car. I fed him the story Harley told me to, feeling sick as I lied but knowing on a gut level that it was the right thing to do. All I can hope is that Ripper will get bitch-slapped by karma one day. Bitch-slapped hard.

I hitch my bag up on my shoulder, ambling to my locker. The tennis match argument in my head has been going for days: Text her. Don't text her. Text her. Don't text her.

It's infuriating.

Swiveling around two girls, I raise my head and see Jonah hustling towards me. I welcome the distraction and slow to a stop when he reaches me.

"Did you hear about the lovebirds?" He grins like a crocodile.

"Huh?"

"Sky and Craig have just had the biggest bust-up."

"When?"

"About twenty minutes ago. They went into the drama room for some privacy, but their shouting was so loud you could hear it all the way down the corridor."

Great. Skylar will be unbearable after this.

I control the urge to roll my eyes and give Jonah a pointed look. "Well, what happened?"

"I wasn't there for the start, but Noelle told me that Craig was hoping for a little private get-together."

My eyebrows dip into a sharp V.

"Oh come on, man." Jonah lightly slaps my chest with the back of his hand. "You know they've done the dirty at school before."

I swallow and make a face, kind of grossed out by the imagery.

"Anyway, Noelle thinks Craig was wanting some and Skylar wasn't into it. Then this argument started, and he was accusing her of being a cheating skank and that she owed him."

I close my eyes, my shoulders slumping.

I'm gonna kill Craig.

"I arrived in time to hear Skylar shouting, 'You'll never touch me again.'" Then she stormed out of the room, nearly crashing right into me. I grabbed her so she wouldn't fall over, but she just screeched and shoved me off her." Jonah shook his head. "Man, I've never seen her so out of control before. What is up with her lately? She went completely cray at the party, and this week it's like she's been possessed."

Although I'm proud of Sky for putting Craig in his place, Jonah's right. She's been acting differently this week—quiet one minute, savage the next. It's got me worried.

"Has she said anything to you?" Jonah quizzes me, acting more like a gossip queen than a Warrior.

"No," I murmur, shaking my head. "But I better go find her and see if she's okay."

Jonah nods. "Craig's feral, so you might want to avoid him."

I scoff and shake my head again. I'm tempted to tell Jonah that Craig is getting exactly what he deserves and I'm proud of my cousin for standing up to him.

But I don't say anything as I walk away. Jonah's the kind of guy that will pass that information straight back to Craig, and I don't need the fallout.

I'm trying to decide where Skylar might go to lick her wounds, but as I round the corner, I find the one person she'd normally run to in a crisis, and she's walking down the corridor alone.

"Hey." My brow wrinkles as Savannah stops in front of me. "Where's Sky?"

Savvy holds up her phone. "She just ditched with a headache. I'll go check on her after school."

"Were you there for the fight?"

Savannah shakes her head. "I was in the cafeteria with Simon and Michelle. Craig had already warned me that he wanted some alone time with Skylar today and I was to back off during lunchtime." She rolls her eyes. "I really hate that guy sometimes."

I flash her a look of agreement. "I'm glad Skylar stood up to him."

"Me too." Her dimples appear and then disappear.

I recognize her look as worry and quickly ask, "Do you feel like she's been acting weird this week?"

She shrugs. "Maybe. She's been kind of quiet, not really herself, you know? I think the fact that she lost control at the party has really freaked her out. She's usually in charge, but she drank way too much and then made out with that stranger."

My mood turns icy black as I think about Ripper.

Stupid asshole.

"Even she has her boundaries," Savannah keeps talking. "Saturday night she jumped right over them, and maybe she regrets it."

I hate that she did that, but have to concede, "Maybe it's a good thing. I mean, if she's dumped Craig because of it."

"Yeah." Savannah sighs. "I don't know if they're officially over. I wouldn't put it past her to fall straight back into his arms next week. You know what she can be like."

I match Savannah's glum smile and grip my bag strap, suddenly feeling awkward when she looks up at me with her sad, puppy dog eyes. "So, you never called me."

I cringe. "Yeah, sorry about that. I, uh... I've had a lot on my mind this week."

"It's okay." She pulls in a breath but doesn't release it.

It's hard to know what to do. When we were together, I'd pull her into a hug and kiss the side of her neck. She always loved it when I did that.

Damn, it'd be so easy.

I could do it right now and we'd be right back to where we were. But something's holding me back.

Not just something.

I know exactly what's holding me back. I just don't know if it should.

"I know these things take time," Savannah whispers. "I guess I just miss you, and maybe regret..." Her eyes glass with tears and I reach out, gently squeezing her shoulder before she starts to cry.

"It's okay." I smile at her, scrambling to think of something, *anything*, to stop the tears. "Hey, um, why don't we just start the way we did before? You know, last summer? Let's just be friends and see what it turns into."

I'm not sure I mean that, but I've said it now and it's scored me a smile. I grin at her cute dimples but feel like I've just jumped into a vat of hot water. I'll get burned alive trying to swim out of it.

Savannah is the easiest option. She wants me. I could have her in a heartbeat, but for some reason that doesn't excite me the way it did a few weeks back. I was pining for this moment, and now that I've got it I just...

The bell rings and a sense of relief washes over me.

At this point I'd usually offer to walk her to class. We're in the friend zone again, it's the right thing to do, but I really have to force the words out. "Want me to walk you to class?"

She grins, then shakes her head. "No, it's the opposite direction from where you need to go."

Again, relief.

"But I'll catch you later, though?" Her voice pitches at the end, so hopeful and sweet.

I can't let her down, so I force a smile and say, "Yeah. I'll see you around."

I'm rewarded with her full-beam smile. She does a little spin, then walks away from me. I watch her for a second before turning towards my own class.

Confusion is a hurricane inside of me, battering my brain and heart.

What do I want?

The girl I thought I loved is practically begging me to get back with her.

But all I can think about is the girl I can't text.

32

A FLASHING YELLOW ARROW

HARLEY

So maybe I've been waiting for a text from Aidan.

I'm not sure.

It's Thursday afternoon, and our Sunday fight feels like a millennium ago.

I can't stop thinking about him, which is driving me crazy. I did go kind of savage on the guy, and there's a strong possibility he's written me off.

Maybe that's fair.

I pull in a shaky breath as I stare at my phone. The surf report is on the screen, but all I can see is a blurry image of Aidan's face as he consumes my mind's eye.

How much longer can I go like this?

"Just text him," I mutter for the hundredth time since Monday.

But every time I say it, I cringe and recoil at the idea of not one but *two* apology texts on record.

"He called you an old hag." I throw my phone on the bed and assure myself that I don't want that kind of bullshit in my life. *He* should be sending an apology text to *me*!

Which he hasn't.

Probably because he thinks I won't respond to it.

I did tell him I didn't need him.

"Which I don't!" I snap, then let out a sigh that seems to deflate my entire body.

Last time I tried to get all stubborn about this, an overwhelming sadness swamped me. And it's happening again. I don't want to be without anymore. Maybe trying to be everything I need all by myself just isn't working.

"But it has to work," I whisper, my throat thick and aching. "It's the only way."

Jed will roll his eyes at me. Accuse me of being a scaredy-cat.

He's right.

I am scared.

I'm hella scared.

What if I put myself out there and he turns into…"that guy"?

"What if he doesn't?" I whisper, liking the sound of the question. Liking the way it feels inside my chest when I imagine me with Aidan, Aidan with me, neither of us being anything but exactly who we are.

Jerking off the bed before I can stop myself, I walk away from my phone and head through the house.

Mom is in the kitchen, a cigarette teetering between her lips while she makes herself a PB & J. Smoke swirls around her head as she pulls the ciggy out and releases that stinky white cloud from the side of her mouth.

I wrinkle my nose and stay back in the clear, breathable air. "I'm out. Not sure what time I'll get home."

"'Kay," she mumbles.

"You working tonight?"

She looks at the clock above the stove. "Doing the late shift. Won't be home 'til around two, so don't wake me in the morning. Got it?" She points a red nail at me and I nod.

"See ya."

She gives me a halfhearted wave and I slip out the door. My nerves are on fire right now. I purposely left my phone behind so I'd be forced to do this face-to-face. I wouldn't be able to cower behind some text message that could be ignored.

It's a little insane, skating to the north beach and just looking around.

Who knows what I'll encounter up there?

But it's Aidan's turf, and if there's even a chance of bumping into him, then I have to take it.

"He's probably not going to be there," I mutter, already doubting myself as I hit the sidewalk and start to skate.

It'll take me a while, but maybe that's a good thing.

I need time to figure out what I'm going to say to him.

Why am I doing this again?

I shake my head, annoyed with my lame self, but I don't turn back.

By the time I reach the north end, my nerves are like frayed rope. The only way to stop my head from literally exploding is to give myself an ultimatum—if I see Aidan on the beach, it's a sign to go for it. If he's *not* there, then I just need to forget the whole thing, rip him from my mind and pretend like I never met him.

That resolve feels good. Like it takes the pressure off me having to make a decision and leaves it up to the universe.

I glide down the hill, smiling as the wind whips the hair off my shoulders. Leaning into the curve, I bend my knees and enjoy the ride, momentarily forgetting about my palpitating heart and sweaty palms.

Putting pressure on my back foot, I slow the board down when I hit the bottom of the hill and kick my board up. It's tucked under my arm as I amble along the grassy stretch before I hit the stairs.

The beach isn't overly crowded. There's a father playing Frisbee with his daughter and their dog, an older woman strolling along the shore, her feet splashing in the water as she looks out towards the sun. It'll be setting soon enough.

I glance left and notice a young couple walking through the sand, their fingers interlaced. She's pregnant, her hand rubbing her belly as she talks to her partner. He's smiling at whatever she's saying, and then he lifts their joined hands and kisses her knuckles. This makes her giggle.

A yearning I don't understand rockets through me. I frown. I don't want that. Those two look super young, and they're about to have a kid. No thank you!

But it's not the round belly that's getting to me.

I think it's the hand-holding, the sweet intimacy of laced fingers. The idle chatter as they stroll along the beach together, oblivious to everything but each other.

Will I ever get that?

Will I ever be special enough to be someone's number one?

"That guy" doesn't count. I was never his number one. Not really.

But could I be Aidan's?

Turning away from the couple, I look right, and that's when my heart stops beating for a second. Time slows around me as the universe flashes a bright yellow arrow at the water's edge. It's blinking on and off, shouting, "Here! Over here!"

I swallow, my fiery nerves now feeling like ice in my veins.

Aidan is standing in the shallow waves, his hands in his pockets and his eyes looking right at me.

33

DISCO PARTIES & OLIVE BRANCHES

AIDAN

I didn't know I could get butterflies this bad, but the second I spotted Harley at the top of the stairs, my stomach started dancing stronger than it ever has before. We're talking full-blown disco.

Rubbing a hand across my belly, I start to walk up the beach, wondering if this was the reason I was so compelled to stop here on my way home from work.

Usually after swim class I'm starving, and I head home for a shower and some chow. Tonight, though, I wanted to wash the chlorine off my skin with salt. I wanted those grains of sand between my toes and that fresh breeze in my face.

Or maybe I didn't.

Because now there's Harley, and the ocean can wait.

I'm not sure I'll ever get this moment again, so I

turn my back on the horizon and make a beeline for her.

We meet in the middle of the sand just as a young couple walks past us. She giggles and rests her head on his shoulder for a second, her shiny black hair draping down his back. They look kind of young to be having a baby, but it's not my place to judge.

I turn my focus to Harley, who is standing in front of me now, her expression puckering as she blurts, "Why didn't you text me?"

"Uh..." I cringe, then hedge. "Why didn't you text *me*?"

"Because I didn't think you'd reply," she murmurs.

I look to the sand, drawing a circle with my big toe. "I would have."

An awkward silence wedges itself between us, and I'm not sure how to break it. The dance party in my stomach is kind of making me nauseous. Or maybe I'm just hungry.

Harley sighs and hugs the skateboard to her chest. "So, I know things didn't end great on Sunday, but I didn't mean for us to stop hanging out. I get it if you don't want to anymore. You know, me being an old hag and everything."

I slap a hand over my eyes and groan. "I never should have said that. I was going to apologize but you told me to shut up."

"I wasn't ready to hear it then." She moves her

board so it's resting against her thighs. "But I'm ready now."

My lips twitch with a grin as I gaze down at her. "I didn't mean it, and I'm sorry."

A small smile flashes across her face. "Your car getting scratched wasn't your fault. And maybe I do need you...just a little bit." Her cute nose wrinkles as she holds her finger and thumb apart by like a quarter-inch.

I grab her hand and squeeze it into a ball, which makes her laugh. And just like that, the tension that has consumed me for the last four days is severed. My shoulders relax as I drop her hand and smile down at her.

"It's good to see you." My words come out softly, my voice suddenly husky as I drink in her freckles and wispy blonde hair, the way it dances around her face in the breeze.

I want to reach out and tuck it behind her ears, but she beats me to it. "Thanks for your help on Sunday."

Say what?

I did not expect that. The fact that she admitted to needing me just a little bit felt huge. But now she's thanking me for my help?

My lips part in surprise before rising into a slow smile. "Excuse me?"

"Don't make me say it again, okay?" I love that pointed look of hers, the way her blue eyes spark. It excites something inside of me that I didn't even know existed.

Laughter bubbles out of my mouth as I tease her, "You gonna let me help you again sometime?"

Her lips purse to the side, her nose wrinkling like she's about to say no, but then she nods. "Actually, I kind of need your help right now."

"Oh yeah?" I take a step closer.

"Yeah, a friend of mine is looking for a surfboard. I thought maybe you could help me look online, see if we can figure out the best kind of board so that when we go shopping, he'll know exactly what he's looking for."

I give her a dry look. It's not exactly *me* helping *her*, but I'll take the olive branch and hold it like a precious gift. A smile grows on my face as I tip my head up to the parking lot. "Let's go."

34

A WHITE MANSION WITH AN OCEAN VIEW

HARLEY

Okay, when I hopped into Aidan's car, I expected to do some surfboard searching on his phone, not drive to his house! He told me as soon as he started the engine and I didn't know how to politely decline, not when we'd just made up. I still felt like we were standing on a glass decking that could splinter and give way at any minute.

Tucking my hands beneath my legs, my knees bob as he drives me into the land of the big white houses. I've never ventured into Clifton Terrace before. This suburb is kind of terrifying for a plebe like me.

"Here we are." He pulls into his driveway, the car angling steeply as it dips beneath the level of the house. He parks in front of a white concrete wall, then waits for me to get out of the car before walking for the steps leading up to his front door. "You coming?"

I shuffle up behind him, my mouth agape as I take in the size of his house. I live in a two-bedroom box. This house is like an apartment block on its own. Crap, I can't believe Aidan has seen my place. It's so tiny compared to his mansion.

He's punching in a code to open the huge double doors. A code! My crappy door has a key that sticks so bad sometimes I don't even bother locking the house. We used to have a screen door, which locked, but the hinges rusted and it fell off last year. Mom's never bothered replacing it.

"Come on in." Aidan holds one of the doors open for me and I step into the entrance, awed—and maybe a little intimidated—by the height of the room.

I still haven't said anything. I'm not sure I'll be capable of words in this house. It's so big, they'll probably echo off all the shiny surfaces.

Aidan trots down some stairs and into an open-plan living area. I follow him, and if I thought my jaw couldn't drop any further, I was wrong.

"Wow," I rasp, my gaze transfixed as I walk up to the glass walls and look out at the ocean.

"Yeah, it's pretty spectacular. It's the reason Mom fell in love with this place."

"I can understand why," I whisper, lightly touching the glass and feeling as if I could fly straight through it and out over the water.

Aidan stands just behind me. I can feel his warmth, and tingles scuttle up my spine. I stiffen my shoulders to counter the sensation.

Maybe Aidan notices, because he takes a step back. "So, uh, yeah. I'll grab my laptop and we can start surfing the web."

I glance over my shoulder in time to see his smile and wink.

Crap, he really is gorgeous.

Scratching my forehead, I keep my eyes on the view while he gets his stuff, almost reluctant to turn my back on it when he pulls out a dining room chair and beckons me to sit.

But I'm here to help him. To mend this bridge. And so I sit beside him and guide him to some of my favorite surf shop sites.

Time disappears as we absorb ourselves in surf talk. We get distracted a couple of times watching YouTube videos, and that soon turns into complete absorption as one video leads to another. I show Aidan some of the pros surfing pipes and the big waves.

He's in awe of their skill.

"You could get that good one day, if you really wanted to." I grin at the adorable expression on his face.

"I don't know." He gives me a rueful smile. "You ever thought about going pro?"

I wrinkle my nose and shake my head. "Don't think

that's the life for me. I love surfing. It's fun, but I wouldn't want the pressure of having to compete."

"What do you want to do after you graduate, then?"

"Not sure." I shrug. "Teaching you to surf has been fun. Maybe I should start up a surf school of my own or something."

"That could be cool." Aidan nods with a smile, but it starts to fade. "I don't know what I'll do either. My dad's an investor and my uncle is in real estate. Knowing my luck, I'll end up in sales of some kind. It seems to run in the family."

I laugh when he rolls his eyes, but the sound is cut off by the clicking of an internal door.

With my breath on hold, I peek over my shoulder and spot a young teen, in soccer gear, and his mother walk through the door. I immediately see where Aidan gets his good looks from.

I don't say anything as she briskly walks into the kitchen, dumping grocery bags and ordering her youngest son into a quick shower.

"Don't you give me that look, Grayson De Beer. You stink. Now go!" Once she's pointed him out of the kitchen, she turns a smile to Aidan and then her mouth pops open in surprise. "Oh, I'm sorry. I only caught a glimpse of you and thought it was Savannah."

The woman walks to the table, extending her hand while throwing Aidan a quizzical frown.

"Mom, this is Harley. She's my..."

I glance at him while shaking his mother's hand.

She isn't letting go, and I don't think she will until she's found out exactly who I am.

I'd kind of like to know who I am too, so I stay quiet and only just manage a smile when he murmurs, "Surf instructor."

"Your what?" she asks, *still* shaking my hand.

I clear my throat and repeat, "Surf instructor. I'm teaching him the basics."

"Wow. Okay." She blinks. "I didn't even know Aidan was taking lessons. I'm Sasha."

"Hi," I squeak, and she finally lets go of my hand. I tuck it under the table and look between mother and son.

Aidan gives her a closed-mouth smile that quickly drops under her silent demand for an explanation. And I thought I had "pointed look" down pat. I've got some things to learn.

I sit uncomfortably between them while Aidan softly explains, "With summer coming, I thought it'd be cool to learn a new sport."

"How are you fitting it in with everything else you have going on?"

He cringes and steals a quick look at me before admitting, "I haven't been going to swim practice *every* morning. And on Sunday afternoon, I wasn't hanging out with Savannah." He looks to the tabletop while his mother obviously struggles to absorb his confession.

"Maybe I should go," I murmur, rising from my chair just as the front door opens.

"Hey-o!" someone calls out.

I flinch and turn to see a man walking into the kitchen.

He's tall like Aidan, with a confident sunshine smile. He stops when he sees me, lowering his brief-case onto the kitchen counter before walking towards me with an extended hand.

"Hello, there."

"Hi." I take his hand and hope this shake is a little quicker. "I'm Harley, a friend of Aidan's."

"You go to school together?"

"No, I go to Ryder Bay High."

"Oh." His dark eyebrows rise. "And how do you know Aidan?"

"She's teaching him how to surf!" Aidan's mother snaps before clipping into the kitchen. Her heels sound like gunshots on the shiny floor.

I give Aidan's dad an awkward smile.

He grins at me and leans forward, whispering, "You can call me Luke, and I can't wait to hear the rest of this one."

He's got a wink just like Aidan's and I can't help a little smile, but then I see Sasha watching me and decide it's time for me to disappear.

"I better go."

"You don't have to." Aidan stands from his chair.

I spin to face him and cringe. "I think I should." His disappointed frown kind of hurts me, so I follow it up with "But I'll see you later, okay? I left my phone at home, but just text or call whenever."

"I can take you home," he offers.

"Actually, he can't." His mother steps between us, giving me a polite smile. "I'm sorry about that, Harley, but you'll have to catch up with Aidan after we've had a chat."

"No problem." I nod and swallow, already inching towards the door. "I'll just grab my board and go."

"The car's unlocked." Aidan gives me a pained smile. I try to make him feel better by mouthing, "Good luck!" and giving him a two-fingered salute.

He salutes back, and I slip out the door, leaving the poor guy to fend for himself...just like I did when his cousin showed up to ruin our dinner.

I sure hope this isn't a sign of things to come.

Every time Aidan and I seem to be enjoying ourselves, something from one of our worlds shows up, like an unexpected grenade landing between us.

Skylar, Axel, now Aidan's parents.

Will it be possible for Aidan and me to just hang out without our two worlds colliding? Causing mini explosions set on tearing us apart?

Grabbing my board from the back seat of his car, I walk up his steep driveway and glance one last time at his house. I wonder what's going on inside those walls right now.

I wonder if, yet again, the thing I want most will become nothing more than an unattainable dream.

35

LIBERATION

AIDAN

As soon as the door clicks shut, Mom turns her heated glare on me. "What is going on? You're lying to us now?"

"Lying?" Dad gets in on the action, pulling off his tie as he walks towards me.

Mom raises her arm in my direction. "He's been taking surfing lessons with this girl when he's supposed to be at swimming or hanging out with his girlfriend." Mom squeezes her eyes shut, pinching the bridge of her nose. "Oh, Aidan, please tell me you're not cheating on sweet Savannah. Is that why she's not coming over anymore? You've just stopped inviting her?"

"Savannah dumped me," I shut Mom up with the truth.

Both my parents look at each other in shock, then turn their gazes back on me. I shove my hands in my pockets, wishing the floor would open up and take me away from this moment.

But it's not.

The bastard's holding me steady.

Forcing me to face this.

"Well, when?" Dad asks.

I sigh, freeing my hands so I can grip the back of the dining room chair. "In April."

"April?" Mom's voice pitches. "That was weeks ago! Were you ever going to tell us?"

"I didn't know how." I spread my arms wide. "I know how much you love her."

Mom's now impersonating a goldfish. It's kind of weird seeing her at a loss for words. She blinks and starts staring out the window, while Dad runs a hand through his hair, making it fluff up at funny angles.

"Did she give you a reason?" Dad can't hide his disappointment, and it hurts to have to tell him.

"She wasn't feeling it anymore," I mumble.

"Not feeling it?" Mom rests her hand on her hip. "What does that even mean?"

"I don't know." I shrug. "She said we weren't going anywhere, so what was the point of staying together." I leave out the part about her regrets and recent attempts to amend things. Instead, I go for the raw, ugly truth— the angst that's been gnawing at me for months. "I've... I've lost it this year, you know? The swimming, my grades—I mean they're not falling, but I feel like I'm only just keeping my head above water. Everything's turned to crap, and I didn't want to give you any more reasons to be disappointed in me."

"Disappointed in you?" Dad's head jerks back like I've just slapped him. "You think we're disappointed in you?"

"Of course you are!" My voice breaks. "I saw your face at that swim meet, Dad. I'm sorry I couldn't come first, okay? I'm just not good enough anymore. Si, Craig, they're all better than me now. I'm not the winning son, all right? I don't know what's happened!"

"That's not..." Dad shakes his head, then looks to the floor as he runs his tie through his hands, finally resting it over the back of the chair. "Bud." He rests his hand on my shoulder, obviously struggling for the right words. His fingers give a little squeeze, and then he looks me right in the face. "I was so incredibly proud of you that day. So you didn't make the podium in that one race. You were still amazing. The Warriors cleaned up, and you were part of that."

I give him a confused frown. "But your face... you looked..."

"I wasn't disappointed in your placing, I was sad because *you* looked so gutted. You didn't seem happy with your team medal. You didn't seem happy with anything. As a kid, I couldn't get you out of the water, but now..." He sighs, his expression wrinkling with sadness. "I don't know how to help you or inspire you.

You just… you've just kind of shut down and lost all your joy. Your motivation."

I blink, emotion overwhelming me as I soak in what he's saying. Glancing at Mom, I see her eyes are glassy, but she's smiling at me, obviously agreeing with everything Dad just said.

"I thought you guys were…disappointed in me."

"We've never said that," my mom whispers.

"You've never said otherwise," I quietly retort. "And when Savannah dumped me, I just… I've been trying to do everything I can to be enough for people, but I just never am."

Mom lets out a little whimpering kind of sound and touches her chest. "You don't have to *be* anything for anyone. Aidan, honey, stop putting so much pressure on yourself."

"How do I not?" I look my mom in the eye. "The pressure is everywhere. The expectations are so damn high! Both of you are so successful and smart. You're good at *everything* and I'm just… I'm not."

"Aidan." Mom stops me, walking around Dad so she can nestle against my side. "Honey, you are amazing. We couldn't ask for a better son. We just want you to be happy."

"She's right." Dad nods, squeezing my shoulder again. "You just need to figure out what makes you happy and we'll support that."

"Is it surfing?" Mom looks up at me. "Because I'm not mad about that, I'm just disappointed that you lied.

It totally threw me off-guard seeing that girl in here, not knowing anything about her." Mom's expression crinkles. "But...you know...as long as you're being safe in the water, then..."

The water.

That girl.

Mom's voice turns to mush in my head as I think about the waves, the rides, the thrill.

A slow smile crests my lips as I relive every moment with Harley.

It's not just the waves and the water.

That's a big a part of it, but...that girl.

I let out a soft laugh, giving Mom a quick kiss on the cheek before walking for the door.

"Where are you going?" Dad calls to me.

I spin at the steps and grin at them. "I gotta go. Don't save me dinner, I'll look after myself."

"Wait! Aidan! We need to work on our communication!" Mom calls as I rush through the door.

Just before I close it behind me, I shout into the house, "I'll tell you everything when I get home. I promise!"

Racing down the steps, I jump into my car and reverse out the driveway, wondering which way Harley has decided to skate home.

I hope I can catch her in time, because all I want to do right now is be with her. I don't even care what we get up to, I just know it'll make me happy...because she'll be there.

36

ILLUMINATION

HARLEY

"Harley!"

I flinch at the sound of my name, nearly coming off my board when I glance over my shoulder and see Aidan driving up beside me.

"What are you doing?" I laugh. He looks kind of adorable with his head popping above the windshield, his usually styled hair tousled and out of place.

He slows to a stop beside me and I jump off my board, catching it with my toe before it runs away from me. "How mad was your mom?" I wince.

"Not too bad." He shrugs. "She wasn't angry about the surfing, just annoyed that I'd been lying about it. We had a chat, and it's all good now."

I tip my head, surprised by how easy that was. Not that I ever have to bother lying to my mom, since she doesn't care what I get up to anyway, but when I piss her off, things are not resolved after a quick chat.

I snicker, once again struck by how different our lives are. Resting my hand against the edge of the window frame, I lean against his car and ask, "What are you doing here?"

"Well…"

Oh man, is he blushing right now?

"I was wondering if you wanted to watch the sunset with me. Or maybe have Mexican food. Or we could walk along the beach, maybe?"

My insides go all warm and fuzzy, the excitement of hanging out with him overriding any of my earlier doubts. "Or maybe we could do all three of those things."

His smile is wide and beautiful as he pops the passenger door open. "Hop in."

―――――――――

Dinner was delicious and uninterrupted by a certain De Beer cousin.

Aidan apologized for that and tried to explain how Skylar can be, but even as he was doing it, he ended up confusing himself.

"To be honest, I don't know why she acts the way she does. Maybe it's the fact that she's a spoiled brat. Only child. Gets whatever she wants."

"Who knows." I shrugged and changed the subject, not really wanting Skylar to spoil the evening.

Before long, Aidan got caught up telling me stories from his childhood. He's traveled to some sweet places, and I lap up every story.

"I want to travel one day," I murmur as we walk along the beach.

The sun set while we were eating our food, and we're now wandering along in the darkness. The moon is a thick thumbnail in the sky, not bright enough to illuminate much, but we can see our way okay.

We're heading for the pier, ambling along at a snail's pace, as if both of us are worried if we walk too fast the evening will be over too soon.

Aidan's walking close enough that our hands keep brushing. I kind of love it so make no move to step away.

"You will." Aidan's knuckle scrapes the back of my hand. "You could travel this whole globe if you wanted to."

With a soft scoff, I shake my head. HRB just doesn't get it. He has the world at his fingertips.

"You don't think you can?" He gently nudges me with his elbow.

I smile, liking our connection. "I don't see how I could ever afford it."

"Stick with me. I'll get you there." He sounds so confident...and I'm not sure how to reply.

The comment is so loaded and could be read a dozen different ways.

Was it casual? Like a joke?

Or did he mean it? And if he meant it, what is that actually implying? That he wants to hang out more, be my travel buddy *and* my surf buddy? Or something else?

Something deeper, potentially better?

My head is going to start hurting if I don't shut these questions up, so I distract myself from the big feels the only way I know how.

Surging to my right, I catch Aidan off-guard, shouldering him right into the water.

He lets out a wail as he loses his balance and crashes into the shallow surf.

Clapping my hands together, I tip back my head and laugh into the sky.

"You little…" He struggles to get out of the water, falling once as he rolls onto his knees.

But as soon as he finds his feet, he's after me.

I yelp and start running, but don't even make it to the pier before his arms are around my waist and he's lifting me off the sand.

I'm laughing too hard to protest and don't even fight him as he wades into the shallows and drops me with a splash. My butt hits the sandy bottom and I'm soaked through.

Saturated and alive.

Bursting to my feet, I chase after him, cupping my

hands in the water and splashing his face. He kicks back at me, his laughter rich and deep as we conduct our epic water fight.

Our playful shouts fill the night air, salty water splashing around our ankles as we run back and forth in the surf.

Laughing and out of breath, I lurch to a stop, resting my hands on my knees and then raising my finger for a quick time-out. Aidan stops beside me, his chest heaving, water dripping off his hair, his chin, his clothing. He bends over, mirroring my stance. His warm breath tickles the side of my face, and I glance at him, our eyes connecting in the dim light.

I can't see the details of his green orbs, but I sense that he's studying me, feeling my breath mingling with his as we slowly stand together. His hand runs down my arm, featherlight but strong enough to inch me closer. His wet shorts hit my thighs, my fingers shaking as I rest them on his arms. His salty skin is cool as I trace my hands gently up to his shoulders and brush my thumb along his neck.

A breath catches in his throat and I still.

Does he want this?

My question is answered in a heartbeat as he leans towards me. But then he stops. He's so close, and so far away. Why'd he stop?

I swallow, nerves attacking me as I struggle to breathe, try to figure out how I'll step away from him when all my body wants to do is push that much closer.

The power of that thought should be freaking me out, but all I can do is stand there and try to read his expression.

"I really want to kiss you right now," Aidan whispers, brushing the tip of my nose with his.

The relief is like a tidal wave surging through me. It nearly makes me laugh, but my palpitating heart stops me. Instead, I let out a shaky breath and rasp, "What are you waiting for?"

His thumb glides up my jaw, brushing across my earlobe and sending tendrils of pleasure curling down my spine. And then any doubts, any fears that may have been lurking beneath the surface, are shot to hell by two simple words.

"Your permission." His husky voice obliterates the knot in my chest, setting my smile free.

No guy has ever bothered to ask me that before.

It's amazing how two small words can hold so much power. So much respect.

I rise on my tiptoes and whisper against the edge of his mouth. "You have it."

His lips curl beneath mine and I press my mouth against his smile. Like turning on a light switch, my entire body illuminates. From the top of my head to the tips of my toes, my senses are reawakened, the blacks and grays from my past torn apart with rainbow colors that simultaneously blind and revive.

Aidan's gentle pressure, the sweet softness of his skin pressed against mine. He starts to pull away, but I dive back for more, gripping his shoulders when his arms glide around my waist, securing me to him. He bends his knees, crouching down to deepen the kiss.

My entire body is trembling as I open my mouth and let him in.

Nerves skitter through me, like restless bats wanting to disturb this moment, but then his tongue finds mine, warm and reassuring. I melt against him, breathing in his scent as we explore the wonders, the tastes, the soft back-and-forth dance that equals kissing.

It's been over two years since I've kissed someone, let them anywhere near my mouth. I'd almost forgotten how good it was.

Or maybe I didn't.

Because what I'm experiencing now is something new entirely.

Something right.

Something beautiful.

Something—

A sharp scream rends the air, annihilating our moment.

As if a blade has been brought down between us, Aidan and I jerk apart and spin to face the pier.

"What was that?" Aidan asks just as I hear something splash into the water.

37

BLOOD IN THE WATER

AIDAN

"Over there." Harley points to the end of the pier and I know she's right.

That scream is running through me, shredding my nerves.

And then came the splash.

Something—or more likely some*one*—just hit the water. And hit it hard.

I'm running into the ocean before I even realize I'm doing it. Jumping forward, I hit the waves and start swimming.

The darkness won't help me find whoever just fell, but I have to try.

That scream didn't ring with exhilaration or delight. It was fear all the way.

Stark.

Cold.

Terrifying.

I kick harder, forcing my body through the choppy water. Stopping once, I get my bearings, angling my body a little to the left before plowing through the water until I reach the first wooden pillar.

Treading water, I scan the surface, the feeble moonlight barely aiding me, and now we have the shadows cast by the pier to contend with.

I hear Harley swimming up behind me. "Do you see anything?"

"Not yet!" I shout back, desperation firing through me.

"Let's go to the end!" Harley starts swimming to the end of the pier and I follow her, quickly overtaking.

The waves are a little stronger out here, pushing us back towards the large posts that have held this pier for years. The moonlight is brighter out in the open and I think I see a body in the water.

I surge towards the floating shape.

"Right there!" Harley shouts behind me.

I crawl forward, keeping my head above the water so I don't lose sight of the white shirt surging back and forth in the waves. Streaks of dark hair billow out around the victim. She's facedown in the water, her body limp. There's a murky darkness around her head, and it's not until I get within a few feet that I figure out what it is.

Blood.

An icy chill races through my body.

Is she already dead?

Ignoring my waning energy, I kick a little harder, my shoulder clipping one of the posts as the water shoves me back. I strain and fight, reaching the girl just as she's pushed into my chest. Flipping her over, I tuck her beneath my arm and start scissor-kicking for shore.

Harley appears beside me. "Is she breathing?"

"Not sure," I puff. "We just need to get her to the sand."

Harley stays with me, riding the waves in and getting to her feet as soon as she hits solid ground. Running back to my side, she takes the girl's arm and helps me drag her up the beach. We're both out of breath, our chests heaving from exertion and maybe a little panic.

I fist my hands for a second, trying to control the shakes, but I have no hope as Harley brushes the dark hair off the girl's face and all I can see is a deep gash, blood dripping over pale white skin...and Skylar's blue lips.

"Shit." I barely breathe the word, lurching forwards and swiping the blood off my cousin's cheek.

Harley presses her fingers into Skylar's neck.

"I've found a pulse. I think." She leans her ear against Skylar's blue lips. "But she's not breathing. You know CPR?"

"Yeah." I nod, rising to my knees and following the protocol that's been drilled into me. I have to do the training twice a year, and thank God it takes over, putting me on autopilot.

I'm still a shaking mess as I tip Skylar's head to the side to drain any excess water from her mouth, then tip her head back and pinch her nose.

Creating a seal, I blow air into my cousin's lungs and silently beg her not to die on me.

"What's happened? Is she okay?" A frantic voice rushes through the darkness towards us. "Skylar!"

I can't look up to make sure, but I think I recognize Wyatt's voice.

What the hell is he doing here?

I don't have time to think about it.

"Come on, Sky," I whisper, checking for a breath and feeling nothing. "Come on!" I urge her, pinching her nose again and blowing two puffs into her mouth.

"Let me past!" Wyatt is yelling.

I glance up to see Harley pushing him back. "Have you got a phone?"

"Is she going to be okay?" He's staring at Skylar with wide eyes and running both hands through his hair. "Shit." He starts wailing. "Shit!"

"Hey!" Harley fists his shirt, yanking him down so she can get in his face. "Gimme your phone. We have to call an ambulance!"

He pulls it out, passing it to her without taking his eyes off Skylar.

I bend over to administer another two breaths, fear building fast and slick inside me.

"Please, Sky. Please breathe." I check for a pulse again and fear clutches my heart when I can't find one. I check again, then shout to Harley, "No pulse! Starting compressions."

She spins to face me, relaying the information to the operator.

Wyatt has dropped to his knees and is now crying into his hands. I want to tell him to shut the hell up, but I'm too focused on trying to keep my cousin alive.

As I count to fifteen compressions, I glance at her face, noticing the deep gash along her hairline. Salty blood continues to stream from the wound. I need something to soak it up, but I can't stop administering CPR.

"Fifteen," I murmur, then pinch Skylar's nose and breathe into her mouth again.

As I sit back up and lock my fingers together, Harley drops to her knees opposite me. "The ambulance is on its way." Whipping off her wet shirt, she ignores the fact that she'll be left in nothing but a black bra and bunches it against Skylar's wound. She's no doubt wondering what happened to my cousin.

Did she slip?

How'd she fall?

Was it a loose railing?

Was she being an idiot and balancing on the top?

Shutting out the questions is nearly impossible.

"That's fifteen," Harley murmurs, and I bend down

to breathe. "Come on. Come on," she whispers, ordering my cousin back to life.

As I blow oxygen into Skylar's lungs, I beg for it to be enough.

If I'm going to succeed at anything in my life, it has to be this.

38

DON'T LET GO

HARLEY

As soon as the paramedics arrived, they took over, pushing Aidan and me aside so they could work on Skylar. It took two shocks to the chest with the portable AED before Skylar's pulse returned. Shortly after that, she started breathing again, but they kept the oxygen mask in place while they rushed her into the ambulance. She was unconscious and pretty much gray as they carried her up the beach.

I wait until the ambulance doors are shut and the sirens are blaring before I take a full breath. Part of me wants to sag to the rough concrete, but Aidan needs to get to the hospital.

I graze my fingers along the palm of his hand and he captures them quickly, gripping tight like he'll fall apart if he doesn't hold on.

"You did good," I rasp, struggling to find my voice.

His expression is numb, his nod robotic.

"We need to get to the hospital." I start leading him towards his car, glancing over my shoulder to see if I can spot the crying guy. He must have taken off while the paramedics were here. I wonder who he is and what he knows about Skylar's fall.

"My parents. Uncle Jeff. Aunt Marlo." Aidan's static voice draws my attention back to him.

He sounds so wooden—an untreated piece of timber that's rough and raw on the edges, splintered and weak in the middle.

"It's okay." I squeeze his hand, noting the pallor of his skin under the parking lot lights. He's going into shock and I need to snap him out of it. We need to keep that adrenaline pumping for just a little longer.

Skylar may have been revived on the beach, but she's still in critical condition. He needs to stay strong right now.

"Your family." I snap my fingers. "Let's call your family." I pull him a little faster to his car. Once we're safely inside, we grab his phone from the cupholder and I help him call everyone he needs to.

He starts with his parents, and as soon as his father answers the phone, Aidan's lips begin to tremble and he can't speak. I snatch the phone from him and relay what information I can. My voice is quaking, but at least it works.

"He saved her life, sir. You can be very proud of your son."

Aidan's father is in obvious shock, but he murmurs his thanks and tells us to meet them at the hospital.

I go to buckle up but pause, taking in Aidan's numb expression. "I'll drive," I murmur, running around and coaxing him out of the driver's seat.

By the time we reach the hospital and I've parked his car, Aidan seems to have found his grounding. He shows me how to put up the roof, and I'm about to lock up the car when he stops me.

"Wait." Flipping down the passenger seat, he reaches into the back and rummages around for a second before producing a wrinkled T-shirt. "Sorry, it kinda smells, but…" He points to my half-naked body and I give him a grateful smile.

"Thanks." I flick it out and slip it on. It's massive on me and basically becomes a baggy dress, but it'll have to do.

Aidan takes my hand and starts walking for the entrance.

We arrive just as two panicked adults run for the door. The woman notices Aidan and starts to cry. "Is she all right? Have you seen her?"

Aidan catches the woman against him, hugging her tight and murmuring, "It's okay. They're gonna look after her."

"Marlo, come on." The man takes her hand and they rush into the emergency room together.

The lady at reception has obviously been expecting them and goes into full comfort mode, guiding them to the waiting chairs and explaining everything in a calm voice that I can't quite hear.

"Aidan!" The emergency room doors have slid open again and Aidan's family rushes in. His little brother looks like he's been yanked out of bed, but he has tears in his eyes and is looking pretty scared right now.

Aidan's father nestles him against his side while Aidan's mother wraps her eldest son in a hug and clings tight, gripping the back of his shirt. "Are you all right? What happened?"

I try to wriggle my hand free of his, but he only tightens his grip and as he pulls away from his mother, I catch the look in his eye.

Don't let go.

I give him a reassuring smile and squeeze his hand back.

I won't let go. I'll stay for as long as he needs me to.

Aidan's father glances at me, then gathers his flock, leading them to the chairs near the other two adults. I have to assume they're Skylar's parents. And I also can assume that Aidan's dad and Skylar's dad are brothers. They look too alike to be anything else.

"Luke." The man stands, his eyes watering as he embraces his brother.

"What'd they say?" Luke asks.

"We're waiting to go in and see her."

"She's breathing. Stable. For now." The woman

rises from the chair to stand beside her husband. Her eyes graze mine and she gives me a confused frown before looking at Aidan. "I hear you saved her life."

"Oh, I just…" Aidan humbly shakes his head, doubt flickering over his expression before he looks at me. "We did. I hope it was enough."

His aunt covers her mouth with her hand and starts crying. Her husband cradles her against him and her knees give out. They fall into the plastic chairs together, and soon everyone around me is fighting tears.

"I'm sure she'll be okay," I whisper, but I'm a nobody in this situation. My comfort isn't enough.

Aidan sniffs and swipes a finger under his nose while we anxiously wait for news.

Thankfully it's not far off, a doctor walking into the room a few minutes later.

"Hey, Kevin." Skylar's father rises from his seat.

"Jeff." The man nods, his eyes skirting mine. A frown flickers across his forehead when he notices my hand in Aidan's, but then he jerks his gaze back to Skylar's parents who are now both standing, their arms around each other's waists as if they're bracing themselves.

"She's stable." Dr. Kevin starts with the good news. "But she'll need monitoring closely. She hasn't gained consciousness yet. Between the fall, the head wound and the time without oxygen, her brain has had a bit of a beating. She's going to need a full work-up—CT and

MRI scans. I want to get a full scope of what we're dealing with."

Skylar's mother pulls in a shaky breath and starts crying again.

The doctor's smile turns sympathetic and he reaches out and squeezes her arm. "It's okay, Marlo. I'm confident she'll get back to her normal self, but it's going to take some time. I'll make sure she gets the best care possible."

"Thank you." Marlo hiccups out the words, then covers her mouth again.

Watching this distraught mother is making me want to cry. She cares so much about her daughter, like if she lost Skylar a part of her would die. I've never really seen that kind of love before.

"Come on, I'll let you sit with her." The doctor with the kind voice extends his arm to show the way. They jerk after him and the rest of us are left to wait it out on the hard plastic chairs.

I look at the shell-shocked family as they slump into seats and stare at the walls, trying to make sense of the unexpected accident. Aidan glances down at me, tugging me over to a chair. He wants me to sit with him, to comfort him, but I don't belong here.

Even though no one has actually said anything, it's so obvious that I'm an outsider.

This is a cohesive family unit.

They have history.

They love each other.

I don't know what that's like, and being around it is incredibly uncomfortable.

"Do you want a drink?" I ask Aidan before I'm forced into the chair beside his. I glance at his brother and parents. "Drink? Anyone? I know Aidan could use the sugar kick. That adrenaline wears off and you just..." My voice trails away when no one seems to notice the fact that I'm talking.

Aidan's father glances up when I stop, then gives me a kind smile and pulls his wallet out. "That'd be great. Thank you." Handing me a twenty, he gives me his order and I memorize it, plus two more.

"Back soon." I drift away from Aidan's side, relieved to be doing something useful. Relieved to get away from a circle of people who seem bound by more than blood. A circle that could be broken if I try to find a place within it.

39

A SAVVY WITHOUT A SKY

AIDAN

I watch Harley's retreat, starkly aware of the fact that she's wearing my shirt, and it looks huge on her. Tie a belt around that thing and she'd have a cotton dress.

I can't take my eyes off her as she disappears from view.

It's weird, but I feel the loss. I felt like I could keep it together when her hand was in mine.

She was my fellow rescuer. The one who drove me here.

My strength when I felt like I was about to break.

Seeing Skylar like that, thinking she was dead, it did me in. I've never faced something like this before, and my insides are raw and shaken.

Harley has a quiet strength about her that seemed to feed into me as she held my hand. But now she's away from me. I rub my thumb and finger together and look across at my family.

That's when I notice Dad's questioning look.

"What?" I frown at him.

"She's wearing your shirt." His comment and dry expression imply so much more than what he's saying.

I work my jaw to the side and strive for calm. "Because she took hers off to try and stop Skylar's bleeding head wound."

"Oh, okay." Dad nods and raises his hands as two white flags.

"We need to get you some dry clothes." Mom reaches out and runs her hand down my saturated shirt. "Were you at the pier? Did you see what happened?"

"No." I shake my head, briefly reliving what I was doing when that scream tore me away from Harley. Her kiss was a mixture of sweetness and fire. My tongue skimming across hers. She tasted good. It was...

"Aidan." Mom snaps her fingers in my direction. "What happened?"

"Uh..." I blow out a breath. "It was dark, so I couldn't really see. I didn't even know it was Skylar until we got her onto the beach."

"What were you doing down there so late? And by the pier? You never go to the south end."

Now would probably be an appropriate time to tell her that I've been hanging out a lot at the south end, but I'm not sure I have the energy for that discussion.

Instead I hedge and mumble, "We just went for a walk after dinner." I can't admit the water fight or the fact that I couldn't remember the last time I'd had so much fun. "Then we heard this scream, and something hit the water. I ran in and started swimming as fast as I could."

Dad gives me a proud smile as he rests his elbows on his knees. "So, you didn't see Skylar fall?"

"No," I croak. "I don't know what happened to her."

It's only then that I remember Wyatt crying on the beach and wonder if he saw something. I store it away, making a mental note to try and catch him at school tomorrow.

Shit. School.

This is going to cause a firestorm.

Gossip will be rife as students try to figure out what Skylar was even doing down at the pier. We never go down there, especially at night. It's creepy and cruddy, and we have way better places to hang out.

So why was she there?

Why was Wyatt there?

My mind instantly answers that question, reminding me of Wyatt's stalker tendencies. Unless they went there together.

Seven minutes in heaven?

My face wrinkles with disgust, but I don't have time to see the thought through because the sliding doors open and Savannah comes rushing into the emergency room.

Her face is streaked with tears, her brown eyes distraught as she hunts the room for answers.

I jerk out of my seat and go to meet her.

The second she spots me, she runs into my chest, wrapping her arms around me and weeping against my shirt.

"Is she okay? Is she gonna be okay?" Savannah whimpers.

I hold her close and kiss the top of her head. "She's gonna be fine." I dish out the promise like it's foolproof, but I don't actually know for sure.

The thought makes me hug Savvy a little harder.

She's already lost so much. Skylar carried her through her mother's death. Those two girls rely on each other for everything. You can't have a Sky without a Savvy or a Savvy without a Sky.

The thought kind of kills me, and I feel Savannah's pain as she weeps against my chest.

Pulling back, I gaze down at her, slashing the tears off her face and trying to think of anything to comfort her.

Sucking in a shaky breath, she whimpers and then lurches for my mouth. Her lips touch mine, feeling all too familiar as she tips her head and wraps her arms around my neck.

It's a kiss to comfort, to distract.

I should pull away, but I'm afraid if I do that, I'll break Savannah's fragile heart clean in half.

40

MISSION ACCOMPLISHED

HARLEY

I jerk to a stop, the soda cans ice cold against my bare skin as I see a girl with wavy brown hair run into Aidan's arms.

I recognize her, my brain matching the pair with a cruel swiftness.

She's the one from Freshmart. Skylar's nice friend who let me keep my job.

What was her name again?

Sav? Savvy?

Sa...vannah?

The knot that Aidan had managed to untie with his sweet kiss quickly tightens in my chest, squeezing hard enough to hurt.

Savannah.

As in Aidan's Savannah. Skylar's best friend.

Shit, it all makes sense now, the links clicking into place like pieces of Lego. Aidan's tight little world just keeps getting smaller. Everyone knows each other. Everyone has a place.

She's the ex. The epicenter of his earthquake.

My suspicion is confirmed when he leans out of the hug and starts wiping tears from her cheeks. And then she lurches towards him, sealing their lips together.

I suck in a sharp breath, like I've just been punched in the stomach.

And then I hold it.

Waiting.

Waiting for him to jerk back, to explain that there's been a mistake. His lips were touching mine less than two hours ago. Is my taste still on him? From the way she's tipping her head and shoving her tongue in his mouth, I'm guessing no.

He's not pulling away.

The knot in my chest is yanked so hard I think my insides are going to flip back to front. The crushing pull is unbearable, but I can't seem to stop watching them.

They look good together.

No wonder he wanted her back.

He doesn't need to crouch down to reach her lips. Their bodies fit like two pieces of a puzzle.

He's still not pulling away.

His hands are holding her waist, but he's not pushing back. They're just there, keeping her against him.

And I'm done.

Why did I let myself believe for even a second that love was a possibility for me?

I should know better.

Have I not already aced this lesson?

People are *never* who they say they are. They act sweet, talk nice and then bam! Betrayal.

Placing the three soda cans on the floor, I line them up in a neat row. Numb precision makes me get them perfectly straight before I lay the change on top of it. Then I turn and find another exit to escape through.

My skateboard is still in Aidan's car, but you know what? I can buy another one.

There's no reason for me to see Aidan De Beer again.

I agreed to teach him how to surf so he could get his girlfriend back.

Well, mission accomplished.

41

SLIPPED INTO THE NIGHT

AIDAN

I pull out of the kiss and bite my lips together, finally understanding what Savannah meant when she broke up with me.

I'm just not feeling it anymore.

I soften my retreat with a smile and brush my knuckles down her cheek.

She's still vulnerable and upset, but I can't kiss her anymore. Harley's taste and touch are still in my brain, and this moment with my ex has only confirmed to me that the surfer girl is the one I want.

My body burns with an intense desire to see her, to kiss her again, to hold her against me. Our first kiss was cut short. Our second kiss won't be.

"My parents are here, if you want to go sit with them for a bit." I start guiding her over to my family.

"I'm sure your dad will be back out with an update soon."

Savannah nods.

Dr. Green has been working at Aviemore Hospital since they moved to Ryder Bay. Skylar's dad helped the family find a home and, in the process, they became best friends. My uncle Jeff is like her uncle Jeff. Our three families are all connected, and I know Savannah will feel safe sitting with my parents.

"Hey, Savvy Sue." Dad gives her a kind smile and makes room for her to sit down between him and Mom. He's the only person in the world who's been allowed to use her middle name—ever. But she's always loved my dad, so he gets away with it.

The second she sits down, he wraps his arm around her shoulders and she starts to cry again.

Mom reaches for her hand, giving it a squeeze and murmuring, "It's going to be okay, honey."

Savannah sniffs and nods, but the tears still flow.

Mom rummages around in her handbag for a tissue.

"Thanks." Savannah takes it and starts mopping up her face.

"Are your brother and sister okay?"

She nods. "Yeah, they're both asleep, so I asked Mrs. O'Neill from next door to watch them for me."

"Good move. That woman's a sweetheart."

"I don't think she appreciated me waking her up, but she understood that I needed to be here. Dad's been on call all week, and him rushing out the door woke me up. I figured it was something pretty serious. And then Marlo called me and I knew right away that Skylar was hurt." Her voice wobbles and she starts crying all over again.

It hurts to watch her. She knows what it's like to lose someone close, and this must be hitting that nerve pretty hard right now.

But still...

I need to go find Harley.

Catching Dad's eye, I tip my head towards the corridor over his shoulder and he nods.

While Savannah is crying against his shoulder, I slip out of the room and hope I can find Harley quickly. I should really be back with my family, but this feels important too.

As soon as I pass through the doors, I start running down the corridor, jerking to a stop when I spot three soda cans lined up on the floor.

Weird.

"Harley?" I look around for her, even scanning out the windows, but there's no sign of her.

With a confused frown, I pull out my phone and send her a text asking if she's okay.

I get crickets.

Bending down to collect the cans and coins, I nestle them against my chest and watch my phone screen, waiting for it to light up with a reply.

It's only then I remember that she left her phone at home.

"Shit," I mutter.

Has she left?

I head down the corridor, searching and softly calling her name, but there's no trace of her anywhere.

It bugs me that she took off without even saying goodbye, but maybe I get it as well.

She's an outsider in some ways. I mean, I don't want her to be, but when we first got to the hospital and everyone kept glancing at her with a frown, she must have felt completely ostracized.

Dammit. I should have gone with her to get the drinks.

I close my eyes with a huff, and nearly jump out of my skin when Dad calls for me.

"Aidan!"

I spin and see him waving me back to the waiting room.

"Dayton and Craig have just showed up. You need to come wait with us. I'm sure Kevin will be out with another update soon, and I want you to be there for that."

With a reluctant nod, I head towards him and try not to worry.

Harley's an independent soul. She knows Ryder Bay better than I do, so it's not like she'll get lost on her way home. I just feel bad that I'm not driving her there.

She probably felt out of place and awkward in this situation and slipped away unnoticed.

I'll text her again when I get home, to make sure she's all right.

It's weird, for someone who's still such a new addition in my life, it's strange that she's the only person I want to be with right now.

42

CRACKS IN THE CONCRETE

HARLEY

Aidan's texted me three times and called twice.

But I'm not responding.

There's been no apology. The messages are all asking if I'm okay.

Well, I'm not okay, and screw him.

He probably docsn't even know I saw him frenching Savannah in the middle of a hospital waiting room. It's not like he's going to admit to it!

Unless he's trying to get in touch with some kind of celebration—*I got Savannah back! Thank you! You're the best for helping me.*

I gag and bury the phone in the bottom of my backpack.

A huge part of me wants to cry, but there's no way in hell Aidan De Beer is getting *any* of my tears. It's stupid to feel this way anyway. We had one kiss. Barely a kiss. Half a kiss...before his life interrupted it. Shoved its finger right through the perfect moment.

I close my eyes with a sigh and shake my head.

"Don't be such a bitch," I reprimand myself.

Skylar did not fall from that pier just to piss me off.

Shit, she nearly died. She could still die, and here I am complaining that she interrupted something special.

I cringe at my serious lack of sensitivity. Curse it, I *am* turning into my mother.

The thought makes me physically shudder, and I scrunch my shoulders before straightening them out and lifting my chin.

I will *not* turn out like her. I am stronger than that.

I'm just thinking bitchy thoughts because I'm pissed off with Aidan.

The big jerk.

I'm so done with those Elites. They can just stay at their end of the beach and leave me the hell alone.

I catch a movement out of the corner of my eye and see Jed loping towards me. He's in blue and yellow stripes today. I don't like them. I look away before I'm tempted to tell him so.

I'm not sure how to feel around him right now.

He told me to go for it with Aidan.

He told me it was a safe bet.

"Morning, HQ." He grins.

I glance at him, then stare at the floor until he stops walking.

"You all right?"

"You were wrong," I quietly mutter.

"What?"

"You told me to let him in. That he was a safe bet. You. Were. Wrong." My voice cracks on the last word and my eyes start to burn. I blink rapidly and look to the cracked concrete between us.

"What ha—"

"He kissed me." I look up and glare at Jed. "And then he kissed her. And I'm done."

Jed blinks, his expression crinkled with confusion. "Hold up. Just take it back a few clicks. I need the details."

I shake my head and step away when he tries to move forward. His arms are open like he wants to give me a hug. To comfort me and make me feel better.

But he can't do that.

Nothing can make this better.

His arms drop to his sides, his expression pained. "Talk to me, girl. I'm here for you."

My head is shaking before he's even finishing speaking. "You're the only person in my life who's never let me down, but it'll happen eventually, because it always does." I swallow, feeling a little bad at the crushed look on Jed's face. "Even if you want to be good and kind, you're gonna hurt me. And I'm done." Okay, the tears are setting in now. His face is going all blurry.

"HQ, come on…"

"Let's just accept reality, man." I take another step back, putting more cracks in the concrete between us. "I'm better off on my own."

"Harley, that's not true." He tries to step forward, but I spin and head into school.

I should be retreating back to my house, but I know he won't follow me into the girls' bathroom, so I run there and lock myself into the back stall.

My tears taste like salt and I lick them off my top lip, not bothering to swipe them off my face.

No one comes to check on me.

And that's just the way I want it.

I can take care of myself.

I've been doing it my whole frickin' life.

43

LIFE CAN BE BLURRY SOMETIMES

AIDAN

I still haven't heard back from Harley and it's bugging me. Big-time.

I'm going to have to find her after school, to make sure she's all right. I'll use returning her skateboard as my excuse, but hey...maybe I don't even need an excuse.

Until Skylar's accident, we were having the best date I'd ever had.

Good food, fun on the beach. A kiss that was still buzzing through my brain.

I want to kiss her again. Laugh with her again. I need to make sure she's okay.

It's tempting to skip out of school early.

Being in the cafeteria for lunch was getting to be too much, so I slipped away from the table and retreated into the corridor. It's way less crowded, and I'm not being circled by the speculation monorail. I feel like it's been rotating around my head since the second I parked my car in the Walton Academy lot.

"What happened to Skylar?"

"How'd she fall?"

"Did you see anything?"

"Wow! You saved her life!"

"Is she going to be okay?"

"What did the doctors say?"

"She's in a coma?"

"Is she going to die?"

I nearly punched Jonah for asking me that one. I don't want to hear the word "die" and "Skylar" in the same sentence. She may drive me nuts sometimes, but she's my cousin. She's an only child. Her death would destroy Aunt Marlo and Uncle Jeff. Shit, it would probably destroy me too. She's been in my life forever, like a sister.

Grayson was quiet this morning. He's worried about his favorite cousin, but he's not about to say it out loud. I tried to ask if he was all right, but he just shrugged and kept playing Candy Crush on his phone. Addict.

With a sigh, I watched him walk into the middle school, and was then bombarded.

Thank God Savannah took the day off. She wouldn't have coped with the onslaught when she was already feeling so fragile. Her dad let her stay with Uncle Jeff and Aunt Marlo at the hospital. I'm waiting on an update.

Last I heard, Skylar was going in for her CT scan.

I amble past my locker but don't stop to exchange any books. I'm all set for the afternoon. I'm just killing time until the bell rings.

"Well, I think she was probably drunk, being an idiot and just slipped," I hear a girl say as she comes around the corner. She and her friend jerk to a stop when they see me, their eyes bulging for a second before they scuttle past. I have no idea who they are. They look young, probably freshmen. They don't know Skylar well enough to say any of that bullshit, but my cousin does have a reputation.

"Shit," I mutter, raking my fingers through my hair and trying to figure it out myself.

The scream hadn't been one of exhilaration.

It was fear.

Cold and stark.

It ran straight through me, like I was watching a horror movie. And then came that splash.

Was she unconscious before she hit the water?

I shake my head. That doesn't feel right. The gash on her head makes me think she hit the water and was then immediately thrown against one of those big wooden pillars. The waves were kind of strong last night. The blow probably knocked her out, and that's why she wasn't swimming or helping herself out of the water.

A shudder runs down my spine.

What if I hadn't been there?

What if the beach had been empty?

I squeeze my eyes shut, warding off those nasty questions...and that's when I remember Wyatt.

I haven't seen him around today. He was pretty distraught when he appeared on the beach. Did he see something?

I stop in my tracks.

Did he *do* something?

My eyebrows bunch together. Surely he wouldn't hurt Skylar on purpose. He's in love with her. Infatuated. Whatever.

I need to find out.

Turning left, I start heading for the sunshine. I'm not sure what I'm going to do once I get outside. Ditch school?

I don't even know where Wyatt lives. I don't have his number, but I could probably find it.

Pulling out my phone, I start looking up his last name when I'm stopped by a deep voice in the doorway.

"Aidan De Beer."

I flinch and look up to see Officer Malloy striding towards me.

"Oh, hey." I raise my chin to acknowledge him.

Craig's father is in uniform today, obviously on official police business. So why does he want to talk to me?

He stops beside me, giving me one of his closed-mouth, serious smiles. "You got a minute?"

"Everything okay?" I slip my phone into my pocket.

"Just wondering if I could quickly debrief about last night. I've checked with your principal. She says it's okay."

I bob my head and follow him outside.

He chooses a white concrete bench seat on the outskirts of the lawn. There are a smattering of students sunbathing around us, and I can feel all eyes on me the second we sit down.

Thankfully none of them are within hearing range, and I'm pretty sure if they try to shuffle closer, they'll get a sharp look from a cop.

"How you doing, son?"

"All right." But I say my answer too softly. It's obvious I'm still kind of shaken up over the whole thing.

"You saved her life. You know that, right?"

I give him a weak smile and rest my elbows on my knees so I don't have to look at him.

He sighs and softly murmurs, "I sure hope she makes it."

"She will," I assure him. Or maybe I'm just assuring myself.

"Yeah. She's a strong girl." Officer Malloy pulls out his notepad. "Craig's really worried about her. I don't think he caught a wink of sleep last night. That's why I let him stay home today."

I nod, suddenly wondering why Grayson and I didn't get a day off too.

Concentrating on schoolwork has been pretty damn impossible. Between Skylar and Harley, my brain is overflowing.

"So, about last night. I'm just needing to follow up with a few questions."

I nod and wait for him to ask.

"Can you run through the events of last night for me? Where were you when you first heard Skylar scream?"

I go through the story again. I kind of told him all of this last night. But last night he was there as a father. Today he's here as a cop.

I describe where Harley and I were on the beach. I'm forced to admit about the kiss because he probes me on exactly what I was doing. He's probably making a note to catch up with Harley at some point. He asks me what her last name is, and I know she'll hate me telling him, but what choice do I have?

Shit, I wish she'd text me back. I need to give her a heads-up. I make a mental note to actually call her once this interview is over.

"Was there anyone else down on the beach?" Officer Malloy asks. "I recall you mentioning someone last night."

"Yeah, Wyatt. Wyatt Mattley. Harley used his phone to call an ambulance."

"Why didn't *he* use his phone?"

"Because he was crying too hard. I think he thought Skylar was dead and it freaked him out."

"Where did he come from?"

"I'm not sure. I was focused on Skylar. He just appeared on the beach, asking if she was okay."

"So, you think he might have seen something on the pier?"

"Maybe." I shrug, then sigh. "Probably. I haven't seen him at school today, but I was thinking about trying to track him down this weekend."

"Hey, you leave the police work to me." Officer Malloy taps my shoulder with his knuckle.

I glance over and see his grim expression. He's serious, and it makes me sit up straighter. "You think he might have done something to her?"

"I'm not saying that." He shakes his head. "But I was on the pier this morning and there's absolutely no damage to the railing. If she fell, she must have been sitting on the top of it or maybe even standing on it."

"Are you saying you think someone pushed her?"

He doesn't say anything for a beat, then murmurs, "Or maybe she jumped."

"Skylar wouldn't jump." I shake my head, emphatic.

"Not even as a dare?"

"Oh, I thought you meant..." I look down at my shaking hands and swallow. "I thought you meant suicide."

His face flushes with a deep look of worry before he runs a hand down his mustache and mouth. "Did she seem to be acting differently over the past few days or weeks? I mean, you don't think she was suffering from depression or anything, do you?"

"I don't think so." I shake my head, then cringe but have to admit it. "She and Craig had a massive blowout on Wednesday. Did he tell you about that?"

The officer's face creases with concern again and he stops writing on his notepad. "No. He didn't mention it."

"I don't want to out him or anything, but maybe he'd have a better idea about that. The last time I really spoke to her was on Sunday, and I think she was feeling pretty bad after you'd seen her."

He lets out a soft snort. "She really hated me challenging her on her behavior. It probably didn't help that she was hung-over, but she needed to hear the truth."

"Yeah, maybe," I mutter.

Officer Malloy lets out a heavy sigh and slips the notepad back into his pocket. "Well, I'll follow up with this Wyatt kid. Hopefully he can shed some light on the situation." He pierces me with a stern look. "How well do you know him?"

"Only a little. I haven't really spoken to him much."

"Is he friends with Skylar?"

I think of Skylar's seven minutes in heaven promise and cringe, then shake my head. "Not really. I mean, they talked sometimes but weren't buds or anything. He was crushing on her big-time, though."

"Hmmm." His lips pucker in thought as he stares

across the grassy quad. "Do you think he'd be capable of hurting her?"

I let out a surprised laugh. "I don't think so. The guy seems pretty harmless. He's one of those quiet loner types, you know?"

He turns to look at me again, silently suggesting that those are the ones you have to keep an even closer eye on.

The thought hits the bottom of my stomach like a boulder.

"Leave it with me, son." Officer Malloy squeezes my shoulder.

I swallow and rasp, "Yeah, well, hopefully she'll wake up soon and can tell us what happened."

He hesitates, then gives me a sad smile that's kind of crushing.

It's hard to breathe for a second.

Does he not think she's going to make it?

I stare down at the grass until the blades merge into a green blur.

"I'll call you if I have any more questions." Officer Malloy pats my shoulder again, then leaves with a soft goodbye.

I thread my fingers together and squeeze until it hurts.

The bell rings, but the sound is muted and fuzzy.

Rising on shaky legs, I numbly walk out of the sunshine but am stopped by my ringing phone just as I enter the shade.

"Hey, Mom." I try to snap out of it, bolster my voice. She'll be worried enough as it is, and I don't want to be another burden for her today.

"Hi, sweetie. Are you still on your lunch break?"

"I'm just heading to class now."

"Okay, I'll be quick. I just heard from Aunt Marlo. Skylar's finished with all her testing."

"What did the tests say?"

"Swelling in the brain and a small bleed. She doesn't need an operation, which is a huge relief, but the doctors don't know how long it will take her to wake up. It's all just a waiting game now."

I slump back against a locker. "How long do comas usually last?"

"Most cases are anywhere from a day to four weeks."

"Four weeks?"

"Dr. Green will monitor her closely. She'll be under the best care."

"So they're keeping her at Aviemore?"

"Yes. That's the decision. It's closer to family and friends. It'll be easier for us to visit her regularly and support her."

I sigh and run a hand down my face.

"Anyway, I'd like you to come to the hospital after school, please."

I think of Harley and my after-school mission to find her. "Actually, Mom—"

"There are no actuallys. There are no buts. You have

to be there."

"Can't I just drop Grayson and then come back? There's something I have to do."

"Whatever it is can't be more important than being there for your family during a crisis!"

I cringe, hating the way her voice gets so screechy when she's stressed.

"Okay, Mom. I'll be there."

"Good. I'll see you soon, then."

She hangs up and I force my body to class. I'll get told off for being late, although maybe Mr. Cooper will show a little mercy today.

As I walk down the corridor, I text Harley again. I probably won't get a reply, but hopefully she'll know I'm thinking about her.

Have to go to the hospital after school, but really want to see you. Can I take you out for dinner tonight? Please reply. I'm worried about you. Really want to see you.

I nearly write *I miss your pretty face* but press Send before I can. Harley doesn't strike me as the kind of girl to get mushy over sweet sentiments.

I kind of like that about her.

She's so tough. Strong. Everything I didn't think I was attracted to.

Yet she's all I want.

44

A PLACE TO HIDE

HARLEY

I read the text about ten times before finally deleting it.

Aidan really wants to see me?

Bullshit!

He's worried about me?

My ass!

If he wants me so bad, why the hell is he making out with his ex?

Two-faced asshole.

I've worked my way up to the fury.

When the text first came in, I'm disgusted to say that I rubbed my thumb over the words, hearing his voice as if he spoke them.

But I couldn't respond.

Minutes became an hour and still I couldn't reply,

my vulnerable emotions riding a rollercoaster until they settled on a safe, protective anger that had me deleting the message.

Why do people have to suck? Why can't they just be who they say they are? Act like the person you think they should be?

I clench my jaw, hating the tingle in my nose.

I'm not crying again.

I spent all of first period crying, then retreated to the nurse's office. She bought my migraine story and sent me home. After spending most of the day in bed, trying to avoid my mother, I snuck out my window and decided to go for a walk.

I've been on the beach since three o'clock.

Why didn't I bring my board?

I could have been surfing.

But the thought of going back and potentially bumping into Mom stops me.

She checked on me once after I got home. "What's your problem?"

"Nothing. Leave me alone." I rolled my back to her.

"Suit yourself," she muttered, slamming my door to let me know she was pissed.

I close my eyes and force air through my nose. The ocean breeze is picking up my hair, making it dance behind me. I focus on the feel of it, the salty tang hitting my nostrils, the afternoon sun warming my skin.

It should be making me feel better, but it doesn't have the same impact it usually does.

For a moment, I'm back in my fourteen-year-old body. Heartbroken. Disillusioned. Alone.

For as long as I can remember, people have always let me down—Mom, her string of boyfriends, even Jacob, the nice one who I thought might stick around. I really liked him.

And then "that guy" and all of his friends who I thought were mine until they took his side and I found myself with no support.

Now Aidan.

Another heartbreaker.

The only person in my life that hasn't hurt me is Jed. But still, he could. And what happens at the end of next year when he leaves for college? After our road trip that probably won't even happen?

I'll be alone again.

"But that's what you want, right?" The words are bitter cocoa in my mouth.

I shake my head and close my eyes, inhaling the fresh breeze through my nose.

Pulling away now is the only thing I can do. I'll save myself the heartbreak of losing him and get used to my solitude before he's even gone.

I open my eyes and keep walking, trying to dodge the memory of Jed's hurt expression when I told him I was better off on my own.

Crossing my arms, I squeeze my right bicep until

it hurts. Until finger marks are branded onto my skin. Tears want to take me again, but I'm not letting them out. It turns into a battle of wills, and I walk all the way under the pier and beyond until I hit the rocks at the very south end of the beach. I scramble over them, finding a safe, private spot where I can hug my knees and watch the sun dip towards the horizon.

I don't know how long I stay there.

I switched my phone off, not wanting another text from Aidan or a call from Jed. Pulling it out, I wonder if I should turn it back on.

But do I really want to face whatever communication might be on there?

What if there's none?

That'll probably hurt just as bad.

I'm tempted to throw the phone into the ocean, but manage to resist the urge and shove it back in my pocket.

Are either of them looking for me?

I hate that I hope they are.

I don't want to be found.

I want to be left alone!

Yet still, I leave my rocky hideaway and climb back out. I can't spend the night there. As much as I want to disappear, I can't make it happen.

Once the sun sets, I'll head back home. Hopefully Mom will have left for work and I can distract myself with TV or something.

I hit the beach and start ambling back to the pier when I spot something to my right.

A group of guys are lounging in the back of a flatbed truck.

Surfers.

Axel's crew.

I recognize Ripper before I see Axel appear behind him. Axel's holding a bottle of amber liquid and takes a swig before noticing me. I glance away and keep walking for the pier.

"Hey, surfer girl!" Axel calls.

I stop walking and turn to watch him running down the beach after me. He's in nothing but a pair of board shorts. I'm sure most girls would swoon. He's like an obsidian masterpiece.

"Hey." He grins.

I give him a halfhearted smile.

"Looking sad. What's up?"

"Nothing." I frown and cross my arms, hating the way he's trying to read me.

I don't say anything as his intense gaze stays on my face.

Finally, after a long beat, he holds out his bottle. "This'll kill the hurt."

It's a bottle of whiskey. I only know this because I read the label. I'm not a big drinker. Mom has kind of put me off over the years. Her drunk is just plain embarrassing. And I never want to be like her.

But the thought of killing this knot in my chest...

That's tempting.

Maybe that burning amber liquid will dissolve it completely.

I snatch the bottle out of his hand and take a pull. The alcohol hits my throat and I'm right about the burn. I start coughing and Axel laughs, patting my back as he takes the bottle off me.

"Come hang out with us, blondie." Shifting his hand to my lower back, he guides me up the beach. "We thought we'd hit the cove tonight."

I nod.

The cove.

No one will think to look for me at the cove.

And that can only be a good thing.

When Axel opens the door for me, I slip into the back seat. Ripper appears on my other side, his gaze bright and hungry. I frown and shift away, nearly changing my mind and getting out of the truck, until Axel reaches through the window and grabs Ripper by the back of the head. His large hand grips Ripper's crew cut like he's holding a basketball.

In a voice deep with warning, he jerks Ripper close and glares at him. "You don't touch this one. Ever."

Ripper growls in his throat and wrestles free of Axel's grip. With a short expletive, he rubs the back of his head, then shouts, "I got it! No touchy!"

"Get in the back," Axel growls, yanking the door open and hauling Ripper out of the cab.

Ripper glares at him, then me, before stalking to the back of the truck.

Axel's lips twitch as he gives me a swift wink, then passes me the bottle. "Look after this for me, will ya?"

I take it with a grin, having another pull before nursing the bottle against my chest like it's my teddy bear. The truck rumbles to life and I shift to the window, letting the wind tousle my hair as we pull away from the beach. The sun will set in the next hour or so and I'll be gone, safely hiding in a cove where no one can find me.

45

THE ONLY GIRL

AIDAN

Skylar is settled into her own private room at Aviemore Hospital. Savannah's dad is doing everything in his power to make sure she's getting the best care possible.

When Grayson and I first arrive, Skylar is being bathed, so we're asked to sit in a small waiting area near the nurses' station.

I find it nothing but frustrating.

All I can think about is Harley and how once again she hasn't replied to my text.

I don't get it.

I thought she was into me. Had I read that completely wrong? Was our kiss just some heat-of-the-moment thing? Was she just pretending to like me?

Raking a hand through my hair, I slump back in my seat, no doubt scowling at the wall.

Grayson is playing on his iPad, and even though Mom's asked him to turn the volume down twice, he still hasn't. I'm tempted to rip the thing from his hands and force him to. I'm sick of hearing the sound effects for Temple Run—some guy grunting as he tries to avoid being eaten by an ugly-looking beast.

Mom's pacing in front of me, talking to Dad on the phone. "Well, when will you get here?" she snaps, then closes her eyes. "Okay. You're right. I'm sorry."

Dr. Green appears around the corner, coming to a stop next to the coffee machine in our waiting area.

"I've gotta go." Mom hangs up and steps around me. "Kevin, how is she?"

Dr. Green gives my mom a quick hug, then pats her on the shoulder. "No change from this morning. I've just gotten off the phone with a neurologist in LA, and he agrees with my diagnosis. It's just going to be a matter of time while we wait for the swelling to decrease. Thankfully she doesn't require surgery."

"Is there anything we can do to help her?"

Dr. Green gives my mom a kind smile. "Talk to her. Hold her hand. Just be a presence in her life. Anything to draw her back to us."

Mom's lips tremble and she bites them together, giving Dr. Green a silent nod.

He rubs his hand between her shoulder blades. "It's

going to be okay, Sasha. She's a strong girl. She'll come back to us when she's ready."

Mom sniffs and gives him a grateful smile.

"You can go through and see her now."

Grayson and I trail after Mom, whose pumps clip on the shiny linoleum floor, alerting the world to the fact that she's coming. People from every corner of the hospital can probably hear her.

Mom slows behind the doctor and sucks in a breath as we turn into room 114. I don't realize I'm doing the same thing, until I step into the room and spot Skylar. She looks so pale and tiny in the mechanical bed, tubes coming out of her arms, a nasty bruised lump on her forehead.

It suddenly hurts to swallow.

The deep gash on her forehead has been stitched and bandaged, but the bruising has spread beneath it, like purple liquid under her skin.

She's so freaking still.

Savannah catches my eye from the other side of the bed and gives me a watery smile. Poor thing. She looks exhausted. Her hair hangs limp around her shoulders, and there are gray smudges under her eyes.

I smile back, hoping to reassure her, and she bites her lips together and starts blinking at tears before moving around the bed and coming to stand beside me.

She wants to snuggle against my side. I can sense it. For a second, it feels like the entire room is watching me, waiting for me to be the good boyfriend.

But I'm not her boyfriend anymore.

With a closed-mouth smile, I rub her back but don't actually pull her against me.

She does that on her own, pressing her body against my side.

I'm not sure what to do.

"You guys must be exhausted." Mom starts talking to Skylar's parents, finding out details that she already knows. There's not really much to report. It's all a waiting game now.

"We need to keep talking to her." Aunt Marlo glances at Savannah, her smile affectionate. "Savannah has been so good at that. You're such an angel. Skylar's lucky to have you."

"Thanks, Marlo," Savannah whispers.

I squeeze her shoulder and drop my arm.

Shit. This sucks. I should be comforting her, being a good person. But all I can think is that I don't want to encourage her, because in the time we've been apart, my heart has started beating for somebody else.

Someone who won't call me back.

Crap!

It'd be so much easier to still be into Savannah. I could slot back into life as I knew it. Everyone would be happy.

Except maybe me. I guess I'd find my groove, but I wouldn't be vibrant, alight, exhilarated by life. That's how Harley makes me feel, and I don't want to give that up.

"Can you excuse me for a second?" I whisper, slipping out of the room and pulling my phone from my pocket. I nearly bump into a chubby black guy. "Sorry," I murmur, veering away from him and around his cleaning cart.

"Aidan!" Mom calls me.

I grit my teeth and spin to face her.

"Where are you going?"

"Bathroom," I lie, then hold up my phone when she glares at me. "And then I need to make a quick phone call."

Her sharp gaze softens, and then she gives me a sad smile. "Okay, but just remember that there are people in here who need you too."

I bite the inside of my cheek and nod.

Mom disappears back into the room and I turn, heading down the corridor and looking for a private spot to call Harley. Man, I hope she answers this time.

I glance over my shoulder and do a double take when I notice the black guy following me. He doesn't have his cart anymore. He's just storming after me with this pissed-off look on his face. I don't even know the guy. Why is he glaring at me?

I pick up my pace and turn left at the vending machine, but when I glance back, he's still on my tail.

This is ridiculous.

Jerking to a stop, I spin and stare down at him. "Can I help you?"

"You Aidan?"

"Yeah." I cross my arms, happy when the guy stops a few feet away and I notice how much taller and stronger I am. He may be chunky, but it's soft chunk and I'm not intimidated by that. "Who are you?"

"Name's Jed. I'm Harley's—"

"BMF!" All my cautious anger evaporates, and I have to resist the urge to grab his shoulders and beg for news. "She told me about you. Is she okay? I've been trying to text her and—"

"No, of course she's not okay!" he snaps, his glare dark and intense. "Why would she be okay?"

"Uh..." My arms drop to my sides as I try to figure out why this guy seems to hate me.

"You're an asshole, you know that?"

"Me? What are you talking about?"

"I told her she should let you in." He jabs a finger at my chest. "I told her you'd be a safe bet! How could you play her like that, man?"

"I didn't play her. I..." What the hell is he talking about?

"You kissed her!" he snaps, then huffs, looking away from me and shaking his head. "Do you have any idea what a huge deal that is? She let you kiss her, and then you go off and start kissing your ex-girlfriend."

The air in my lungs evaporates, the temperature in the room suddenly sky-rocketing.

"Oh, there it is." He points at me. "Yeah, she saw you, and now she's gonna push everyone away again, because love only means hurt to her. Don't you get that? We were gaining ground. She was starting to trust, and now you've gone and screwed it up. You just made everything worse!"

"I didn't mean to." I rush out an explanation. "Savannah kissed me, and she was upset and… shit!" Scraping my hand through my hair, I fist the back. "That's why she won't text me back. I've got to go find her. Where is she?"

Jed's dark eyebrows dip together in confusion. "At the beach, man. Where else would she be? Do you not know her at all?"

I close my eyes with a short laugh, then give Jed a grateful pat on the shoulder. "You're a good friend. She's lucky to have you."

"Right now she doesn't even want *me*. If you don't fix this, I'm gonna kick your ass."

"If I can't make this right, I'll give you permission to kick my ass."

Jed gives me a lopsided grin, then shakes his head. "HRB. You better be good for it."

I have no idea what that means, but I don't really have time to ask, because he starts pointing over his shoulder and ordering me out the door. "Just go! Fix this!"

I don't need to be told again. Hauling ass through the hospital, I run out into the fading daylight and make a beeline for my car.

I can't believe what an idiot I was.

The soda cans lined up in the corridor? I should have worked it out.

I can't believe she saw me kissing Savannah. Shaking my head with a growl, I slip into my car and reverse out of the parking space.

Mom will kill me for ditching, but I can explain when I get back.

All I can think about right now is making it right.

I'd love to know what Jed meant about gaining ground and the whole trust thing, but I can find that out later, after I've convinced Harley that she's the only girl for me.

46

PRESERVATION

HARLEY

I'm drunk.

I've never really been drunk before.

I usually hate the taste of alcohol. Mom has always let me sip her wines and beers. Every time, I've made a face and gagged over them. But tonight, the hot liquid is making me giggle. It's killing the hurt, just the way Axel said it would.

With a silly laugh, I tip sideways and rest my head on Shane's shoulder. He laughs, taking a long pull from his bottle before passing it on to Ripper.

Ripper's creepy.

I want Aidan.

Frowning at the random thought, I forcefully shove it to the back of my mind and focus on Axel's creepy friend. I don't know what it is about the guy, but I feel like his eyes keep having sex with me. Like he's imagining it every time he looks my way.

It's gross. In a weird way it makes me feel dirty, like I need a shower or something.

A shudder runs down my spine and I jerk straight, then struggle to stand up.

"Where are you going?" Shane steadies me, but I flick his hand off my arm with a soft grunt.

I don't want to be touched.

I just want Aidan.

With a sharp snarl, I take a step away from Shane. The world is kind of spinning right now, but I keep my ground and stare out at the water.

Hatchet Cove is pretty.

It's always been pretty.

The sky is getting dark, but it's still that deep, navy hue rather than blackness. I stare across the small fire at Axel. His black skin will disappear soon, fade into the darkness. He'll become a shadow. A tall, strong shadow. One that's helping me tonight. Killing the pain.

I grin at him, swaying slightly to the music coming from his portable speaker.

The lyrics of "Darkside" call to me. "Fall in—to the darksi—de," they sing.

"What are you doing?" His deep voice rumbles. "You dancing?"

"No." I flick my octopus tentacle through the air. I've become boneless. Floppy. "I don't dance. I surf."

It's hard to talk right now. It's like the words are having to be pulled out of my mouth rather than just flowing smoothly. It sounds funny. I don't know what's up with it, but I don't need to talk to surf. I bite my bottom lip as laughter rumbles in my chest.

"Surfing's fun." I giggle. "I love surfing." I swallow, my head too heavy for my body. When I nod it's like the world goes down with me. But then I blink and point around the group. "I'm gonna surf."

Spinning in the sand, I head for Axel's truck.

"That's not a good idea!" Shane calls to me.

Pierce laughs. "It's a shitty idea!"

"Surfing's never a shitty idea!" I argue, resting against the truck for a second. "The water's my haven! It's the only safe place in this whole damn world, so you can all stick it!"

"You're drunk, surfer girl."

"Maybe." I turn to glare at Pierce, my body swaying as I point at him. "But I'm never too drunk to surf."

With that, I stomp to the back of the truck and struggle onto the bed.

I don't know whose surfboard I'm taking, but no one has jumped up to stop me, so I keep going, grunting as I wrestle the blue-and-white board free of its ties.

"This should be entertaining," one of the guys murmurs.

"Are we gonna stop her?"

"She's too drunk to even get out to the water." Axel's deep voice breaks apart with laughter.

It sets everyone off, and they're soon howling at the idea of my drunk ass trying to ride a board.

I'll show those assholes! I'll show everyone!

Surfing's my salvation. And I can do it anytime I damn well please. I don't need any of them to help me or stop me. They can all just go screw themselves.

The water's my only friend in this world. It's the only thing that's never hurt me or let me down. Water can heal, and if I get into that ocean right now, maybe it'll stop my insides from shredding.

47

BAD NEWS FROM MR. DREADLOCKS

AIDAN

I pull into the parking lot and jump out of my car, running to the high point of the path and scanning the beach. It'll be completely dark soon, but there's still enough light for me to make out silhouettes. And none of them are Harley's.

With an irritated huff, I try to figure out where to look next. Do I start walking the beach? Which direction? Past the pier? Or maybe she's at her place.

An intense urgency to find her is building in my chest.

I can't explain why it's getting so strong.

Probably because I'm desperate to right my wrong. To explain why I let Savannah kiss me. To tell her that it was a final goodbye, because I've figured it out now.

I finally know exactly what I want.

Closing my eyes, I berate myself yet again for being such an idiot.

"Aidan?" I spin at the sound of my name and notice Savannah getting out of her car and coming to join me.

I sigh and walk towards her, stopping at the stairs leading down to the beach.

"What are you doing here?" I murmur.

She looks disappointed by my question, but it's time for me to stop pretending.

I sigh and look to the ground between us.

She's wearing her white Adidas sneakers with the three black stripes. I remember going shopping with her to get those.

So much history.

But I don't want history anymore. I want future.

I open my mouth to say it, but she stops me by answering my question. "I needed a break. I've been in the hospital all day. When I saw you take off into the parking lot, I followed you to make sure you were all right. You were running pretty fast. Is everything okay?"

I shove my hands in my uniform pockets, wishing I'd gone home to change before hitting the hospital. At least I ditched my tie and blazer in the car. I've also rolled up the sleeves of my white shirt, but I still feel uncomfortable in these business-style clothes.

I'd rather be in board shorts and a T-shirt.

Or better yet, a rash guard, and out on the water with Harley.

With a heavy sigh, I quietly confess, "I'm looking for someone."

"Who?"

Glancing out at the water, I scan the waves for her, knowing she won't be there. Instead I see that guy with the dreads, walking up the beach.

"Is it a girl?" Savannah asks, her voice trembling.

I let out another heavy sigh and nod.

"Who is she?"

"My surf instructor. We've...grown close."

Savannah tips to the outer edges of her feet, a sure sign she's feeling nervous. I hate that I'm gonna hurt her with this.

"I really care about her. A lot. I mean, I'm falling for her."

"Oh."

I glance up in time to see Savannah's face bunch with sadness.

"I'm sorry." I brush my finger lightly down her arm. "I shouldn't have kissed you yesterday. That was wrong of me. I just wanted you to feel better, but it probably did more damage than good."

"I thought we were maybe getting back together." Her voice is so weak and miserable.

"That's what I wanted for so long." I blink, my chest tight as I let her down. "But then I met Harley, and things started to change. She..." I don't know what else to say.

Does Savannah really want to know that Harley

makes me feel more alive than anyone ever has? That she's not afraid to challenge me? That I feel like a better person when I'm with her?

That'll just hurt Savannah's feelings even more, but damn, I wish there was a nice way of explaining how my feelings have done a complete 180.

"Savvy, I—" I lick my lips as a tear slips down the side of her face.

She quickly swipes it away and swivels her body when someone appears at the top of the stairs.

I glance over and see it's the Ryder Rental guy.

He looks right at me, his expression dented with concern. "Aidan, right?"

I nod. "Griffin?"

"Yeah." He nods, takes a quick look at Savannah, and then his intense gaze is back on me. I don't know why he's looking at me like that. "You still friends with the blonde surfer girl?"

I want to say *more than*, but all I can manage is a nod, because hell, I don't know. If I can't find her and make it right, we might be a big fat pile of nothing.

The idea burns, but not as much as Griffin's worried expression. "I think she might be in trouble."

"What?" My heart does a painful squeeze, then starts drumming out of control, fear burning the edges of my brain.

"I saw her drinking with that guy Axel, and then she jumped into his truck with all his friends and they took off." Griffin hisses and shakes his head. "I don't know. Maybe I'm reading it wrong, but I just got a bad feeling in my gut. If I'd been able to get to my truck fast enough, I would have followed them. But..." He sighs. "I don't suppose you have any idea where they might have taken her?"

"Shit." Panic sets in, thick and fast. After my encounter with those jerks at Hatchet Cove, all my imagination can conjure is ugly ways of them hurting Harley. Without a word, I sprint to my car, nearly tripping as I jump off the sidewalk and land against the door.

"Where are you going?" Savannah chases after me.

"I think I know where they might have taken her. At least I hope I do." I wrench my door open and am just starting the engine when Savannah jumps in next to me.

"What are you doing?"

"I'm coming with you."

"What? No you're not. It could be dangerous."

"Then you're going to need all the help you can get," she retorts.

"I agree." Griffin leans down to speak through my car window, then gives Savannah a little smile. "I'll jump in the back."

"Okay." She seems excited by this little adventure, but she's freaking crazy.

She doesn't even know Axel or any of his crew.

And what the hell is Griffin doing? I don't even know this guy!

He plunks into the back seat while Savannah snaps the passenger seat back into place and slams the door shut. "Let's go."

I seriously don't have time for this shit.

With a dubious scoff, I reverse out of the lot and start figuring out how I can ditch Savannah at the entrance to Hatchet Cove.

Shit, what are those guys doing to Harley?

Fear roils through me as I accelerate out of the parking lot and head south.

Maybe having Griffin with me isn't a completely terrible idea. I may not know the guy, but I trust him more than I trust those surfers. I think I trust *anyone* more than I trust those guys.

If they've hurt Harley, I'm gonna kill them.

I grip the wheel, trying to dodge the pain of knowing this is partly my fault. If I hadn't let Savannah kiss me, Harley wouldn't have seen. She'd still trust me, be on her way to becoming my girlfriend. I wouldn't be hauling ass out of Ryder Bay to reach her, because she'd be sitting where Savannah is, not hanging out with a bunch of assholes who are doing who knows what with her.

48

A REALLY BAD IDEA

HARLEY

Of course no one's helping me.

With my jelly fingers and octopus limbs, it takes me five tries before I finally win over the bungy ties holding the surfboards against the side of Axel's truck.

Task one: done.

Now I have to get the board out of the truck and into the water.

I can do this.

I jump—more like kind of fall—out of the truck, and have to take three fumbling steps before the world stops moving. Giggles continue to rumble in my belly. Spinning back to the truck, I grab the end of the board and pull it out.

It's so much heavier than usual—I don't understand

why—but finally manage to secure it under my arm and start walking for the shore.

The guys are all laughing and pointing at me now.

I flip them the bird and trip over in the sand, landing on my knees.

This only makes them laugh harder. They topple against each other, obviously enjoying the show.

With a humph, I stand up and forget about carrying the board. Flipping it over, I just drag it across the sand until I reach the shoreline.

The water tickles my feet and I feel instantly better. Its cold touch is a welcome home. With a sloppy smile, I flop to my butt and wrestle the lead out from under the board. It takes a couple of tries, but I finally get it free. Wrapping it around my ankle, I secure it firmly.

"Never surf without your lead attached." I murmur the words that have been drummed into me.

By "that guy."

A heavy rock forms in my gut and tears threaten to overwhelm me.

I clench my jaw, warding off the memories, and force my body up.

My jean shorts are sticking to my butt cheeks and I probably have two big wet patches. Maybe that's why the guys are laughing so hard.

Ignoring them, I drag the board into the water, until it starts to float on its own. And then I jump on and start paddling.

Wow. It's harder than I remember.

The water feels thicker tonight, like I'm trying to paddle through chowder. I grunt and push a little harder, my tentacles complaining at the workout. A wave rolls in the farther I get out and I brace for a duck dive but screw it up. My board ends up tipping and I get swallowed by the wave, churning in its power until I can kick my way to the top.

Spluttering against the salty sting in my throat, I gulp in some air and rest my arms against the board. Another wave is rolling in, and I quickly dip below the surface before it can attack me.

Popping back up, I feel my senses struggling to align. It's like they want to switch on, alert and ready for action, but this thick fog is getting in the way. Goose bumps rise over my skin as the cold water sends spikes of awareness through the cloud cover.

With a grunt, I struggle back onto my board. I should probably turn back for the shore.

But I don't want to be on the sand with those guys.

I want to be here.

Riding these waves.

Liberated from the pain of the past. The things that haunt me. The people who have let me down. I want to eradicate the ache in my chest. The new burn that Aidan inflicted.

The water can heal it.

Cool it.

Paddling farther out, I see a new set building in the dim light. Darkness is nearly complete, hindering my view, but the moon is a pale spotlight and I can sense the energy in the water.

Closing my eyes, I listen to the faint roar as the wave begins to mount in front of me.

This is it.

Riding time.

With a sleepy grin, I wrestle my board in the right direction and wait for it. Wait for it.

As the wave rises beneath me, I force my arms to paddle. Order my body to do what is automatic.

And just as I rise to my feet, a thought hits me sharp and clear.

Harley, this is a really bad idea.

49

DRUNKEN DISORDER AT THE COVE

AIDAN

By the time we reach the turn off to the cove, my muscles are wound so tight, my brain so consumed by worry, that I totally forget about kicking Savannah out of the car.

It's not until I reach the end of the road and spot the bonfire in the sand, hear the drunken laughter, that I remember she's with me.

"Stay in the car," I bark as my car skids to a stop beside Axel's truck. I shoulder the door open, fired up and maybe just a touch scared. These guys could pummel me where I stand, but not until I've made sure Harley is safe.

"Hey!" someone shouts at me. I can't see who it is in the fading light. "Get the fuck out of here!"

I ignore the warning and race around the truck,

grabbing the first guy who tries to stop me and roughly demanding, "Where is she?"

The guy snickers, spurting his putrid breath all over me. He's so drunk that when I shove him back, he crumples to the ground with a stupid laugh.

"Axel!" I roar, about to race over to the guy when the asshole who messed up my car appears on my left.

His fist is poised and ready to deliver a blow. I duck, ready to defend myself, but I don't have to bother because Griffin is right behind me, capturing the guy's fist and pushing it back. I glance over my shoulder in surprise, my eyebrows rising as I see the heated warning on Griffin's face.

Turns out Mr. Dreadlocks can look scary as hell when he wants to.

I duck around Ripper, leaving Griffin to keep him in check, and run to Axel's side.

For some reason he's staring out at the water. He looks a little unsteady on his feet, but he's not laughing. His arms are crossed and he's frowning at the waves.

And that's when I know.

She's in the water.

I run up to Axel's side, scanning the dark waves for any sign of Harley.

There she is! My heart lurches out to her, fear catapulting up my throat when I spot the blonde, murky flash teetering back and forth on the board.

"She's drunk!"

It wouldn't take a rocket scientist to figure that out. The smell of alcohol is ripe in the air.

"You let her in the water?" I shout, grabbing Axel's shirt and wanting to demolish the guy.

He doesn't respond. Doesn't even look at me. All he can do is stare at my surfer girl, his face etched with fear.

I glance back to the water as the wave takes control of the rider, powerfully surging over her and toppling the board sideways.

The wipeout is a nasty one, and I don't even hesitate.

Ripping off my shoes, I sprint into the Pacific, begging my body to be the champion it used to be.

Harley's head hasn't popped into view. She's still below the water, no doubt fighting the washing machine as the waves topple over each other.

Diving into the salty spray, I start my crawl. I've never wanted to swim faster in my entire life. Even rescuing Skylar the night before didn't feel as desperate as this.

I didn't know who was in the water then.

But I do this time.

And I have to reach her before she never surfaces again.

50

TASTING DEATH

HARLEY

My lungs burn as I scrape the water, trying to propel myself to the surface. My jelly legs have no power, and it takes way too long for my head to breach the surface.

As soon as it does, a second wave is over me, crashing into my face and forcing me below the surface again.

Something heavy is dragging on my right ankle. My fuzzy head can't figure it out, and as I fight the churning water, I try to kick it off. But it won't leave me. It's tugging, pulling, making it hard to fight.

The water, usually so friendly, has turned into my enemy as I grapple to figure out which way is up.

Air.

I need air.

And I can't reach it.

The realization that I could drown hits me like a brick to the back of the head. My flailing arms falter as a circle of clarity grows in my brain.

I'm alone.

Helpless.

No one is going to rescue me, because I have pushed everyone away. In an attempt to protect myself, I've made myself vulnerable. Isolated.

I have no friends.

I open my eyes in the salty blackness. Fear laughs in my face, mocking me.

This is it, Harley. You've dug your own grave.

Now drown in it.

My lungs are screaming, begging me to open my mouth and take in air. As my floppy limbs lose power, I tip my head back and let my lips ooze apart. I have to release the pressure inside of me. I have to breathe.

And then a blur appears.

I flinch.

Shark!

It's my first thought and I flail, trying to get away from it. I open my mouth to scream, air bubbles spewing forth like foam in the water.

It grabs me. Yanking hard.

It's taking my arm!

I'm gonna die. I'm gonna die!

But I'm not.

As a solid arm encircles my waist, propelling me to

the surface, I realize that I haven't been robbed of a limb. I'm not in pain. I'm not going to die.

I'm being saved by some kind of guardian angel.

When we breach the surface, the air hits me like a slap to the face and I start sucking oxygen in big gasping breaths.

"I've got you." The strong arm pulls me close. "I've got you." He's repeating the words over and over like he needs them for life support.

Aidan.

He's here.

Clinging to his shoulders, I let him support my full weight as he rests his other arm on the board.

He came for me.

I'm alive because he's here.

I blink at that reality, my body too shocked to laugh or cry or do anything other than hold tight to something more than water.

Something more than just me.

51

WORLDS CHANGE

AIDAN

I use the surfboard to help get us back in, gripping tight to the side while holding Harley against me and riding the waves back into shore. They take us there easily, and as soon as I feel sand beneath my feet, I let the board go.

Harley's body is acting like seaweed, flopping against me as I wrestle her ankle strap off.

"Harley." I shake her, worried that she's suddenly blacked out on me.

"I'm fine," she mumbles.

"Bullshit," I mutter, flinging the lead aside and then scooping her into my arms when her knees buckle after only one step.

She feels so lightweight and fragile, her head knocking against my shoulder as I carry her past Axel and his drunken buddies. I glare in their direction, a growl rising in my throat when one of them makes a move to block me.

"Back off!" Axel barks.

The guy stumbles back and sways a little on his feet but doesn't take his laser-beam glare off me. I focus on my car and getting Harley into it as quickly as I can.

Griffin is waiting for me, his arms crossed as he guards Savannah, who totally ignored my order and got out of the car anyway.

I want to tell her off. Shout at her.

Anger is raging through me. Or maybe it's just fear.

Harley—the super-strong, tough surfer chick—is cradled against my chest, weak and barely lucid.

I could have lost her tonight.

The thought is an actual pain in my gut.

As I approach the car, Griffin leads Savannah into the back seat and I carefully set Harley down, buckling her up in spite of her slurred protests.

"You can't do it," I snap. "Let me help you."

Her hand slips off my arm, thumping onto her lap as her breath tickles my face.

Surfing while drunk. When she's better, we're having serious words about that.

I was racing to Hatchet Cove because I thought she was being held there against her will. I was expecting to drive up and rescue her from drunken idiots who were messing with her.

I didn't think she'd be stupid enough to get drunk and go surfing.

Anger and fear churn together, creating a storm in my chest that is taking too long to ease.

"Let's go to the hospital so you can get checked out." I reverse the car in the sand, my wheels spinning as I floor it to get out of Hatchet Cove as quickly as possible.

"No." Harley smacks my arm with the back of her hand. "I'm fine."

"You're not fine!" I retort, my voice cracking. "You nearly drowned!"

She blinks, her head popping off the back of the seat like she's suddenly sober. Her swallow is thick and audible as we bump along the unpaved road. And then she sniffs. Just a quiet one, but it sounds like she's about to cry.

I wince, not sure I can cope with her falling apart on me. I'm barely holding it together. One little whimper from her will undo me completely.

Softening my voice, I glance at her. "I just want to make sure you're okay."

"I am," she whispers. "I don't need to go to the hospital. I just want bed. My bed. Please." Her voice starts to break apart and wobble.

How can I argue with that?

She's breathing, not injured. She's just drunk and probably feels like shit right now.

Bed is probably the best place for her.

We reach the main road and I turn towards Ryder Bay, watching my speed and making sure Harley gets home in one piece.

The drive back is quiet and awkward.

Savannah and Griffin are squished together in the back, not saying anything.

Harley rests her head against the glass and stares out into the night.

I don't know what to say to her. How to make this better.

I think I'm in a little shock myself. As the adrenaline drains out of me, I'm swamped by a tired sadness that I can't even explain.

Pulling onto her street, I thankfully remember which house is hers and stop outside the carport.

Harley fumbles with the door handle as I unbuckle my seat belt.

She says she's fine, but she's not. She's too drunk to even open a door.

I run around to the passenger side and ease it open, catching her as she flops against my legs.

"Come on." I help her out of the car.

She groans and leans against me. "I feel sick."

"I bet you do," I murmur.

I've never been drunk enough to puke before, but I've been drunk enough to remember how hideous the nausea can be. If Harley was drinking straight from those bottles, she wouldn't have needed much to intoxicate her small body.

I'm guiding her towards the front door when her body jerks and she suddenly starts heaving. With a soft yelp, I direct her to the uncut weeds alongside the house and stop her from toppling over while she pukes. Wrapping my arm around her side, I hold her up and scoop the hair over her shoulder before she gets sick all through it. The vomit splashes onto the side of the house, reeking of recklessness and regret.

"It'll make her feel better," Griffin calls out to me.

I glance over my shoulder. He's leaning against my car with his arms and feet crossed, looking way too relaxed for what tonight has been.

I scowl at him, then turn back to Harley as she wipes a shaking hand across her mouth and starts to stand. She's trembling, and I sweep her into my arms again. I don't know how I'm supposed to get her into the house.

"Do you have a key?"

"In my pocket."

I glance down at her saturated clothing and won't be shocked if the key is now sitting on the ocean floor.

With a grunt, I lift her higher into my arms and try the door before having to squirm my fingers into her jean shorts.

The handle creaks but then pops open.

"Is your mom home?"

"I don't know." Harley's head flops against my shoulder and I creep into the house.

"Ms. Quinn?" I softly call.

But no one answers. I try two more times, only to confirm that the house is empty.

Stepping over a pile of unfolded laundry in the middle of the living room floor, I turn sideways through the door which I assume leads to the bedrooms.

The place is tiny, with old decor that's peeling and frayed at the edges. Burnt orange and yellow carpet with brown swirls, patterned wallpaper that makes you feel cross-eyed. This house is like an acid trip. An old, fading acid trip that hasn't been shown an ounce of love and care in years.

I swallow, suddenly understanding why Harley was so quiet and awestruck when she walked into my pristine white house.

Spotting a bathroom at the end of the hall, I head in that direction. I know Harley wants bed, but I can't lay her down on her mattress soaking wet and reeking of puke. I need to clean her up first, but as I place her down on the bathroom floor, I wonder how comfortable she'll be with me undressing her. She's basically falling asleep at my feet and I'd be completely justified, but how will Harley feel when she wakes up in the morning and knows I've seen her naked?

"I'll clean her up." I glance over my shoulder and see Savannah standing in the doorway. She tips her head sideways, silently ordering me out of the bathroom. "Can you find her some dry clothes?"

"Sure." I give her a grateful smile, then quickly find what has to be Harley's bedroom. The door is open already, the walls covered with surfing posters. Her bed is unmade, her desk in disarray. One of the bookshelves is broken and sitting askew, with books piled up beside it.

I notice a pale yellow T-shirt sticking out from under her pillow. Assuming it's her pajamas, I race over and tug it out, then unearth a pair of cotton boxer shorts. I run them back to Savannah, who is crouched over Harley with a damp cloth in her hand.

"Thanks," she murmurs.

"I'll just wait outside. Call me when you're done."

She nods and gives me a sad smile before flicking the door closed with her foot.

I pace the narrow hallway, biting the inside of my cheek as I walk to what is probably Ms. Quinn's room. The door is shut, so I can't really tell. The place is so tiny, it only takes me about five strides to get from one end of the hallway to the other.

Man, this little box is so different to my house.

Harley no doubt felt intimidated as I walked her through what I thought was a simple, modern kitchen and living area. Shit, I really have no idea. Me in my sheltered little world.

The bathroom door clicks and I spin.

"She's asleep." Savannah points over her shoulder. "You want to carry her to bed?"

I nod and slip past Savvy, crouching down to cradle Harley against me. She's softly snoring, which has to be the sweetest sound I've heard all day.

Savannah straightens the covers while I lay Harley down and graze my lips against her forehead. Brushing a wet tendril of hair back off her face, I stare down at her and am overwhelmed with relief.

Tonight could have gone so differently.

Thank God for Jed.

Thank God for Griffin.

Savannah clears her throat and I turn to look at her. "Thank you," I whisper.

"You're welcome," she rasps, then points over her shoulder. "Can you take me back to my car, please?"

"Sure." I follow her out through the kitchen, locking the door behind me. Surely Harley's mother has a key. Even if she doesn't, I don't care. I'm not leaving her alone in an unlocked house.

The trip back to the beach is silent. My phone screen lights up with a message from my mom. Savannah texted her for me when we were heading to Hatchet Cove. She took my suggestion and lied:

With Sav. She needs a break. We'll be back soon.

"Your mom wants to know how much longer we'll be." Savannah's voice is so quiet tonight.

"Tell her we're heading back now."

Savannah replies for me, her fingers flying over my screen. The only sound in the car is the click of the message being formed, then the swoop of the message sending.

"She's already replying," Savannah murmurs. "They're heading home. She wants you to do the same."

"Okay." I nod, and then the silence descends again.

No one has anything to say. I glance in the rearview mirror to check on Griffin. He seems content enough in the back, staring out the window. He strikes me as a very mellow guy. Unlike me, he seemed completely unflustered by the shit that went down at Hatchet Cove. Unless he's just really good at hiding his emotions.

As I pull the car into a parking space, I look over my shoulder and hold out my hand to him. "Thanks for your help tonight."

"I didn't do much, man." He takes my hand and gives it a shake. "You were the one who rescued her."

I let out an embarrassed scoff and shake my head, opening my door and flipping the front seat down so he can get out.

"Two rescues in two days." Griffin smirks as he stands straight. "You ever considered a career in lifeguarding?" I open my mouth, not sure what to say, but he just chuckles and lightly smacks my chest with the back of his hand. "You should think about it, man. I'm pretty sure Marshall would be all over that." He looks across my car and grins. "'Night, Savannah."

"Good night." She swallows and looks down, picking at some invisible spot on the car roof.

Griffin gives me one last nod, then jogs away.

I slump against the car, my mind whirring over his comments, then racing back to the argument I had with Harley about finding something that ignites me. I stop and make myself think about what it felt like to rescue both Skylar and Harley.

Maybe I don't have to have a future in finance or sales.

"So this is what it feels like."

I spin at the sound of Savannah's soft voice. "Huh?"

Her smile is sad as she looks over at me, I can see that much under the orange boardwalk lights. "Rejection. This is what rejection feels like."

My expression crumples, and I don't know what to say.

"The way you looked after her tonight, it's so obvious." Savannah blinks, sucks in a ragged breath, then starts picking at the roof again. "We never had that."

"Savvy, come on. You were my world."

"And I thought you were mine for a while too, but that feeling just kind of faded, which is why I broke it off." She sniffs and shrugs, like she's trying to tell herself it's no big deal.

But it is.

She's fighting tears right now.

And I can't stop them.

"I just didn't expect to miss you so much." Her

forehead creases and she looks at me again, her beautiful brown eyes glassy with tears.

I give her a pained smile and wish I could do more.

But there's nothing more to say or do.

We're over.

Our chapter is done.

52

BMF RESTORATION

HARLEY

Starting a new day has never been so hard.

The light piercing my bedroom wall is like a laser beam, and opening my eyes is a new brand of torture I've never felt before.

Every one of my senses is thick and sludgy. My tongue has grown mold overnight, and the furry, putrid taste is what pulls me out of bed. Someone's gone and filled my body with concrete. Even making it to the bathroom to pee is an effort. I bend over the sink with a groan and put my mouth under the faucet, sucking in water and trying to figure out why I feel so bad.

And then the memories come.

Flashes of knowledge that break through my swollen brain and remind me that I acted like the world's biggest idiot last night.

Drinking whiskey straight from the bottle?

Surfing?

Nearly drowning under a double hold-down?

I grip the porcelain sink, my arms shaking.

Death opened its mouth to me last night, its teeth nearly cutting me in half until Aidan dragged me away.

Aidan.

I look into the mirror, grimacing at my reflection. I don't usually care too much about my appearance, but the thought of Aidan seeing me like this is kind of horrifying. Brushing the fur off my teeth, I then stumble to the shower, flick it on and peel off my clothes. The water cleanses me somewhat, rousing my senses and tempering the painful thud in the back of my head.

Opening my mouth, I drink the spray and think about what lies ahead.

I have to find Aidan today.

I have to thank him. Maybe tell him why I acted like such an idiot.

I know he's back with Savannah now, but he saved my life, and the least I can do is explain how much I'll miss hanging out with him.

Who knows, maybe we can figure out how to be friends somehow.

With a hard scoff, I flick the water off and get ready for what will no doubt be a taxing day.

And I'm right.

The second I walk into the kitchen, my mother orders me to clean the puke off the side of the house.

"What puke?" I frown at her, desperate for some of that juice she's pouring.

"Of course you don't remember." She shakes her head and starts to laugh at me. "Shit, girl, you must have a thumping headache today. I don't think I've ever seen you wasted. Kind of sad I missed it."

She hands me the glass of orange juice and I snatch it off her, downing the liquid. The tangy coldness soothes my throat as I try to figure out what puke she's talking about.

I must have thrown up last night.

Oh crap, right in front of Aidan. Talk about humiliating.

I have vague memories of sitting in his car, fighting the urge to vomit. I thought I'd made it.

Then there was me on the bathroom floor and someone was cleaning me up, helping me out of my wet clothes.

Was it Aidan?

I shake my head and instantly regret it. My brain sloshes from one side of my skull to the other.

Biting my lips against a groan, I rest my elbows on the counter and try to figure out who got me changed into my pjs.

Aidan wouldn't have undressed me like that. He asks for permission before kissing a girl. Which means it must have been...

I swallow, hating the answer. Vague memories of a girl with long brown hair and gentle eyes make me shudder.

Mom holds out a bucket and cloth. "Clean the house and I'll make you my hangover smoothie."

"Sounds disgusting," I grumble, reluctantly taking the bucket from her hands and stalking outside.

The puke isn't too bad. I got most of it into the grass, but there is a fair spray of yellow on the house. I grab the garden hose and get to work, the entire time promising myself that I will never drink like this again.

Once I'm done, I trudge back inside and am forced to down some green sludge that Mom tells me will kick the headache and get me back to normal.

I sure as shit hope so.

After chugging down the gloop, I press the back of my hand against my mouth and try not to throw it up. As I hand her the glass, Mom smirks at me. "I'm guessing you'll want to spend the day in bed."

I shake my head. "I have some things I need to do."

"Well, you're gonna have to walk to wherever you want to go." She pulls out a cigarette and perches it between her lips to light it. "I need the car today, and I didn't see your skateboard in the carport."

I cringe. That's right. Aidan still has my board.

"Walking will be good for you anyway. Just take it easy, all right?" She pulls a pack of gum from her bag and hands me a piece of sugar-free peppermint.

I take it with a small smile. It's not often that Mom

takes care of me, and she hardly ever tells me to look after myself. I can't explain the warmth in my chest right now or the sudden urge to cry. Looking over my shoulder into the living room, I hide my expression and manage to fight off the tears before they show.

"Harley?"

"Yeah." I turn back, forcing my eyes wide so she can't see how much they're burning.

"Don't get drunk like that again, okay?"

I nod. "Promise."

She sucks her cigarette, then blows the smoke away from my face. And suddenly the warmth between us is awkward. We both seem to sense it at the same moment and she walks out of the kitchen to get away from me, while I shove the gum in my mouth and head to my room to find my most comfortable pair of sneakers.

I can't find my phone anywhere and have to conclude that I probably left it at Hatchet Cove. I'll likely not get it back. Not that Axel would steal it, but everyone was pretty wasted last night and it's probably smashed or buried in the sand. If by chance it's in his truck, he might return it to me, but I'll probably have to seek him out to ask for it, and I don't feel like seeing any of those guys today. Or possibly ever again.

It takes me forty minutes to walk to the hospital.

I figure Aidan will probably be there with his family, or if he's not there, someone who knows him will be, and I can find out where he is. Before I do anything else, I have to get that apology over with.

The first thing that hits me as I walk into Aviemore is the icy, fake air. Goose bumps ripple over my skin as my body adjusts from the heat of outside. The waiting area has a few minor injuries to be seen, but it's pretty quiet today. I walk past reception and into the bowels of the hospital.

It's visiting hours, so no one looks at me twice or asks me who I am.

I'm not sure which room Skylar is in, but I walk the corridors, my courage waning as I pass a room with family surrounding a bed. It's not the De Beers, but it still makes me realize that I'm about to knock on a door and have everyone turn and look at me. Their gazes will remind me that I don't belong.

Clenching my jaw, I turn the next corner and run straight into a cleaning cart, banging my knee and nearly tipping it over. I grab it and help the cleaner right it before things topple all over the floor. As soon as the cart is stable again, I glance up and see Jed smiling at me.

"She lives," he murmurs.

My eyebrows flicker with confusion as his introductory smile fades away and is replaced with a sharp frown.

"What?" My voice is mouse-like as I step back from his angry expression.

Jed angry is weird. I'm not used to seeing it. He

shakes his head and slaps his cleaning cloth down on the cart. "Surfing drunk? Are you out of your mind? You could have died, HQ! Do you have any idea how much that kills me? How horrible my life would be without you in it? How dare you go and do something so stupid! And what were you thinking, hanging out with those jerks? You should have come to see me instead of pushing me away. I'm your boy. The one you run to when you're sad. You made a big mistake last night. Big mistake."

"I know," I whisper, thoroughly reprimanded.

Jed rests his hands on his hips and huffs, his chin trembling just a little.

I smile at his sweet angst and try to make it better. "I love you too, BMF."

His head jerks in my direction and he gives me a stunned look, blinking a few times before finally saying, "I am talking to Harley Quinn right now, aren't I? Because I'm pretty sure she's allergic to the L-word."

I snicker. "It felt like an appropriate time to use it."

"It sounded nice." He starts to smile, and I realize how much I do love him.

My insides tremble with regret and it shows in my voice. "I'm sorry I pushed you away. You're my best friend, and I seriously don't want to live without you. I'm your HQ, right?"

He shifts around the cleaning cart, pulling me into a tight bear hug. "Always and forever."

I squeeze him back and don't let go until he kisses

my cheek.

Holding me at arm's length, he studies my face and laughs. "Nearly dying has worked out well for you. I'm liking this girl...although I'll love you no matter how you behave. It's kind of my duty as your BMF."

I grin. "Thank you, Jed."

He nods, then lets me go, moving back around to grab the handles of his cart. "Well, as much as I hate to say this, I'm supposed to be working."

"Yeah, you better get back to it." I point my thumb over my shoulder. "I was just looking for..."

"The guy who saved your ass?"

I stop, a thought suddenly hitting me. "How'd you even know about last night?"

"I saw him here. Maybe an hour ago?" He shrugs. "We talked. He's worried about you. Once I got over the shock of finding out what happened, I told him not to stress, because you're the toughest chick I know." I give Jed a grateful smile, but it fades as he keeps talking. "Anyway, he looked kind of sad or angry. I couldn't quite tell. All I know is that you have to go make it right. I like the HRB...and so do you."

"OTD." I grin.

He laughs and points at me, obviously stoked that one of his acronyms is catching on.

"I don't suppose you know which room Skylar's in?"

"He's left already."

"Oh." My shoulders slump.

"But I'd start with the beach if I were you. My guess is...he wants to find you as bad as you want to find him."

I give Jed a nervous grimace.

His expression softens, his brown eyes throwing off waves of kindness that I want to wrap myself in. Maybe I could spend my day cleaning the hospital with him instead.

No, Harley. Stop being so chicken!

Jed reaches out and brushes his hand down my arm. "All you can do is try. Be honest with him and then see what happens. No matter what, remember this always..." He steps back and points at me with a serious expression, then bursts into the chorus of "Two Is Better Than One."

I roll my eyes and start to laugh.

"Thank you, Jed!" I try to talk over his singing, but he just keeps going.

With a shake of my head, I walk away from my crazy friend and head into the sunshine to find the guy who owns my heart. No matter what happens after I talk to him, no matter how the conversation ends, I'm happy to let him keep a small piece of it.

Aidan may have just been a short season in my life, but it's been a precious one.

One I can hold onto for the rest of my life.

It's time to stop being so afraid.

At least if I tell him the truth, I can walk away knowing I did the right thing.

53

MY SURFER GIRL FROM THE SOUTH END

AIDAN

I've been on the beach for nearly an hour and still Harley hasn't appeared. Having walked up and down the length of it, I'm taking a break near Marshall's lifeguard tower.

He's sitting high up on his chair, watching the swimmers in the water. Weekends are always busier, and he'll have a full-on day ensuring people's safety. I then spot Griffin walking past him. He stops at the base to have a quick chat before heading to the Ryder Rentals shed.

I wonder if I should apply for that summer job. I could watch Marshall work in between hiring out boards, see what being a lifeguard is really all about. Those two rescues, although harrowing, had a certain element of satisfaction to them. I saved both lives. I was good at it.

I still have one more year of school left, but knowing what direction to take after graduation would be kind of cool.

"Lifeguarding," I murmur to myself, trying to imagine myself doing it.

Maybe the ocean has really been my water all along —salt vs. chlorine.

Salt wins!

The comparison makes me smile as I think of Harley and how she told me I should change my water. She's opened up a whole new world for me. Meeting her on this beach, although it complicated so much, was the best thing that could have happened to me.

Glancing over my shoulder, I push my shades up and scan the beach behind me.

Still no Harley.

I guess it's a fool's hope to think she'll show up.

Part of me wants to turn up on her doorstep, but if she's hungover she'll be feeling gross, and I don't want to wake her.

What if her mom's there?

As far as I know, the woman has no idea who I am, and I don't want to land Harley in any hot water by admitting I drove her daughter home. After saving her life. Because she went surfing while off-her-ass drunk.

I grimace, reliving that moment where she crashed into the water and failed to surface.

Shit, she could have died.

Sliding my shades back on, I don't know whether to cry or shout. Part of me is raging that she'd do something so stupid, while the other part of me is overcome with relief that I managed to find her in the water.

Man, I hope I get to see her today.

I've texted her and am just waiting on a reply, but Harley doesn't have a great track record with that. I'll just sit here in the sand until I can't stand it, and then no doubt drive past her house until her mom's car is no longer in the driveway.

But surely she'll show up. The beach is Harley's haven. Unless last night put her off. It better not have. I'll just have to help her fall in love with the water again, if that's the case.

I'll—

"Hey."

I whip around to find Harley standing behind me. She's holding a pair of beat-up white sneakers between her fingers and is dressed in her standard T-shirt and cut-off denim shorts. Her blonde hair is dancing in the breeze, and I lift my shades to get a decent look at her brilliant blue eyes.

"Hi." It's all I can manage. Emotions are charging through me thick and fast.

She's here.

She's alive.

She's so freaking beautiful.

With a heavy sigh, she plunks down next to me and

buries her toes in the sand. "Surf's looking good today."

I follow her line of sight and nod. "Yep. You going out in it?"

"Not today," she murmurs, then gives me a pained smile.

If I'm reading her expression right, the edges are tinted with dark shades of regret.

I scoff.

I can't help it.

"What were you thinking?" I rake a hand through my hair. "Night surfing. Drunk. It's just so...insane!"

"I know," she counters. *In other words, shut up!*

Biting my lips together, I hold back my lecture, although it's busting to get out of me. I need her to promise that she'll never do anything that stupid again.

"I don't normally get drunk, swear," she mumbles.

"Oh yeah? Downing bottles of whiskey isn't your style?" My tone is sharp and scathing. I don't mean for it to be. She just makes me so crazy. I want to be mad at her and making out with her in the same breath. I want to grab her shoulders and shake some sense into her, but then the feel of her cradled in my arms last night was so freaking fantastic...I want that again too.

"Okay, fine. You're right," she snaps. "I get that you're mad. If you need to tell me off, just get it over with!"

"I don't want to tell you off." I angle my body to face her, perching the shades on top of my head so she's forced to look me in the eye. "I just don't want you to ever do that again. You scared the hell out of me. It was stupid. What you did could have gotten you killed. I just don't understand why you did it. Why did you go with Axel? That has trouble written all over it."

"Maybe I wanted trouble," she mumbles.

My eyebrows shoot up in surprise. "You wanted to kill yourself?"

"No!" She cringes, then rubs her forehead and looks out to the horizon. "Axel told me it would kill the hurt, and when he handed me that bottle... I just wanted to stop feeling for a while."

She goes quiet, her lips pursing as she so obviously fights tears.

My gut wrenches uncomfortably. I always hate it when girls cry. It does my heart in.

"I just like you so much." Harley's voice wobbles. "I mean, I know we argue sometimes and get pissy with each other, but being with you is so much fun. I'm happier with you than I am with anyone! And now it's over." She sucks in a sharp breath and slashes the tears off her cheeks. "I want to keep hanging out with you, like all the time. You're smart and funny. Easy to talk to. Smoking hot." She blushes, but her lips don't curl into a smile. If anything, my "hotness" seems to irritate her. Like she wants to like me but doesn't think she should. "I'm just gonna miss you so much."

I don't think my heart could grow any bigger right now if I wanted it to.

A smile rises on my face, but she's not looking at me.

She can't see.

She doesn't know.

"I'd miss you too."

She sniffs and bobs her head. "I guess I was just trying to process in a really stupid way, but last night was a good lesson. I won't do it again, and you can trust me not to be an idiot. If I care about you as much as I think I do, then your happiness comes first, right? And then maybe we can be friends. I'm sure if Savannah's cool with it, then we can keep hanging out. Hey, maybe I can learn to like her too? We can hang out all together? Or, no..." She shakes her head. "That'll be way too awkward. Do you think she'd be okay with us still surfing together?"

She finally looks at me and I've never felt such strong affection for anyone. Ever.

Brushing my fingers down her cheek, I then capture her wind-blown hair and tuck it behind her ear.

She leans away from my touch. "I don't think Savannah will like that."

"I'm not with Savannah," I whisper, my voice thick and husky. "I'm sorry that you saw us kiss. I never intended to do that, but she was sad and hurting and when she kissed me, I didn't want to make her feel bad. I shouldn't have done it, though. I... It was a mistake. I told her last night that there was no chance of us getting back together. It's over."

"But...I thought she was what you wanted?"

"She was." I brush my thumb along Harley's cheek-bone. "For a really long time, but then you...changed my mind." Her lips part with surprise and a smile curls the edges of my lips. "When I found out you were in danger last night, it just confirmed it all for me, you know? The idea that you were hurt, or in trouble..." I shake my head, the emotions stealing my voice for a second. "I don't want to be without you, Just Harley. You're the only girl I want. And you never have to miss me, because I'm not going anywhere."

"You want me?" she squeaks.

I grin and capture the tear leaving her left eye. "You're the best thing that's ever happened to me. Of course I want you."

She lets out a surprised laugh and a few more tears slip free. I gently wipe them away and gaze at her. "Your eyes are so bright blue right now. I could look at them all day."

Her swallow is thick, her lips trembling just a little before breaking into a grin. "You have my permission."

I snicker. "To look at your eyes all day?"

"No, you idiot." She sniffs. "To kiss me, and I swear if you don't in like the next ten seconds, I'm gonna have to kick your ass."

With a soft chuckle, I lean towards her mouth and don't even hesitate before sinking into a kiss that turns my world on its axis. Harley's fingers curl into my shirt as she tugs me a little closer. Her sweet, minty taste is intoxicating; her soft lips and warm tongue send my senses reeling. Running my hand around the back of her neck, I deepen the kiss again and figure that the rest of my day is now figured out.

I've got sand, sun, surf...and Harley.

Of all those things, she's the only one I really need.

My surfer girl from the south end.

54

THE BEGINNING

HARLEY

S ummer has officially begun.

Woot!

School got out three days ago, and I'm ready to spend the next couple months surfing, working—blech —and hanging out with my boyfriend.

My boyfriend.

A sizzle runs through me. I have a boyfriend. Sometimes that makes me nervous. Past experience warns me to be careful. But then, Aidan is *nothing* like "that guy." He's sweet and thoughtful, seems to really care about me. I don't feel like he's with me for anything other than the pleasure of my company. There's no ulterior motive or secret plan to do me over down the track. At least I don't think there is.

Yeah, I'm pretty sure with Aidan De Beer, what I see is what I get.

And I'm more than happy with that.

Because I like what I see.

I glance to my left and study Aidan's profile. His jaw is clenching and unclenching. Yeah, the poor guy is nervous. He starts his new job today. In like an hour. It's kind of funny that he's so nervous about working at Ryder Rentals. It's not like it's going to be hard, but I guess the first day on any job can be a little nerve-racking.

We're currently sitting in his convertible. He's driving me to Freshmart for my morning shift. We met at the beach early to fit in a surf and will meet up again after work for an afternoon session.

I already can't wait.

Aidan's thumb rubs over my knuckles in a steady rhythm. He's not saying anything and I'm happy to just sit with him, my fingers linked through his, the breeze kicking up our hair as we drive the final few blocks.

The last week and a half have gone by in a whirlwind.

Aidan applied for the Ryder Rentals job the same afternoon we made up. He decided that working on the beach for the summer would be a really good way to check out lifeguarding. I was stoked. He's thinking of being a lifeguard! He'd be so incredibly awesome at that.

I found the courage to admit my jealousy about the

fact that he'd get to work on the beach over summer, while I'd be stuck at Freshmart. He told me I should apply for the Ryder Rental job instead, which then started up a mini-argument between us.

It was resolved quickly when Aidan finally relented and said that he'd go for the Ryder Rental job on the condition that I had some business cards made up and he could offer my services as a private surf instructor.

Damn, how the hell could I argue with that?

I spent the Sunday afternoon hanging out at his place while his kid brother, Grayson, designed this wicked logo and business card for me. The kid has skills.

So Aidan got the job after like a five-minute interview. It may have helped that Aidan's dad is good friends with Marshall Swinton—the owner of Ryder Rentals—but I like to think he got the job on his own merit. He'll be great. He's good-looking, friendly, smart —people will no doubt flock to the board shed with two gorgeous guys manning it.

On Monday, we celebrated with dinner at Aidan's place, where Grayson presented me with a stack of one hundred beautifully printed business cards.

I swear I nearly cried.

I was so nervous over dinner that I could barely eat, but by the end of the meal, I started to relax. Luke is a pretty funny guy, and Sasha is actually really sweet. A total mother. She even gave me a hug before I left and sent me home with a goody bag of food. I thought I was going to cry—again.

The rest of this week has gone by in a blur. We wanted to make the most of every spare second we could find, so we've been meeting up early before school and staying out until sunset each evening. The only day I haven't seen Aidan is when he went to his friend Simon's graduation.

Other than that, I've seen Aidan more than I have my own mother.

I helped him find a new board and he's been testing it out. He's wiped out a few too many times for his liking, but he'll get there. His surfing has come a long way in a short space of time. He's definitely got an affinity with the water.

I love that about him.

"You're gonna be great today." I squeeze his fingers as he pulls into the Freshmart lot.

He grips back and lets out a shaky breath.

It makes me laugh. "Don't be so nervous. You've got this. It's renting out surfboards and getting people to sign disclosures. It's a piece of cake."

Parking the car, he turns to look at me, his lips twitching with a grin. "And handing out business cards."

I rest my hand on his cheek, so tempted to tell him I love him, but it's too soon. I don't want to be in love with him yet. That's still just a little too scary to process. Instead, I lean over and kiss him.

He breathes in through his nose, like he's trying to absorb all of me, and cups the side of my face. I love how he does that. Aidan's kisses make my toes curl, and I like to think I have the same effect on him.

As much as I could happily spend the rest of the day making out in his car, I force my mouth off his. Work is just behind me, and it's hard not to make a face as I think about how painful my six-hour shift will be.

"We'll be surfing the waves again before you know it." He gives me a tender smile. The look in his eyes says so much, and the warmth inside of me makes my stomach tingle and dance. "I'm gonna do my best to get you as much business as possible. Hopefully you can quit this place soon and come hang out on the beach with me."

I snicker and give Aidan one more peck on the lips. "Do that, and you'll become the world's best boyfriend."

"What? You mean I'm not already?" He winks and I laugh, unable to resist the urge to kiss him again.

Wrapping my hand around the back of his neck, I deepen the kiss until we're both out of breath.

His eyes are still closed as he rests his forehead against mine and puffs, "No matter what I am, you're the world's best girlfriend."

A giggle spurts out of me before I can stop it. "Why? Because I leave you breathless?"

His eyes pop open and his green gaze drinks me in. "That's only one of the many, many reasons."

I swear the look on his face is going to turn my heart to custard…or maybe even melted honey.

I swallow and bite my lips together, forcing myself to open the door and get out of the car.

"You got your phone?" he asks. "Text me when you're done and I'll come back and get you."

"Sure thing." I pull my bag from the floor and hitch it onto my shoulder. My phone is inside it. My new phone, which Aidan bought me, and then had to spend an hour persuading me to keep. Yes, the argument was real and borderline savage, but we resolved it in the end. I scored myself a new phone and a very sweet makeup session before the evening was up.

I hover by his car door, not wanting to leave him or spend most of a good day inside Freshmart.

With a soft snicker, Aidan unbuckles his seat belt and leans across the car. I bend down so he can brush his hand lightly down my cheek. "It'll be over before you know it, and then it's just you, me and the water, babe."

I grin, steal one final kiss, then force my body to walk away from him.

I can sense him watching me and turn one last time when I reach the doors, blowing him a little kiss before disappearing inside.

Pulling in a breath, I try to think about the afternoon. If I can just focus on what's ahead, then the time will tick by and I'll be back in Aidan's car and heading for the waves.

I'm already anticipating an awesome afternoon.

As long as Axel and his crew aren't around.

I saw him this morning.

He was at the beach before Aidan got there, obviously doing an early surf while the waves were good. He was getting out of the water while I was waxing my board.

Water was running down his head and he swiped a hand over his crown and face. I was relieved he was getting out. I've been avoiding him and his crew like the plague and didn't really want to be surfing the same waves.

Thank God Aidan hadn't arrived yet.

Ripper is still pissed that Aidan showed up at Hatchet Cove and got in his way. But Axel hasn't said anything. I wonder if he feels bad about what happened to me.

He caught me staring at him and stopped walking. His gaze was intense, but I couldn't seem to break contact. I really didn't want him coming over to talk to me.

Thankfully Shane came running down the beach to distract him. "You surfing without me? You asshole!"

Axel grinned at his friend, and I was off the hook.

For then, anyway. I don't know if he'll try to talk to me.

I don't always understand Axel. He's mean, but seems to tolerate me. I don't know how he feels about my connection with Aidan. But I can't care, because I'm not giving up Aidan for anything.

Dumping my stuff in the back room, I sign in for the day and am told I'll be working checkout number five. Holding in my sigh, I take my key and change drawer, then head in that direction.

I've only been sitting here for about ten minutes when someone slaps a packet of gum down on the belt.

I glance up and my insides freeze.

It's a girl.

A pretty one, named Savannah Green.

She's staring at me with this hard determination that's making it impossible to move.

I have to reach for that gum. I have to scan it and tell her the price, but there's this giant rock in my throat, so talking's off the table.

Why I am reacting like this?

She's just a girl.

No she's not, she's Aidan's ex! And she looks like she wants to eat you alive.

With a sharp huff, she rests her hand against the edge of the counter and abruptly says, "We need to talk."

TO BE CONTINUED…

Keep reading to find out what Savannah has to say in *The Impact Zone*.

And if you want to find out more about Harley's "that guy," you're welcome to download her diary entries from when she was fourteen...or you can wait until the final book in this trilogy to learn more.

DEAR READER...

Thank you so much for reading Aidan and Harley's story. I hope you enjoyed it, because I loved every moment of writing this book.

Harley is such a strong, independent character, and I love that about her. But I also love how Aidan challenges her. They challenge each other, and watching them grow together was so much fun. I can't wait to see more of them in the coming novels.

But what's up with Savannah?
Sweet, shy Savannah who doesn't like to make waves or cause any problems.

With her best friend in a coma and her relationship with Aidan most definitely over, Savannah is feeling completely lost.

https://www.subscribepage.com/JF_RyderBay_signup

ALSO BY JORDAN FORD

BIG PLAY NOVELS

The Playmaker

The Red Zone

The Handoff

Shoot The Gap

THE BROTHERHOOD TRILOGY

See No Evil

Speak No Evil

Hear No Evil

THE BARLOW SISTERS TRILOGY

Curveball

Strike Out

Foul Play

RYDER BAY NOVELS

Over the Falls

The Impact Zone (releasing March 2019)

Face of the Wave (releasing April 2019)

ABOUT THE AUTHOR

Jordan Ford is a New Zealand author who has spent her life traveling with her family, attending international schools, and growing up in a variety of cultures. Although it was sometimes hard shifting between schools and lifestyles, she doesn't regret it for a moment. Her experiences have enriched her life and given her amazing insights into the human race.

She believes that everyone has a back story...and that story is fundamental in how people cope and react to life around them. Telling stories that are filled with heart-felt emotion and realistic characters is an absolute passion of Jordan's. Since her earliest memories, she has been making up tales to entertain herself. It wasn't until she reached her teen years that she first considered writing one. A computer failure and lost files put a major glitch in her journey, and it took until she graduated university with a teaching degree before she took up the dream once more. Since then, she hasn't been able to stop.

"Writing high school romances brings me the greatest joy. My heart bubbles, my insides zing, and I am at my happiest when immersed in a great scene with characters who have become real to me."

CONNECT ONLINE

Jordan loves to hear from her readers. Please feel free to contact her through any of the following means:

WEBSITE:
www.jordanfordbooks.com

FACEBOOK:
www.facebook.com/jordanfordbooks/

INSTAGRAM:
www.instagram.com/jordanfordbooks/

NEWSLETTER:
This is the best way to stay in touch with Jordan's work and have access to special giveaways and sales.
www.subscribepage.com/JF_RyderBay_signup